See Jane Run!

A West River Mystery

Jolene Stratton Philo

Midwestern Books
MB

ISBN-13: 979-8-9857175-0-1

Library of Congress Control Number 1-11149300671

Cover design by: eBook Cover Designs

Published by Midwestern Books
801 W Washington Ave, Polk City, IA 50226

Contact: info@midwesternbooks.com

Dedicated to the memory of Shawn Burghduff, who as a six-year-old, drove away and left his teacher to tramp down the hill and across the prairie all by her lonesome.

It's a long way to Tipperary,
It's a long way to go.
It's a long way to Tipperary
To the sweetest girl I know!
Goodbye, Piccadilly,
Farewell, Leicester Square!
It's a long, long way to
Tipperary,
But my heart's right there.

–Jack Judge

Chapter 1

I slammed on the brakes. My car fishtailed. I fought to keep the Beetle from careening into the Black Angus herd loitering on the highway. The car shuddered and stopped, its bumper inches from the back end of a steer. I released the steering wheel and sat on my hands to stop their shaking. I had almost died, and the steer had almost become hamburger. All because some rancher let his cattle wander all over the road. What kind of country was this? In the rearview mirror I watched the trailer hitched to Uncle Tim's Chevy truck swing from side to side. Uncle Tim wrestled the steering wheel until the truck glided between two steers as slick as you please. The trailer swung perpendicular to the road, and the back wheels slid toward the ditch.

This couldn't be happening! We'd driven twelve hours without a single problem. The trailer, which held everything I owned, was about to be ruined. It inched closer to the ditch. And closer. And closer.

I couldn't watch. I closed my eyes. I had to watch. I

opened my eyes as the back wheels gave in to gravity and slid into the ditch. The cattle lounging on the road stood and sauntered away. Stupid animals.

Uncle Tim opened the driver's side door and stepped out. The brisk breeze ruffled his cropped black hair and pushed at his polo shirt and jeans. When Mom got out on her side, the wind flattened her bouffant hairdo and set the sleeves and legs of her homemade polyester knit blouse and shorts to flapping.

Shaking, I joined them beside the stranded trailer. Uncle Tim's presence would temper but not quash Mom's reaction so I stood behind him and braced for what was coming.

Her eyes were on fire. "I absolutely cannot believe that South Dakota considers a twenty-three mile gravel road to be a state highway! And whoever thought of letting an entire herd of cattle graze next to it?"

As always, my mother didn't disappoint.

Uncle Tim cleared his throat. "I prefer to think of it as an adventure, Doris. Perhaps we should table this discussion in the interest of saving the trailer. Jane, you watch for vehicles at the top of that rise." He pointed to the hill where I'd stared death in the face. "Doris and I will stand over there." He pointed to the west.

The more distance between Mom and me the better. I held my nose and picked my way between the cattle chewing their cud and their cow pies. Ugh!

"If I'd known how primitive this corner of South Dakota was"—Mom pointed a finger at the landscape as they walked away—"I would never have allowed Jane to move here."

This was 1977 and I was twenty-one. The proud owner

of a newly-minted elementary education degree. Allow me, my foot. I was about to grab hold of life and make it on my own. And no one was going to stop me. Not cattle on the road. Not a stranded trailer.

Not my mother.

A dust devil appeared on the road to the east, traveling in our direction. Maybe I should flash a bit of leg. No, it was better to wave in my best imitation of a country schoolteacher about to arrive in a new town. Except I wasn't pretending.

The dust devil slowed and a brown Ford truck, more rust than paint, appeared as the grit settled. The driver rolled down his window and rested a tan arm on the sill. Dark brown eyes studied me. The door opened, and a pair of low-heeled cowboy boots appeared.

I gasped. They were like my dad's boots, though the soles of his rested on the footrests of his wheelchair and not the ground.

The sight of those boots transported me to the shoe store where Mom took my sister, brother, and me to buy school shoes when they went on sale each August.

The salesman gathered up the boxes with our new shoes and set them on the counter. Then he placed a boot box on top of the stack.

"Give them to Harold." He patted the carton. "With my compliments."

On the way to our car I glanced over my shoulder, certain the police were on their way to arrest Mom for stealing. Who would take care of us then? When Mom set the boxes in the backseat beside me, I hid the boots under the seat. Just in case the police showed up.

When we arrived home, Dad was sitting outside in his wheelchair.

I crawled onto his lap and pressed my face against his shirt. The aroma of pipe tobacco and Aqua Velva aftershave soothed my fears.

"Dad, why did the man at the shoe store give you new boots when you never wear out your old ones?"

He took his pipe from his mouth and held it with a shaky hand. "I think it's because boots are what he has to give, Janie-Jo." He puffed at his pipe and chuckled. "If only the guy at the bakery would give me doughnuts."

The shoe salesman still gave Dad new boots whenever he felt like it. Dad still sat outside in his wheelchair in good weather. He still smoked a pipe, though his hand had grown wobblier and Mom often threatened to cut off his supply of tobacco. I had watched Dad's health fail gradually for years. Saying good-bye to him, leaving him to take a job so far from home almost broke me.

"Ma'am?"

His question wrenched me away from Dad again.

"Need some help?"

The man in front of me had a friendly face. He wore grimy blue jeans, a white T-shirt, and a battered cowboy hat.

"I'm Junior Wentworth." He flipped on the truck's hazard lights. "You folks look like you could use some help."

Wow. A cowboy and a gentleman.

Uncle Tim joined us. "Janie-Jo, drive up to your mom and turn on your flashers. Stay there and watch for traffic."

When I reached my car, I checked my appearance in the mirror. After twelve hours in the Beetle my clothes were wrinkled. My hair was tangled. As scratchy as my eyes were, they had to be bloodshot. I sniffed an armpit and grimaced. So much for making a good impression. I slicked on some lipstick anyway.

Mr. Wentworth and Uncle Tim took the Ford to the beached trailer, and Mr. Wentworth maneuvered his truck until its tailgate was a few feet from the Chevy's front bumper. They climbed out and together they pulled a stout chain from the truck bed. Uncle Tim wasn't a tall man, five feet eight at the most, and Mr. Wentworth towered over him. But not for long.

Our Good Samaritan dropped to the ground, crawled under his back bumper, and fastened the chain somewhere underneath the Ford and then under the front of the Chevy.

He stood. "This oughta do the trick."

The men climbed into their vehicles. Mr. Wentworth nosed forward until the chain pulled taut. He stuck his head out the window and yelled, "Put it in neutral!"

Uncle Tim hollered back. "Ready when you are!"

The tires on Mr. Wentworth's truck fought to gain traction. As the Ford inched forward, the Chevy shuddered. The trailer bucked, and its back tires rolled onto the road.

Uncle Tim waved. "We're good!"

I raised my arms over my head and hummed the theme song from *Rocky*.

Mom elbowed me in the ribs. "Jane, you're making a spectacle of yourself."

I hummed louder.

Mr. Wentworth poked his head out his open window. "I'll tow you into the lane up that direction. We can unhitch there."

Uncle Tim gave a thumbs-up. The tiny caravan wove around the placid cattle and parked in the lane. Mom and I followed in the Beetle. The men got out and unwound the chain. They were stowing it in his truck bed when another dust devil appeared in the east. Lights flashed and a siren blared as it crested the hill and slowed to a stop.

"Our sheriff likes to make his presence known." Junior squinted and wiped his forehead. "In case you hadn't noticed."

The door of the patrol car swung open. The man who stepped out was shorter than Junior and young, much younger than I'd expected. A badge was pinned to his tan uniform shirt. From the waist down, his belt, jeans, and boots were pure cowboy.

He removed his wide-brimmed brown hat before the wind could do it for him. "You need any help?"

"Nah." Junior crossed his arms and leaned against his pickup truck. "Their trailer had a run in with the ditch, but we took care of it."

The sheriff brushed a hand over his dark blond hair before putting on his hat and getting into the patrol car. "In that case, I'll get out of your way."

"Thank you kindly for your concern," Uncle Tim said.

The sheriff gave an expressionless tip of his hat and closed the door.

Mom shaded her eyes and watched him drive off. "My goodness, he's not a conversationalist, is he?"

"He and his deputy have to keep moving. They have a lot of ground to cover." Junior turned his attention to me. "Where you headed?"

I quit poking at the gravel with my shoe. "Little Missouri."

Mom squeezed my shoulder. "She'll be working at the school."

He gave me the once over. "You must be the new teacher everybody's been talking about."

Were there sweat stains on my blouse? Did I have lipstick on my front teeth? I crossed my arms and flashed a toothless smile.

"Welcome to Tipperary County. How long you been driving?"

"We left Sioux City at dawn," Uncle Tim said.

"Then I'll be on my way." He caught my eye. "I didn't get your name?"

"Jane Newell. Thanks again for your help, Mr. Wentworth."

"That's way too formal for these parts. Call me Junior." He offered a hand to Uncle Tim. "I'll leave you to escort your daughter to her new apartment."

Uncle Tim gave Junior's hand a firm shake. "Tim Moy. But I'm not her father."

"He's her uncle. I'm her mother. My husband Harold is Jane's father, but he doesn't travel like he used to. Multiple sclerosis."

Those two words set my teeth on edge. Before he became ill, Dad would have relished being stuck in the middle of nowhere surrounded by cattle. He would have embroidered the tale and commanded the room each time he told it. Multiple sclerosis left a hollowed-out version of that father. "I'm sorry to hear that," Mr. Wentworth—make that Junior—said.

"He was a cattleman in his day." Mom's tone was half proud, half wistful. "And a county extension agent."

"Your husband was a county extension agent?" Junior ran a hand through his hair and put on his hat. "With a pretty woman like you at his side, I bet people thought highly of him."

Her face went soft and sweet. "Very highly."

"Who's meeting you at the apartment? I can call from my place and let them know you're coming." His smile was kind.

"Oh, don't bother. The principal mailed me a key."

His jaw tightened like Mom's had when I refused to eat liver as a kid. He kept smiling, but the kindness was gone. He shrugged and walked to his truck. "Be seeing you around."

Mom stepped toward him. "Tell your wife we are sorry for delaying your return home."

Oh my word! Could my mother be any more obvious?

"If I had a wife, I'd tell her." He settled in the driver's seat, slammed the door, and drove away.

"Honestly, Jane." Mom glared at me. "I know he looks like he doesn't have two dimes to rub together, but would it hurt you to act the least bit sociable? He's the first man we've seen in this entire county. Plus he's got gumption and good manners on his side. That counts for a lot, you know. Besides, he was interested in you."

"He was just being polite." Guys were always polite to me. My last boyfriend, the one I'd dated for three years in college, had been as polite as Emily Post until graduation. That day he took me out for coffee. He held my chair as polite as could be. He ordered my favorite maple-iced doughnuts. Then he politely broke up with me. I knew polite, and I was over it.

"I saw the way he looked at you. He was very interested. At least until you were rude."

I was too tired to argue. "Interested or not, I'm thankful that he pulled the trailer out of the ditch."

After Mom and Uncle Tim climbed into the truck, I got into the Beetle and pulled onto the highway. Uncle Tim followed close behind. Bumper-to-bumper, we inched through the scattered cattle on the road.

The view from the top of the hill could have been the backdrop to a Kodachrome western from the 1950s. The sun hung red in the August sky, hovering above the rugged, tree-covered buttes on the western horizon. The Little Missouri River snaked through the valley. Tall cottonwoods lined the narrow riverbed, their bright green foliage a sharp contrast to the broad expanse of fawn-colored prairie stretching in every direction. Other than the river and the buttes, the only break in the brown landscape was the town of Little Missouri, a tiny cluster of buildings huddled on the far side of the river.

We crossed the bridge, and I led the way past the well-kept Forest Service Ranger Station and around the corner where a gas station struggled to stay upright. Turning onto Main Street, we drove past vacant storefronts, the Round The Bend Bar and Cafe, a tiny grocery store, some tired-looking frame houses, and several overgrown empty lots before we pulled into the gravel parking area beside the schoolyard.

Uncle Tim jumped out of the truck and raised an

eyebrow. Mom emerged, her square face as disgusted as it had been the day a mole emerged from the entrance of his tunnel in her side yard. She'd whacked him to death with the garden hose in record time.

She turned in a circle, taking in the unkempt schoolyard and the snaggletoothed chicken -wire fence surrounding two sides of the playground. The school consisted of two tan, double-wide, double-long trailers. One ran along the northern edge of the playground and the other along the western edge. The play area sported a dilapidated swing set, a ramshackle metal slide, and two ancient teeter-totters.

"What were you thinking when you accepted a job in the middle of nowhere, Jane Newell? These people don't even own lawn mowers! I can't believe my little girl is going to live here." Mom crawled into the truck, slammed the door, and began to sob.

Uncle Tim held up a hand in warning. "Don't say a word, Jane. You're about to begin a new life. She'll return to a sick husband in a few days. Have a heart."

His words hurt like a slap. I whirled around and stomped up the apartment landing stairs. Tears obscured my vision as I jabbed the key into the lock. I yanked the door open, stepped inside, and banged it shut. The cattle. The trailer. The schoolyard. Mom's revulsion. Uncle Tim's admonition. The events of this horrid day hammered at my resolve. I placed my palms on the door and pressed against it with all my weight to keep from rushing out and begging Mom and Uncle Tim to take me home.

Chapter 2

You can do this. Dad's voice rose from somewhere inside me. Or was he beside me? My eyes popped open, and I scanned the empty apartment. He wasn't there, but he spoke again. *You can do this, Janie-Jo. Now, wash your face and get going.*

I straightened and his presence accompanied me to the kitchen sink. I splashed cold water on my face, dried it on my sleeve, and joined Uncle Tim and Mom. We hauled in sleeping bags, pillows, the cooler, and our suitcases. We were too tired to do more than eat sandwiches from the cooler and bed down on the living room floor.

In the morning we lugged boxes and furniture into the apartment, which was in the southern half of the trailer that ran along the west side of the schoolyard. Mom lifted a heavy box from the Beetle's trunk. "Where do you want this one?"

"It's stuff for school." I snatched the box away and took it into my classroom in the northern half of the trailer. I shoved it on the bottom shelf of a cupboard behind a mountain of art supplies so my mother couldn't find it.

Once the truck bed and trailer were empty, Mom and I started to put the kitchen to rights.

She fiddled with the knobs on the stove. "The burners aren't working." Mom spoke with the gravity of a national evening news anchor.

I sighed. Not even eight o'clock and she was at it again. This was going to be another long day.

Next, she yanked open a kitchen drawer, and the handle came off in her palm. She waved it under my nose. "This cabinet is a piece of junk." She tossed the handle on the counter, and it pinged against the phone sitting by the refrigerator. "And someone needs to hook up this antique. I haven't seen one of those since my folks moved to town twenty years ago!"

The black phone was an outdated version of my parents' desk phone. This one had a metal case instead of plastic and a crank handle where the rotary dial should have been. I didn't have a clue about how to make it work. The run-down apartment bothered me too, but I wasn't about to tell Mom. If I showed the slightest hint of weakness, she would pounce like a barn cat and drag me back to Iowa.

Uncle Tim inched past the boxes in the kitchen and returned a few minutes later. "There's a leak under the bathroom sink. I stuck a bucket under it and mopped up the water. You'd better call the school maintenance man and get it fixed toot suite."

Ah, there was the rub. "He's a she, and she lives here in town. The principal told me her name, but I can't remember it. It began with V. Vivian, maybe? Venice? Or Vida?"

Mom took a pencil and notepad from her purse and plunked them on the counter. "Start a list of repairs for this mystery woman so you don't forget them too."

My fingers curled around the pencil and I started the list.

She peeked in the refrigerator. "Absolutely filthy!"

The tip of the pencil broke and I hid it in my pocket. No need to add fodder to Mom's fire.

Uncle Tim pulled me aside. "Your mom'll be fine in a few days. This is your chance to sit in the catbird seat, little girl. Make the most of it. And don't you worry about your dad. Your brother's still at home. Me and your Aunt Wanda and the kids'll stop by to keep him company. Don't you ever feel guilty about starting your own life, Janie-Jo."

"Thank you," I whispered, "for everything."

"Doris, put down those pans and grab your purse. We're going to that cafe down the street for lunch." He winked. "My treat!"

The mention of a free meal sent Mom searching for her purse, a brush, and a mirror. Five minutes later, we were walking down Main Street. A dozen dirty pickup trucks sat helter-skelter along the north side of the bar and cafe, and more were parked along the building's Main Street side. From the looks of things, the entire population of Little Missouri, and perhaps Tipperary County, was inside.

A Ford pickup with a crew cab pulled into a vacant space. The passenger door opened and a boy tumbled out. His mop of dark blond hair fell into his eyes. A man and woman in their mid-forties climbed out after him. He was tall, broad, and hearty, the picture of a hard-working rancher. She was so small and fine featured she looked as though a stiff prairie wind would blow her away.

The man lifted his Stetson to reveal a thick shock of gray hair and a wind-burned face. She ran rough fingers through blond hair fading toward gray.

"Miss Newell? Is that you?"

I stared at her. How did she know my name?

"Good to see you again." She held out a hand.

My face turned hot. "I'm so sorry. Do I know you?"

"I'm Cookie. Cookie Sternquist. We met during your interview in March."

"Yes, I remember now. You and your husband Brett were there."

"Bud."

Oh dear.

"Bud." I turned to him and stifled a yelp as he squeezed my fingers. Then I turned toward the boy. "And this is?"

"Tiege, our youngest." Cookie ruffled his hair. "This is Miss Newell, your new teacher and . . ."

"My mother, Doris Newell, and my uncle, Tim Moy."

Tiege tugged at his father's arm. "Can we go inside? I'm starving."

My stomach growled.

Tiege's eyes widened. "Didn't you eat breakfast?"

"Tiege, where are your manners?" Bud thumped his son's head. "You're welcome to sit with us."

Mom waved away the offer. "Oh, we don't want to impose."

Bud laid a hand on her shoulder. "Mrs. Newell—"

"Doris," she corrected him.

"Doris, the cafe's gonna be packed tighter than cows in a semi. You got no business taking 'em on without reinforcement. You sit with us and remember, most everybody in this county is relation to most everybody else. So keep your head down and your mouth shut 'til you figure out who belongs to who."

Uncle Tim chuckled. "Sound advice."

Tiege trotted to the door, held it open, and waved everyone in. A blast of chilled air laced with the heavy scent of fried food greeted us. The din of voices competed with the pop and sizzle of food on the grill. Three Formica-topped tables and four booths, straight out of the 1950s, were crowded into the small room.

The woman at the register caught Bud's eye. "We're full up in here." She jerked her head toward the doorway in the north wall. "There's room in the bar if you want to eat there."

A black-haired woman, wrinkled, rail thin, and short, rose from her seat at one of the tables. She shouted above the clamor, "They can have this spot. I'll settle up."

A slim boy with dark hair parted and slicked into place sat at the table the woman had vacated. He stood and threaded his way toward the door while she paid at the cash register.

Cookie steered me toward him. "Beau, come meet Miss Newell."

He stared at the ground until the older woman walked over.

Cookie tried again, her green eyes gentle in her weather-beaten face. "Beau, say hello to the new teacher."

"Hi." He met my gaze, but his eyes were devoid of expression.

His blank face made my heart sink. "Hello."

The woman dug a pack of cigarettes from her pocket and led him out the door. His bony shoulders drooped like Atlas bearing the weight of the world on his shoulders.

What had happened to him? What had extinguished his spark?

"Jane!" Mom pointed to an empty chair. "I saved you a seat."

"Hey, Trudy." Cookie gestured the waitress over. "Have you met Jane Newell?"

Trudy shook her head. "Not yet. My boy Renny is in your class. So's my niece and nephew, Elva and Stig Borgeson." She motioned toward the other room. "Renny's in the bar playing pool."

Tiege sprang from his chair. "Can I go play?"

"Much as you bellyached about being near starved to death?" Bud gave him a sharp gaze. "Playing can wait until after you eat."

Tiege sat down with a thud. After Trudy took our orders, he dug something from his pocket. "Look what I got."

He held it so close, my eyes crossed. I lowered his hand. In his palm were what looked like six interlocking vertebrae made of a translucent material. Each one was smaller than the previous one and had a small gray pebble at its center. The final vertebra tapered to a dull point.

"What are they?"

"Oh, nothin' to write home about." Bud reached over and poked at them with a finger. "Just the rattles from the snake Cookie found on the welcome mat this mornin'."

Mom choked on her water. She coughed until her

face turned red and tears streamed down her cheeks. Uncle Tim grabbed a wad of napkins from the dispenser and shoved them at her while I thumped her back. Her coughing fit subsided.

"Are you okay?" I asked.

"Yes. Water down my windpipe."

Bud winked at Uncle Tim. "Cookie killed it with the spade, and Tiege cut off the rattles once the body quit thrashing around. He was supposed to put them in the mason jar where they belong. But somehow"—he raised his voice and his eyebrows—"they ended up in his pocket."

Tiege stared at the floor.

Mom wiped her eyes. "There was a rattlesnake on your welcome mat?"

"Not on the mat *inside* the door, Doris." Bud scooped the rattles from Tiege's palm and dropped them in his front pocket. "The one on the deck. *Outside.*"

"Bud," Cookie scolded, "you make it sound like we find rattlers on the deck once a day, not once every ten years."

Trudy arrived with our orders and all talk of rattlesnakes ceased. We tended to our food. My burger and fries were half-eaten when Tiege pushed his empty plate away. "Mom, can I go in the bar and play pool with Renny now?"

Cookie wiped a ketchup smear off his cheek. "Manners, please."

"Mom, may I please be excused to play with Renny?"

"Yes, you may."

He sprinted across the room and through the barroom door.

A barrel-chested man in his mid-thirties stopped by our table. "I'm Trudy's better half, Glen Berthold. We own this place." He gave my hand a quick pump. "You ever have trouble with Renny, he'll have a sore backside, and your supper will be on the house."

I pulled my hand away. If this man thought I would ever give him a reason to lay a hand on his son, he had another think coming.

Next, a man with a full head of white hair and soft brown eyes and a woman in a hot pink, polyester pantsuit came over. "Frost McDonald. And my wife, Fannie. We own the gas station down the street."

"Our granddaughter will be one of your kindeegart'ners," Fannie said. "She's smart as a whip, is our little Keeva."

More strangers came by to introduce themselves and their relatives. My food had gone cold by the time the other tables were empty. When we were the last customers remaining, I brought up the little boy I'd met earlier. "What happened to Beau?"

Cookie sighed. "That's an awful deal and we hate to talk about it. But you're his teacher and you ought to hear the whole story."

Bud tucked a toothpick into the corner of his mouth and began. "The boy's mom, Twila, she and our oldest boy was in grade school together. She went wild in high school, drinking pretty steady. Never graduated. Ran away from home after her sophomore year. She showed up pregnant a few years later on her parents' doorstep. Burt and Iva Kelly. They own the grocery store across the street. You met them yet?"

"No."

"Good people." He drained his half-empty water glass. "A week after Beau was born, she lit out again. He's been living with 'em ever since."

"So the woman with Beau was Iva?"

"Oh, heavens no." Cookie swiped at a smear of ketchup on the table with her napkin. "That's his great-aunt. Iva's sister, Velma Albright."

I banged a fist on the table and the silverware danced. "That's it!"

"What's 'it'?" Uncle Tim asked.

"The janitor's name is Velma."

Cookie plucked another napkin from the dispenser on the table. "That's right. She lives in the red-and-white trailer east of the cafe. She takes a while warming up to people. Just so you know."

"Where's Twila now?"

Cookie dipped the napkin in her water glass. "She died a week ago. The funeral was yesterday."

Mom's fork clattered to the floor.

Cookie wiped the mustard bottle. "She called Beau shortly before she died. Said she'd straightened up and gotten a job about thirty miles north of here in Marmarth, North Dakota. She was coming to get him. The next day, her body was found on the Marmarth Road."

Uncle Tim sat up straight. "She was on foot?"

"Yes." Bud took the bottle of mustard from Cookie and grasped her hand. "Best they can piece together, she went out drinking after she called. When the bartender took her keys, she decided to walk to Little Missouri. Made it twenty miles when she got hit. There was fragments of broken headlights around her body, so the sheriff declared it a hit-and-run accident. Most likely a pickup truck, considering the point of impact. So far, the investigation is going nowhere. Like Cookie said, it's an awful bad deal."

I closed my eyes and saw Beau's drooping shoulders. His loss pressed on my chest. It was my loss too. His mother was gone in an instant. My father had been disappearing inch by inch all my life. But my sister and brother and I shared the loss. We leaned on each other. Who did Beau have?

Me. Beau had me.

As soon as Mom was on her way home, I would pull out the box tucked behind the art supplies. I would use my carefully packed criminal justice text books, my notes, and forensic supplies to find the coward responsible for Twila's death. Until then, even Mom couldn't fault me for asking about the tragedy surrounding a student. I leaned forward. "Where's the Marmarth Road?"

Bud traced an imaginary line on the tabletop with a toothpick. "Take Main Street north from here, past the school straight out of town, and you're on it."

Uncle Tim stood. "Does the road get much use?"

"Just locals, mostly." Bud put the toothpick back in his mouth.

Mom put her silverware on her plate. "So whoever killed Twila is from Marmarth?"

Bud's eyes darted first to Cookie, then to me, and then to Mom. "Or from right here in Little Missouri."

I yanked a napkin from the dispenser and shredded it to bits. Bud chewed his toothpick. Cookie stacked dishes. Mom gathered more silverware. Uncle Tim paid our bill at the register.

Mom's voice was high and unnatural as she thanked

the Sternquists for their company. Then she gripped my elbow hard enough to leave bruises, forced me to my feet, and pushed me out the door.

"That does it. You will call the principal, resign your position, and we'll go home tomorrow." She steered me along Main Street. "If not sooner."

Chapter 3

"Stop packing my things. I am not going back to Iowa." I intercepted Mom carrying an armload of cookie sheets and muffin tins. "Put them back in the cupboard."

She faked to the left and made a quick right around the kitchen table. Uncle Tim blocked her path.

"Don't try to stop me." Mom spit the words.

As if anyone could stop Mom when she acted like this.

"Doris." Uncle Tim put his hands on her shoulders. "Quit."

"You go ahead and quit. But I won't." Her words came out low and cold. "I had my misgivings about Jane taking a job at the end of the world. I held my tongue about the roads and the state of this town."

My jaw dropped. Did the woman have amnesia?

"I haven't said a word about rattlesnakes on welcome mats or children playing in a barroom. But I cannot remain silent about a crime committed just a few miles away. When I found out you were taking criminal justice classes in college behind my back, I told you there was no future in it." She took a step forward until we were nose to nose. "I want you to listen to me loud and clear, Jane Newell. Even though your student lost his mother, even though she may have been intentionally killed, there is no reason for you to get involved in the investigation. But I know you will. So the best thing for everyone involved is for us to pack you up and take you home."

She dropped the baking pans on the table and sank into a chair. "I can't bear the thought of something happening to you, Jane. I just can't." She covered her eyes. Her shoulders shook. She took the hankie Uncle Tim offered and pressed it to her face.

I knelt beside her. "You saw Beau. He must feel like his mother abandoned him. If I go home, he might think I'm leaving him too. I can't do that."

She lowered the hankie. "You can't save every child, Jane Josephine Newell."

"Hmm." Uncle Tim stroked his chin. "Isn't that what Harold says when you fret about your students?"

"It's not the same." Mom gave him the handkerchief. "Sioux City doesn't have murderers running free or rattlesnakes on every doorstep."

"You've got a point there." Uncle Tim stuffed the hankie in his back pocket. "And I've got a solution for the snakes. Tomorrow I'll purchase a blunt-end spade for Janie to keep in her entryway." He turned my direction. "Any time you open the door, thump the spade on the landing and count to ten. That'll give the snakes time to vacate the premises. If they stick around, you can decapitate them."

"A rattlesnake guillotine for a housewarming gift." Mom drummed her fingers on the table. "Never in my wildest dreams."

I stood. "But Mom, this isn't your dream. It's mine." I grabbed my purse. "And I'm going to chase it with everything I've got. Now, I'm going to rent a box at the post office and stop by Velma Albright's trailer. You're welcome to come along, but there's to be no more talk about me going back to Iowa." I met her gaze. "Well?"

***

Ten minutes later we arrived at the post office. It clung to the west wall of the gas station like an afterthought. The effect of the aluminum siding's jaunty red and white stripes was marred by the building's slight tilt to the east. I pushed the post office door open, expecting the inside to be a sorry affair. It was anything but.

Rows of ornately decorated, brass post office boxes covered one wall. The other walls sported fresh, white paint, and the patterned linoleum was polished to a high shine. The room was cool and smelled of ink, stamps, and paper with a hint of motor oil underneath.

Mom hissed in my ear. "Did it occur to anyone that attaching the post office to the gas station might be a fire hazard?"

"Be right with you!" A man appeared behind the counter . He had a lined, tan face and black eyes under a head of salt and pepper hair cut short. He wore a crisp regulation uniform, and the name tag pinned an inch above his shirt pocket read "Dale Cunningham."

"Good morning, ladies." He leaned against the wide counter. "What can I do ya for?"

"I'd like to rent a post office box."

"Okeydoke." He gave me a paper and a pen. "Fill this out and I'll get you set up in no time."

He chatted with Mom while I completed the form. "Where you from?"

"Sioux City."

"That's a bit of a drive. What brings you here?"

"My daughter is the new teacher."

He coughed. "I don't suppose your college taught you much about what to do when a kid loses his mother."

My hand jerked, and the tip of the pen squiggled. Doggone it!

"It's all anybody can talk about." Mr. Cunningham passed me a bottle of correction fluid. "You know the McDonalds? They own the gas station on the other side of the wall"—he jerked a thumb over his shoulder, "—and they found Twila. Scared both of them half to death. Frost stayed to watch over the body while Fannie drove to town to raise the alarm. He got a good look at the broken bits of headlight and brake light covers on the road and is one hundred percent certain they come from a truck, not a car."

Mom stiffened and put a hand on my elbow. If I showed the least interest in the postmaster's patter she would drag me away. I painted correction fluid over my pen squiggles with careful, deliberate strokes.

"Broken headlights are a dime a dozen in this county. But Frost said some of the shards on the road had blood on them, and he figures the broken headlight does too." Mr. Cunningham lowered his voice and raised his eyebrows. "I guess the sheriff doesn't think it's worth his time to look for broken headlights with blood on them."

I angled away from Mom so she couldn't see the smile playing at my lips. It might not be worth the sheriff's time, but it was worth mine.

"Good heavens, Jane, how long does correction fluid take to dry?" Mom craned her neck to see the form in my hand.

I touched a fingertip to the paper. "What do you know? It's ready." I paid for the box rental and Mr. Cunningham presented my key with a little flourish.

Mom paused at the door before we left. "One more thing. Who do we contact about getting the phone hooked up?"

"That would be Gus and Betty Yarborough. I'll let Gus know."

Mom shut the door and fell into step beside me. "That postmaster likes to pass along gossip. Maybe that's why he doesn't ask for a transfer to somewhere respectable." Her nose wrinkled as we passed the frame buildings on Main Street. "For heaven's sake, someone could take a paintbrush to these buildings every fifty years or so."

"The Bertholds keep Round the Bend looking good." We turned the corner toward Velma Albright's trailer.

"How comforting to know the most respectable business in town is the local bar."

She was right, so I kept my mouth shut. When we arrived at Velma's, we climbed her rickety stairs, and I knocked.

She opened the door, her dark eyes squinting in the sunlight. "Yes?" Her voice lacked warmth.

"Hi, Velma. I'm Jane Newell, the new teacher. We met at the cafe last night. This is my mother, Doris."

Velma took a drag on her cigarette. "What do you want?"

"The principal said I should let you know about any problems at the apartment."

She crossed her arms. "What's wrong?"

"One of the kitchen drawer handles fell off."

"Wull, I'll be darned."

"And the bathroom sink is leaking."

"Wull, I'll be darned."

"And there's a strong smell of natural gas in the kitchen."

"Wull, I'll be darned."

Mom bristled like a bull terrier with its hackles up. "We expect you to look into it while we're in Tipperary tomorrow morning."

Velma frowned. "Can't make any promises."

"That natural gas smell might be dangerous."

Velma gazed at the school. "Don't look like nothing's exploded."

Mom glared at Velma.

Velma glared back.

Mom narrowed her eyes.

Velma blinked first. "I'll see what I can do."

She slammed the door so hard I lost my balance. Mom caught my arm. "You steer clear of that woman. She's the kind that could make your life miserable."

We both knew Mom was right, but I wasn't about to admit it. After all, I had my pride.

Chapter 4

We were in the apartment breaking down cardboard boxes when someone knocked. I went to the door. A man stood there, white hair peeking out from under a straw hat. He wore striped overalls over a faded shirt. He smelled like my farmer uncles, a mixture of manure and woodsmoke and dirt. He wiped his forehead with a red bandana. "You my new neighbor?"

"Well, that depends on where you live."

"Over there." He jerked a thumb in the direction of the house behind the school.

"Then we're neighbors."

"Hello, neighbor." He stuck out a hand. "Merle Laird."

"Jane Newell." I stepped back and bumped into my personal guard dog. "This is my mother, Doris."

Would she growl at him?

He took off his hat. "Ma'am."

She bristled, but remained silent.

He replaced his hat. "You 'et supper yet?"

"No. It's been a busy day."

"I'm fixin' to make non-skid pancakes, and you're invited to join me."

"Non-skid pancakes?"

His blue eyes danced. "Waffles."

I liked him already. "Is my uncle invited too?"

"The more the merrier. It'll be ready in fifteen minutes."

***

"I can't believe you accepted an invitation from a total stranger." Mom trotted to keep up with us on the short walk to Merle's house.

"Get a move on, Doris. Jane and I are hungry. Think of this as another family adventure."

"Do you mean like when Harold's wheelchair nearly rolled into the lake?"

That had been hilarious.

"Or the camping trip when he almost choked to death on an apple?"

That hadn't been funny at all.

"Obstacles breed adventure, Doris." When Uncle Tim knocked on the door, flakes of white paint shook loose and wafted to the ground.

"Come in."

We stepped into a mudroom crammed with egg cartons, a gaggle of cats, a cream separator, and rows of glass gallon milk jugs.

"I'm in the kitchen."

We followed the smell of fresh waffles and frying bacon into a tiny kitchen. The table was shoved under the window so close to the stove that bacon grease from the frying pan spattered the table top. A counter butted against the stove and ran the length of the narrow room. An old-fashioned sink and drainboard occupied the opposite wall. Baking pans, condiment bottles, canning jars, and kitchen paraphernalia covered every inch of the counter. The clutter was covered with a thin layer of gray, greasy grime.

Merle tended the waffle iron on the counter. He gestured to the chairs around the table. "Have a seat."

Bile rose in my throat at the thought of eating anything prepared in this salmonella playground. From the way Mom perched on the edge of her chair, her stomach was doing cartwheels too.

Uncle Tim rubbed his hands together with relish. "I'm hungry enough to eat a bear."

Merle forked waffles and bacon onto our plates. "Eat up. There's plenty."

Mom took a bite. "These are delicious."

Had I heard right? Merle's cooking passed Mom's muster?

I spread butter and poured syrup on the waffles and dug in. They were fluffy on the inside and crisp on the outside. The bacon was cooked to perfection. "Marvelous!"

Merle sat down and picked up his knife. "You met Velma Albright?"

Mom and I exchanged glances. "Yes," I said.

Merle buttered his waffles and drowned them in syrup. "She bit your head off yet?"

Mom snapped a piece of bacon in two. "More than once."

"Sounds 'bout right. She's had a burr under her saddle for forty years. You don't want to get on the wrong side of her.

"Me and Velma and Arvid Drent—you met Arvid yet?" Merle didn't wait for an answer. "We three was all in the same grade at Slick Creek School north a town. Went through eight grades together. Arvid still lives on his family's homestead. Velma moved into town for high school, and she don't never let me and Arvid forget she got a dee-ploma, and we don't."

Mom cocked her head. "Little Missouri had a high school?"

"Yes, ma'am." Merle rubbed his ear. "Straight east of my kitchen. This was a big town after the US government opened it to homesteaders in aught nine. It had close to four hunnert cit-ee-zens before the Dust Bowl drove 'em out. That's when I bought this place for next to nothin'. Quit ranching and started trucking instead. I don't think Arvid forgive me yet for movin' to town. Me and him, we played some awful tricks on Velma when we was kids. She give you any trouble, me and Arvid'll set her straight."

I licked at a droplet of syrup on my thumb. "Aren't you being a little hard on her considering her niece's funeral was yesterday?"

"I oughta knowed you heard about that. The number one hobby of most everbody in this town is flappin' their gums." Merle rubbed the hair on his ear. "Velma's got every reason to mourn Twila's death. But her contrariness is a mixture of natural mean-spiritedness and three packs of Lucky Strikes a day since FDR was pres-ee-dent."

Mom carried plates to the sink and balanced them on a stack of dishes on the counter.

"You folks got time for a peek at my garden and my milk cow Snippy?"

Mom yawned. "It will have to wait. It's been a long day and we are ready for bed."

Merle walked us to the mudroom. "Got a little something for you." He handed a carton of eggs to Uncle Tim and another to me before giving Mom a glass gallon jar of milk. "Fresh from the cow. It'll have a quart of cream on top come morning. Bring the empty jug and cartons when you need more. Two bits a dozen for eggs and four bits for a gallon of milk."

I eyed the full jug. "Is it safe to drink?"

Mom cradled the jar like a baby. "Don't be such a worrywart, Jane. I drank milk fresh from the cow every day growing up on my parents' farm. In my day, I'd give the cats a squirt and then take one myself."

Merle rubbed his ear. "You milked a cow?"

"I milked nine cows. Every day, twice a day for six years. When I finished high school, my hands were so big I needed a boy's graduation ring."

We said goodbye and carried Merle's gifts home. I dawdled in front of his truck, but it was too dark to see light covers. Shucks! I should have brought a flashlight.

"Mark my words," Mom said, "you give that man a foot in the door, and he'll talk your leg off. You keep him at arm's length and Velma Albright and that Arvid Drent fellow too—what kind of name is that anyway?—or they'll commandeer your time and destroy your social life."

When we got home, Mom tucked the eggs and milk

in the refrigerator. "I'll show you how to skim off the cream in the morning. I haven't done that in years."

Uncle Tim licked his lips. "I'm having fresh cream sprinkled with brown sugar on toast for breakfast."

A few minutes later, Uncle Tim lay in his sleeping bag on the couch. Mom and I shared my double bed. I was drifting off to sleep when the howl of a coyote set every dog in town barking. Once the clamor died down, I punched my pillow and relaxed, but was jerked awake when the coyote howled and roused the dogs again.

Mom didn't begin whimpering until the coyotes had yowled a half-dozen times or so. "I'm leaving my baby in a hell hole." She held my hand so hard I almost whimpered too. A few rounds of howling later, she rolled to my side of the bed and locked her arms around my neck while she sobbed, "Oh, my baby . . . my baby."

I closed my eyes and clamped my mouth shut on the words I wanted to hurl at her. It took all my willpower not to push her away. I waited until she was sleeping, then slid free, rolled over, and covered my head with a pillow.

I pressed the pillow harder against my head, aching for who my mother used to be. For crying out loud, she took on the Sioux City school board in 1962! My mother faced them all down. I could still remember her telling us about it at supper.

Right there at the school board meeting, I stood up and started in. "I'd like to know why men in this district get more pay than women."

"It's quite simple," the board president explained, looking at me like I was stupid. "Men are heads of the household, and women aren't."

"I've been the head of our household since my husband became ill," I told him.

The lone female board member piped up. "I'm sure everyone has heard about your family's situation and makes allowances."

Allowances! I almost threw something at her.

I could see my mother —the mother she usually was—doing that. The image of her chucking a book at that woman's head made me want to applaud.

"But I didn't throw anything. I just looked at our eye doctor, who was also a board member. "Dr. Barkley, do you give us a discount for eye exams?" He shook his head. "How about eye glasses?" Then he looked at me like I was crazy and said, "No."

I took my time, looking at each board member in turn. "I rest my case."' Then I turned and left.

The next year the board raised the pay of women teachers in the district to match what men earned.

Tears trickled down my cheeks. That was my mother, and I missed her. Memories of that mother ushered me to sleep. When I woke at dawn, I found that mother's imposter curled in a fetal position on her side of the bed, still whispering, "My baby, my poor little baby."

"Rise and shine, Mom." I shook her by the shoulder. "This is the day you're going to watch me sign my contract for a salary equal what the male teachers earn." I rolled out of bed and grabbed my clothes. I left the room, closing the door to block out her whimpers.

Chapter 5

"Morning, Janie," Uncle Tim greeted me from the couch.

"Morning, Uncle Tim," I yawned.

"Long night?"

"Don't ask." I plodded to the bathroom.

I showered and changed into a denim skirt and a sleeveless red blouse. I corralled my hair in a ponytail holder and put on some lipstick. I wanted to make a good impression with the principal, Mrs. Dremstein. I hadn't been her first choice to fill this teaching position, and I wanted her to see she'd hired the right person for the job.

Uncle Tim drove his truck to Tipperary with Mom and me wedged in beside him. We chatted until we reached city limits where twenty-three miles of winding, washboard gravel turned to pavement. Uncle Tim dropped us off in front of the Tipperary County school building, which housed grades kindergarten through twelve. “You two go in and sign the contract while I buy a rattlesnake shovel.”

My heart pounded. I broke into a cold sweat as we entered the building and walked to the office. Inside the principal handed me my contract. My knees began to shake when I read through it. Once I signed this, there was no turning back. I’d be on my own. In a town full of strangers. I breathed in and out until my knees stopped knocking. I wrote my name with the care and concentration of a kid completing a penmanship lesson.

Mom insisted on a snapshot of Mrs. Dremstein and me. “This is a momentous occasion and one day you’ll be glad you have a photograph.”

I gritted my teeth and said cheese.

When Uncle Tim returned, he drove to the bank where I opened a checking account. The next stop was grocery shopping for Mom and me while Uncle Tim poked around in the drugstore next door.

I was steering a shopping cart toward the produce section when a woman in the next aisle said Twila Kelly’s name. I stopped in front of a bin of apples and began putting Granny Smiths in a paper bag. Very slowly.

“Her death was a crying shame. Did you hear the sheriff removed the crime tape and opened Marmarth Road yesterday?”

A man’s voice replied. “It’s about time. People were getting mighty tired of driving the long way to town while he poked around.”

“He finally finished the castings of the tire tracks near her body,” the woman said. “Or were they footprints?”

"He found tracks on a hard-packed gravel road? Are you sure?"

"I'm simply reporting what Sonja told me." The woman sounded miffed.

My bag was full. Much as I wanted to keep eavesdropping, Mom would get suspicious if I lingered any longer. I would have to be content with the tidbit I'd picked up. The Marmarth Road was open, so I could scope out the place where Twila's body had been found.

We finished shopping and paid for the groceries. Uncle Tim met us outside and loaded our purchases and my new rattlesnake spade in the truck bed.

Mom opened the passenger door. "Jane Josephine Newell, don't even think about visiting that crime scene after Tim and I leave. You signed a contract to teach school and nothing more. Do you understand?"

"I do."

I also knew that understanding and obeying were totally different animals.

Next we stopped at the courthouse. Mom and Tim waited in the car while I went into the motor vehicle department. The woman at the counter—Anna Marie Baumgartner according to the placard in front of her—explained that drivers' licenses were issued between the hours of eight and five on the second Tuesday of each month.

I took out my pocket calendar and wrote a reminder for August ninth. "I just moved to Little Missouri and want to explore the area. Somebody told me Marmarth Road was closed. Do you know when it will open again?"

She shifted a wad of gum from one side of her mouth

to the other. "You picked the right time to ask. It opened this morning. You going up to see the oil derricks?"

"Just to explore the countryside. But now that you've piqued my interest, I've got to find them."

"Go north toward Marmarth, and you can't miss them. The oil field'll be over to the east."

I pretended to scribble the directions in the margin of the calendar. But I wrote something quite different. *Visit the crime scene. Make headlight chart.* Then I tucked the calendar in my purse, thanked Anna Marie, and joined Mom and Uncle Tim in his truck.

The twenty-three miles back to Little Missouri felt more like a hundred. Though the speed limit was fifty-five, the road was such a roller coaster of twists, turns, steep inclines, and plunging descents that the speedometer needle never got above forty-five. We were halfway to Little Missouri when Mom pointed at a butte towering above the road. "That was in the background when your nice Junior Wentworth rescued us."

My Junior Wentworth?

"He looked just like the Marlboro Man with that butte rising in the distance behind him. Don't worry, though. I didn't catch so much as a whiff of smoke or the scent of tobacco, so when he kisses you, that won't be a problem."

"Mom, will you please give it a rest!"

Junior Wentworth was handsome. Mom was right about that. But I was stuck between a rock and a hard place if he ever did ask me out. Saying no meant surrendering any chance of getting to know Junior. And boy, I wanted to get to know him. Saying yes meant hearing Mom crow "I told you so" when I told her we'd gone out.

Which meant never telling her about Junior. Easy-peasy. If my dating track record held true, there wouldn't be anything to tell.

Lunchtime was long past when we arrived in Little Missouri. I would make sandwiches, peanut butter and jelly for everyone. Except—I hit my forehead with my palm—I didn't have peanut butter. How had I spent a small fortune on groceries and forgotten to buy any?

"Uncle Tim, I need peanut butter. Would you stop at the store?"

He parked in front of the small grocery store kitty-corner from Round the Bend. "Do you mind if I join you?"

Mom unbuckled her seatbelt. "I'll come in too."

Inside, I scanned the shelves holding only the basics, the produce department stocked with wizened apples and oranges, the miniature dairy case, and the gleaming meat counter.

Mom and Uncle Tim wandered around while I picked up a jar of peanut butter and checked its sticker.

Two dollars? I cringed all the way to the cash register.

A compact, gray-haired clerk introduced himself. "Burt Kelly. Me and my wife Iva own the store. Live down the street about a block west of here. Our grandson Beau, he'll be in your class this year."

"I met him last night at the cafe. I'm so sorry about his mom. Would you like to meet before school starts to discuss anything?"

His eyes were as flat and devoid of expression as Beau's had been the night before. "The only thing to do is move on."

I wanted to grab his shoulders and shake some sense

into him. There were better ways to help Beau than to just move on. The sadness Burt wore like a cloak stopped me. Beau had lost a mother. Burt and his wife had lost a daughter. Tears welled in my eyes. I sniffed and willed them away as I set the peanut butter on the counter.

Burt keyed the price into the register. "Do you know if Velma got them repairs made at your apartment?"

How did he know about that?

A woman spoke from the back of the store. "Uh-huh. She took care of everything."

Burt raised his voice. "What'd she do?"

"She put new screws in the drawer handle and relit the stove's pilot light. That's what made the kitchen smell so gassy. Then she smeared plumbers' glue on the crack in the pipe under the bathroom sink."

A Velma look-alike, with the rough edges sanded away, came to the counter. "I'm Iva. Velma says it's a temporary fix, so go easy on the water until the new pipe comes on the mail truck from Belle Fourche." She pronounced the second part of the town's name so it rhymed with "whoosh."

I paid for the peanut butter and turned to leave. Uncle Tim and Mom stood near the door, their lips twitching. We left and as soon as we were outside, they burst into laughter.

Mom regained control first. "My little girl is the talk of the town."

Uncle Tim wiped his eyes. "Harold's going to fall out of his wheelchair in hysterics when he hears about this."

"Wull, I'll be darned." I imitated Velma's raspy voice.

With that, we gave into the giggles again and chuckled all the way home.

***

I was clearing up after lunch when loud knocking made me jump.

"I'll get it." Uncle Tim disappeared into the entryway and reappeared with our caller.

The man's head tilted at a peculiar angle, and he gazed at the soffit above the kitchen cabinets. His dark hair, gray at the temples, was clipped and combed. The skin around his eyes was pitted and scarred. He wore a plaid wool shirt too hot for the weather, and the kind of trousers Dad wore before he got sick.

He shifted his white cane to his left hand and extended his right one. "Gus Yarborough. Me and my wife Betty, we own and operate the Little Missouri Phone Company. We are at the center of this community, and nothing gets past me and my lovely bride. If you have a question about anything or anyone, you give us a call."

Mom stopped scrubbing the countertop and stared. Uncle Tim's eyes sparkled.

"Dale Cunningham says you want your phone hooked up. I did the outside work already. You want me to show you how to use it?"

I nodded.

Gus acted like he hadn't seen me.

It took me a few seconds to realize he hadn't seen me. He couldn't see me or anyone else. He was blind. I cleared my throat. "I'd appreciate that."

Gus tapped his way to the kitchen and felt for the phone. "To make a call, pick up the receiver and give the crank a twirl." He demonstrated. "When Betty answers—she runs the switchboard—you tell her who you want to talk to and she'll put the call through. Think you can do that?"

"It sounds easy enough."

"Just remember, you're on a party line with the phone in your classroom, the one in the classroom in the other trailer, and a few other houses on this side of the street. You answer the apartment phone when you hear two longs and a short. Your classroom's ring is three longs and a short. The one across the way is four longs and a short. Got it?"

"I think so."

"Why don't you use the school phone and give it a try? Tell Betty to call the apartment."

I trotted to the classroom phone, lifted the receiver, and gave the crank a tentative twirl.

A reedy voice came through loud and clear. "Wittwe Missowi switchboard. How can I hep you?"

I held out the receiver and stared at it. What had she said?

I put it to my ear again. "I beg your pardon?"

"I'm the switchboad operator. How can I hep you?"

Gus bellowed from the kitchen. "Tell her to connect you to the apartment."

"Would you please connect me to the school apartment phone?"

"My pweasure. Nice to make your acquaintance, Miss Newew."

"Nice to meet you too."

A click and a ring later, Gus picked up the apartment phone. "You want to practice again?"

"No need. I think I've got it." I put the receiver in the cradle and went back to the apartment.

Gus led us outside and pointed to the telephone pole near my car. "A bad wind from the northwest'll tangle those wires and make your phone worse than useless. When that happens, you make a beeline to our place. I'll get here quick as I can to climb the pole and put things right." He extended his cane, descended the landing steps, and crossed the playground.

As he crossed the playground, I cupped my hands around my mouth. "Where do you live?"

He waved with his free hand. "In the shack near the Forest Service. The one with the mule out front."

I waited for Mom's comment.

"The one with the mule out front. Why am I not surprised?"

I had to agree with her. Just this once.

Chapter 6

Uncle Tim ushered us inside. "Anyone ready for another adventure?"

I tripped on the throw rug in the entryway and bent to straighten it. "Can you top a blind telephone lineman and a phone operator with a speech impediment?"

Mom put her hands on her hips. "Murderers and rattlesnake spades."

"You can stay here and worry, Doris. But I'm going exploring. Merle said the buttes west of town are full of hiking trails and picnic areas."

I pointed to the bulging garbage bags in the kitchen. "Do we have time to go to the dump first?"

Uncle Tim checked his watch. "Sure, if you don't mind a late supper. Or we could roast hot dogs at the buttes."

I was packing the cooler when Merle hallooed outside. I let him in.

"You got a Kodak?"

A Kodak? "You mean a camera?"

"That's what I said, a Kodak."

"What for?"

"I been wantin' a picture of my Snippy. Best milker I ever had."

"Well, we're just leaving for a hike in the buttes."

"The Long Pines?" He limped outside and squinted at the cloudless sky. "Blamed arthritis in my hip's acting up. You best get on your way and shut them windows before you go. It'll storm 'fore nightfall." He descended the landing stairs and made his slow way home.

Uncle Tim came out with the cooler. "Get in the driver's seat, Jane. You could use a little more practice driving around this country."

I got behind the wheel. Mom scooted in next to me, the rattlesnake spade between her knees.

Uncle Tim got in beside her. "You're gonna do just fine, Jane. Just take it slow."

When we arrived at the dump, Uncle Tim hopped out and directed me as I backed up to the edge of the pit. I cut the engine and got out. Mounds of trash bags, broken furniture, and lumber were piled in a hole about as long and wide as my apartment. Rats scurried among the refuse.

Mom shuddered. "When we get home, we'll need to burn our clothes."

"Are you overreacting a little, Mom?"

"All right, then. We'll wash them. With bleach. At the highest temperature setting."

"It's a deal."

Mom handed out work gloves. Uncle Tim climbed into the truck bed and handed us cardboard boxes, packing materials, and other odd bits that hadn't survived the move. I was sweating hard when an ancient pickup truck approached, circled around, and began to back up.

Uncle Tim jumped down, waved the driver closer, and gestured for him to stop when the truck's rear end was three feet from the pit's edge.

A very tall, very thin man stepped from the cab. Gray temples peeked from the edge of his feed cap. His long-sleeved, plaid flannel shirt was buttoned to the throat. His heavy-duty dungarees, and thick boots made me start sweating again.

"I thank you, sir." His voice was too deep for his thin frame. "Arvid Drent."

"Tim Moy. This is my sister-in-law, Doris Newell, and her daughter, Jane."

"You be the new schoolteacher. Merle Laird's been singing your praises." Arvid shook our hands in turn.

I wagged a finger. "We've heard about you too. From what Merle said about how you tormented Velma Albright when she was a girl, I'm surprised her hair didn't turn white."

"It did." Arvid heaved a bag into the pit. "She dyes it."

We made short work of dumping our trash and then helped Arvid. A bag slipped through my hands and split open at my feet. A wrinkled scrap of paper fell out, and I picked it up. It was a letter written with a shaky hand and splotched with water stains. I brought the paper closer and examined it. A few lines down, an old-fashioned capital "T" sat in front of a cursive "w." A stain obscured the letters behind the "Tw". The first letter after the stain was "a."

"Tw—a" Twila?

I glanced around. Mom wasn't watching.

I folded the paper and pushed it into the back pocket of my jeans.

When Arvid's truck bed was empty, Mom opened a paper grocery sack. "Drop your gloves in this."

I detoured in front of Arvid's truck and checked his lights. Not a crack in them. I joined the others and tossed my gloves in the sack.

Mom threw it into the dump and distributed disinfectant wipes. "Scrub between your fingers and under your nails. I doubt we'll be able to wash our hands at the picnic grounds."

I turned to Arvid. "You're welcome to join us. We're roasting hot dogs and making s'mores. There's plenty."

"Where's yur picnic gonna be?"

"The Long Pines."

Arvid's face lit up like a sunrise. "I know every inch of them buttes. Spent purt near every summer I was a kid tramping through 'em hunting for lost calves."

Uncle Tim whistled. "You must have some stories to tell! How about I ride with you?"

"Git on in." The men walked to Arvid's truck. Mom and I took our places in Uncle Tim's vehicle and trailed them into the Long Pines.

"You are a mystery, Jane Newell." Mom crossed her arms. "You won't give the time of day to that nice Junior Wentworth—you know he reminded me of your father, the way he put me right at ease and kept the conversation going—but when a washed-up, old rancher shows up at the dump, you invite him to supper like he's your long lost friend."

"I invited Arvid because he reminded me of Dad."

"What in the world do you mean?"

"They're both lonely."

She remained silent for the rest of the drive.

At the picnic grounds, the scent of pines filled the air. Cactus and prairie grass mingled at our feet.

Uncle Tim nudged me. "This place remind you of anything, Janie-Jo?"

"It sure does."

I pictured my uncle behind the wheel of his Pontiac Catalina. Aunt Wanda sat beside him in front.

Their three daughters, my brother, my sister, and I bounced on the seat behind them. The orange and white pop-up camper hitched to the car swayed in the wind.

"Look to your left, kids." Uncle Tim tapped on the window and pulled into a campsite. "That's where we're staying tonight. Everybody out."

We poured out of the backseat. My brother and our cousins ran to the play area. My sister and I stayed behind to help Aunt Wanda make sandwiches.

I could still taste the bologna on white bread. With mayonnaise. And tomatoes. Far more exotic fare than what Mom served at home. And I could still smell the air as Aunt Wanda tucked me in at night in their pop-up camper nestled in a pine grove.

But camping with my uncle and aunt was more than bologna sandwiches and sleeping in the woods. For my sister, brother, and me it was trip to a different world. One not limited to places where Mom could push Dad's wheelchair.

My heart swelled with love for my uncle and his

family. A thousand thank you notes would be but a drop in a bucket compared to what they had given me. I groped for the right words and came up short. But they would have to do.

"It reminds me of the best summer of my childhood." I squeezed his hand. "The very best."

Arvid suggested we climb Capitol Rock. "General Crook's soldiers named it after the Capitol Building in Washington, D.C. They carved their initials all over it during the Indian wars in the 1800s."

Mom picked up the spade. "In case of rattlesnakes."

Arvid nodded. "You be a wise woman, Mrs. Newell."

When we reached the summit of Capitol Rock, Uncle Tim rubbed a finger against it. "Is this limestone?"

"That's what I've heard, but I ain't no ge-ol-ee-gist." Arvid scrambled to his feet. "I do know the view from the top be the purtiest thing I ever saw."

He was right. The town of Little Missouri huddled near the river to the east. Stands of gnarled cottonwoods followed the path of the river. To the south, dark hills covered with evergreens swallowed the river whole. Miles and miles of rolling prairie stretched into Montana and melted into the west.

The distance made me dizzy. "How far away is the horizon?"

Mom guessed twenty miles. Uncle Tim thought it was closer forty or fifty.

Arvid sat on a boulder. "At least that. Some folks claim they can see seventy on a clear day."

Gray shadows shrouded the horizon. I backed away from the edge. Nooks and crannies dotted the landscape, a multitude of hiding places for a vehicle with a cracked headlight. The wind freshened, chill and brisk. I shivered.

Uncle Tim started down the path. "Time for supper."

The others followed him. Still dizzy, I sat and scooted down on my backside. Balance had never been my strong suit, but it hadn't caused my vertigo. The vastness of the landscape was messing with my equilibrium. A butt full of cactus spines was a small price to pay to get away from it.

My equilibrium returned in the glow of our campfire. Exercise and dry air whetted our appetites. Before long we were devouring half-burned hot dogs and s'mores. The first raindrop fell while I roasted a marshmallow for Arvid.

Uncle Tim took one look at the black clouds rolling above the treetops and began stuffing food into the cooler. Arvid doused the fire. Mom and I collected trash, matches, and the spade.

The abrupt shift from sun to storm made me jumpy again. Goosebumps prickled my skin. Arvid dashed to his truck, and we ducked into Uncle Tim's as the rain began in earnest.

When we got home I ran to the apartment and shut the windows. I should have listened to Merle.

A half hour later, Uncle Tim was asleep on the couch and Mom and I were in bed. The rain drumming on the roof drowned out the coyotes. Mom's breathing slowed and she began to snore.

Unable to sleep, I rolled out of bed and took the pocket calendar from my purse. I crept into my classroom and turned on the desk lamp. I added *talk to the Yarboroughs* to the notes in the margin and *examine*

Arvid's letter with magnifying glass from box behind art supplies. I found paper, a ruler, and a pencil in the desk and fashioned a headlight chart. I put Arvid's name in the first row of the first column and wrote "headlights intact" in the second column, secured it to a clipboard, and put it face down in a desk drawer.

I switched off the light and stared into the darkness. Mom and Uncle Tim were leaving in the morning. Tomorrow I would be on my own in a town where store clerks knew more about my comings and goings than I did. Where my mother had taken a fancy to the Marlboro Man. Where a lonely bachelor rancher penned indecipherable letters to a dead woman. Where a boy had been orphaned. Where his mother's killer had yet to answer for her death.

Tomorrow I'd start the headlight chart in earnest. I'd have to be careful not to make the gossips in Little Missouri suspicious. Beau was worth the risk.

CHAPTER 7

The sun was an orange ball on the eastern horizon when I opened the living room windows the next morning. Fresh air poured into the apartment and chased away the dark thoughts from the night before. Rain had scrubbed the leaves clean and coaxed green shoots to sprout from brown clumps of grass. The sky was a clear, dazzling blue.

I served bacon and eggs for breakfast and whisked away Mom and Uncle Tim's plates as soon as they finished. "You should pack up and hit the road soon. You know Dad'll be watching the clock until you get home."

A few minutes later, their suitcases were the lone occupants of the trailer hitched to Uncle Tim's pick up. We stood beside the truck, gripped by an awkward silence.

Mom blew her nose. "You'll be so far from home. We'll lose touch."

"I'll call every weekend when the rates are low."

"What if the phone system is too old to handle long distance?"

"I'll write letters. You'll write back. And I'll be home for Thanksgiving."

"What if your car breaks down?"

"I'll call Junior Wentworth."

Mom's face paled. "Promise to thump the rattlesnake spade on the landing before you set one foot outside."

"I promise."

"And to lock your apartment and your car at all times."

"I promise."

She loosed her final arrow. "And to leave the investigating to the sheriff."

I couldn't promise that, so I deflected instead. "You know what teaching is like. It will keep me busy."

"Probably too busy to make any friends. Or have a social life." Mom pulled me close, buried her face in my shoulder, and wept until my shirt was damp. I never knew what to do when she got like this.

"Doris, we have to get going. Otherwise, you won't be home in time to take care of Harold. You promised Jeff you'd be there to relieve him before he goes to work."

Bless you, Uncle Tim. Bless you, bless you, bless you for mentioning my little brother.

Mom squeezed me hard and let go.

"Doris, you and Harold raised Jane right. She's gonna be just fine." Uncle Tim nudged Mom toward the passenger door and shut it after she got in.

Uncle Tim and I walked to the driver's side. He rested a hand on the door handle. "Mark my words, Janie-Jo. You'll have plenty of friends before you know it." He cocked his head in the direction of Merle's house. "You already have an old rancher half-smitten with you. The young ones will start coming around once they get wind of you."

His expression changed to the one he reserved for talking politics, religion, and protecting his family. "That spade's heavy enough to ward off more than snakes. You'd be wise to pack it along whenever you're driving alone. Will you promise me that?"

"I promise."

He got in, saluted, and started the engine. I watched until the truck turned the corner by the gas station and vanished from sight. Then I went to my classroom, grabbed my clipboard, and hurried outside to take a survey of all the headlights in town. If people asked what I was doing, I could say I was sorting out who lived where and ask for their names. Nothing could go wrong with a simple plan like that, right?

Chapter 8

The town consisted of only five blocks, and canvasing them took less than a half hour. I walked along the street that went by Merle's house. I rounded the corner beyond it and passed a couple tired-looking houses. A block later on the edge of town, I came upon a clapboard church in good repair. Its steeple was easily the tallest structure in Little Missouri, but it had no sign to indicate when services were or what denomination it was.

More curious than the church was the lot across the alley. Chickens clucked behind the tall, board fence surrounding of the lot. Crossed sticks draped with old shirts had been nailed to the boards like crucified scare-crows. The fence on the far side of the property butted up against a tiny, tar-paper shack. Too small to be a house. More like a gardening shed. A curl of smoke rose from a metal pipe in the roof.

Someone lived there? I almost dropped my clipboard.

I reversed course and headed east past another church, this one with a sign identifying it as the Catholic church, but with no mention of when Mass was held. I circled the few remaining blocks dotted with trailer homes and small frame houses in need of paint, their yards in need of mowing. Along the way I recorded the license plate numbers of three trucks with broken and discolored headlights. I saw no one, but from the number of curtains that twitched in houses as I walked by, whoever lived in them had seen me.

Next I walked toward the Forest Service compound on the southeast edge of town. Government vehicles sat in the parking lot on one side of the Ranger Station building. On the other side, a driveway led to the garages behind the ranger houses. While no one had stopped me on my trek around town, the Forest Service staff might not appreciate me walking around their premises without permission. So much for my foolproof plan.

The Ranger Station door opened, and I didn't hang around to see who it was. I headed east and crossed the bridge at a brisk pace. My muscles, knotted after days of driving and unpacking, relaxed. When the nape of my neck began to sweat, I turned toward town. Halfway to the bridge I noticed a lane on the north side of the road. A lush lilac hedge and a row of well-tended Russian olive trees lined the lane's east side. Beyond the windbreak, a low, ranch-style house of tan brick nestled beneath tall cottonwoods. I wanted to walk down the lane for a closer look, not to check headlights, but because the house's tidy charm made me homesick for Iowa.

My bare arms tingled. If I stayed outside much longer, I'd be sporting a sunburn tomorrow. I headed for town and heard children whooping and hollering as I crossed the river. The commotion came from the yard of the house on the corner of the Forest Service compound. A short, plump woman was hanging jeans on a clothesline, and a half-dozen kids were chasing each other around the fenced yard.

I knew her! Pam Barkley and her husband Dan put me up when I came for my interview. They treated me like royalty and wrote to congratulate me when I got the job. Maybe I could talk her into a tour of the Forest Service campus.

I waved and she came to the fence.

"I'm so glad you accepted the position on such short notice. The other gal was moving into the school apartment one day, and she moved out the next. Word around town is that some ski bum in Aspen got her pregnant, but who knows? Do you have time for a glass of iced tea and a look around the compound?"

This was way too easy. "Yes, please."

The iced tea hit the spot. After a second glass, Pam took me around the compound. She didn't question the clipboard or my scribbling. Not that there was much to scribble. The vehicles, with National Forest Service logos prominently displayed on their doors, were in pristine condition. Not a broken headlight in the bunch.

"Why is this one different?" I circled a truck with a South Dakota Games, Fish, & Parks seal on the driver's side door. The paint was dinged up, but the headlights were not.

"Oh, that belongs to the state trapper. He's employed by the state, but does a lot with the rangers here. Don't ask me what, though."

After the tour ended, I declined Pam's offer of more tea.

"Would you join us at church tomorrow and come to Sunday dinner?"

I wanted to say no. After all, I had wasted years going to church, following every "thou shalt" and "thou shalt not" in the Bible. Every night at bedtime, I asked God to heal my father. I prayed the same prayer night after night. But Dad didn't get better. He got worse. Even so, I prayed up a storm. Until the day I walked into the bathroom and found him huddled on the floor by the toilet, feces smearing the floor.

He gazed at the wall and spoke in a monotone. "I fell off the toilet."

"It's okay, Dad. I'll call Uncle Tim."

His jaw clenched. "It's not okay. A daughter shouldn't see her father like this."

Uncle Tim got there as fast as he could and took over. While he gave Dad a bath, I went to my bedroom, found my Bible, and threw it away.

I opened my mouth to say I didn't go to church, but opted for Iowa nice. "I don't want to put you out."

"Put us out? Dan's grilling hamburgers, and I'm making potato salad."

My mouth watered.

"Bring your clipboard and write down the names of everyone who comes to church."

And get a look at their headlights. "What time?"

"Ten-thirty." She pointed to where the tiny steeple of the church stabbed the sky near the tar paper shack. "Right over there."

A ruckus broke out beside the sandbox. Two boys

rolled in the grass, fists flailing. Dogs barked. Kids screamed, "Fight! Fight!"

Pam ran toward the fracas and I walked to my apartment, studying the meager notes recorded on the chart. Maybe I was barking up the wrong tree. In the apartment, I opened the pocket calendar to August and reviewed what I'd written.

What should I do next? I could examine Arvid's letter from the dump. But until I had more than one lead to follow up on, there was no reason to stir things up by asking questions.

Which left a visit to the crime scene. Why hadn't I asked Bud Sternquist where it happened on Marmarth Road exactly? I was out of practice and my investigative skills were rusty.

I set the clipboard and calendar on the table, dug Arvid's letter from my jeans pocket, and took everything into my classroom. I dragged the box from behind the art supplies and opened it. My fingers twitched as I laid the clipboard, the calendar, and the letter on top of the items I'd packed with exquisite care before leaving Iowa.

Hang on a little longer. I shut the flaps of the box and gave it a pat before returning it to its hiding place. *We'll be working again before you know it.* Then I marched into my classroom with single-minded purpose. It was high time to tend to my paying job.

Chapter 9

I stood in the doorway and breathed in the odors of crayon wax, textbooks, chalk dust, construction paper, mimeograph fluid, and rubber playground balls. Those smells had thrilled me since the first day of kindergarten. My teacher, Mrs. Fischer, distributed scratch paper and scotch tape with a free hand, commodities my mother hoarded at home. Then and there I decided to be a teacher, a choice that didn't waver until a child psychology class led to a new interest. Today however, the heady aroma of my classroom—*my classroom*—wove its spell and drew me in.

I found cleaning supplies in a cupboard under the sink and filled a bucket with water. I made steady progress wiping down desks and scrubbing shelves until my stomach protested. A glance at the clock said it was four-thirty. No wonder I was hungry. My last meal had been breakfast with Mom and Tim.

A knock sounded at the door and I went to see who it was. Liv McDonald, the upper grade teacher who had attended my interview last spring, stood outside. She was stout and short with dark hair pulled back in a ponytail, striking dark brown eyes and a tan, ageless face. She could have been thirty-five. Or she could have been fifty.

A little girl peeked out from behind her. Her hair was scraped into tight pigtails. Her blue eyes met mine before she lowered her head.

"This is Keeva. She's been wanting to meet you since her grandparents said they saw you at the cafe the other day." She tugged at her daughter's arm. "Say hi to your new teacher."

Keeva stepped forward, but didn't look up.

"Come on now. Say hello. Just like we practiced."

The girl raised her head. "Good afternoon, Miss Newell."

Miss Newell. Would I ever get used to being called that?

"Good afternoon, Keeva. I'm happy to meet you."

She ducked behind her mom again.

"You were all she could talk about the entire way from our place to town, and now she wants to hide. She can't wait until kindergarten starts in January." Liv sighed. "I stopped by to ask you to come to supper out at our place tonight around six."

My stomach growled and my face went hot.

Liv laughed, her beautiful brown eyes sparkling. "Is that a yes?"

"It's a yes. What can I bring?"

"My other daughter made a pie. Could you bring ice cream?"

"Of course. Where's your ranch?"

"Head north out of town on the Marmarth Road.

We're about six miles out, on the east side of the road. Name's on the mailbox."

"So you're on the same road where Twi. . ."—I glanced at Keeva—"where there was an accident?"

"You heard about her already? That didn't take long. We're the first mailbox beyond the fence posts with crime tape blowing every which way. You can't miss it. See you soon."

So now I knew the location of the accident. I was about to drive right by it.

First, a shower and clean clothes. Next, the grocery store. Then I'd be off with time and daylight to spare. I was about to poke around the crime scene. For what, I wasn't sure. But why should that stop me?

***

Clipboard in hand, I studied the road. A flashlight dangled from my belt loop and the rattlesnake spade leaned against the Beetle's front bumper. Nothing conspicuous about me. No siree bob.

I'd been standing here too long. Any minute someone would drive by and see me. I had two options. Go to the McDonald's ranch now. Or come up with a plausible reason to be here.

I checked my watch. Five-forty. Too early to go to Liv's. I scanned my surroundings for a reason to hang around. The fence posts on the west side of the road looked promising. They weren't manufactured posts, but a hodgepodge of salvaged tree limbs, a procession of twisted, knobby wooden soldiers standing sentry next to the pasture.

I opened the glove box and hung my camera around my neck. Using the spade for a walking stick, I inched down and across the ditch. I chose a post riddled with knobs and twists, framed a shot, and squeezed the shutter. The camera flashed and light bounced off something at the base of the post. I reached down to see what it was.

Don't be stupid!

I snatched my hand away. I had almost stuck it into what could be the den of a snake or some other disgusting critter. I scrambled up the side of the ditch and rummaged in the Beetle's backseat. When I found a metal coat hanger, I bent it into a long-handled hook. I returned to my fencepost, thumped the ground with the spade, and counted to ten. Nothing happened. I did it again. Same result. I poked at the base of the post with the tip of the hanger, and it slipped inside.

Well, well, well. I'd found a hidey hole. I steadied my grip and went fishing. After a few tries I reeled in a wrinkled pack of Lucky Strikes. Its cellophane wrapper must have reflected the camera flash. I lifted the lid. Inside were four cigarettes and a piece of paper. I pulled it out and read what was written on it. TK 7012795556.

I climbed out of the ditch and got into my car. I switched on the flashlight and reread the note. TK for Twila Kelly. Ten digits, most likely a phone number. Was it her phone number or someone else's? Who had hidden it? And why so close to where she'd been killed?

I took the cigarette pack to my car and laid it on the passenger seat. Then I started the Beetle and made a U-turn. When I arrived at home I would call Liv, say something had come up, and call this phone number. She would understand. But would Keeva? Or her sister, the pie maker? I couldn't disappoint them.

I slowed, made another U-ie and headed north again hoping the pie would be cherry and that it would be delicious.

Chapter 10

I turned onto the McDonald's lane and parked beside their mailbox. I shoved the cigarette pack into a mitten I'd found under the front seat and stuffed the mitten in the glove box. I drove down the lane to where Keeva sat perched on a huge horse in front of a white frame house. When I got out of the car she dismounted and looped the reins around a fence post.

She stroked the horse. "Miss Newell, you gotta meet Baby. Baby, this is Miss Newell. She's gonna be my teacher in one hunnert and thirty-nine days."

"You know how many days until kindergarten starts?"

"Uh-huh. I count them on the calendar every day. It is a lot of days." Her pigtails quivered. "Wanna see my kitties?"

Liv appeared in the doorway, pushing strands of dark hair that had escaped from her ponytail away from her face. "Keeva, don't you dare take Miss Newell to the barn before supper. Come inside and wash your hands."

Keeva escorted me inside. I gave Liv the square of ice cream and sniffed the air before speaking to the heavy-set man at the stove. "Whatever is in that pot, I want some."

"I'm Axel, Liv's husband. Hope you like your chili spicy." His blue eyes twinkled with welcome. He was average height and lifted the pot off the burner with muscular, meaty hands. His hair was already going grey, though he couldn't have been more than forty.

We exchanged small talk while their children—Brock, a cocky blond of fourteen, Rosalie, who surely was the spitting image of her dark-haired mother at age eight, and Keeva—quibbled about where to move the jumble of books and papers on the table and who would carry the dishes from the kitchen.

"Stop arguing and get it done now!" Axel's tone was steely.

Before long, we were at the table eating eye-watering chili and mouth-watering cornbread.

I refused second helpings. "I'm saving room for dessert."

Rosalie slipped into the kitchen and returned with a cherry pie.

Yes!

"Teacher brought ice cream too." Keeva jumped up. "I'll get it."

"Your pie looks like it could win a blue ribbon." I tasted it. "Make that grand champion purple."

The kids scattered after dessert and Axel cleared the dishes. Liv and I sat at the table and talked shop. She offered to drive me to Tipperary for the inservice the Thursday before school started.

I said yes before she finished her sentence.

Careful, Jane. You don't want her to think you're desperate.

Next, she showed me how she did her lesson plans and organized her grade book. She waited while I made sketches of her forms.

"Do you have any tips about how to get on Velma's good side? She seems a little"—I searched for the right word—"crusty."

Liv snorted. "She's never been the friendliest person. But she turned real disagreeable after Twila Kelly died. I saw her driving to Marmarth and back more than once. Always way too fast. Sometimes I wonder if she hit Twila." The light left her brown eyes and she looked tired.

Keeva wandered in. "Mommy, can I take Miss Newell to see the kitties now?"

Liv went into the kitchen and returned with a pan of table scraps. Keeva took it and led me to the barn. She set the pan on the floor. Six kittens appeared as if by magic.

My mind wandered as she picked them up one by one and recited their names. Could Liv's suspicion possibly be true? Would she dare say such a thing without good reason?

"Miss Newell, are you paying attention?"

"Absolutely." I made a show of checking my watch. "It's getting late. We better go in."

Twilight enveloped us when we left the barn. "Who lives there?" I pointed at lights twinkling to the north and west.

"Um, the Sternquists, I think."

More lights glowed directly across the road to the west. "How about over there?"

"Oh, that's where Arvid lives. Mom says he's a lonely old man. Rosalie and me used to ride over to see him, but not anymore."

"Why not?"

"Mommy says it's too dangerous because somebody hit Beau's mommy on the road between our lane and Arvid's."

I shuddered and took Keeva's fuzzy-with-cat-hair hand. "Your mom's right. The road is dangerous."

The blare of a horn, a dull thud, and the tinkle of breaking glass invaded the darkness. Keeva pulled away, rushed to the house, and ran inside. I was right behind her.

"Mom! Dad! We heard a crash."

Her parents came running.

Axel snatched a jacket from a hook. "What direction?"

Keeva pointed toward the road.

"Brock's checking stock out that way. Hope he ain't done something crazy." He ran for the truck.

"I'll come too." Liv grabbed her coat and looked at me. "Will you stay with the girls?" She left without waiting for an answer.

"Brock's always doing something crazy." Keeva closed the door. "He likes crashing into stuff."

"Are you exaggerating a little?"

"No, she's not." Rosalie came in and wiped the table with a damp cloth. "Brock acts like the ranch truck is a bumper car. He's been banging it up pretty regular since I was a little kid. Dad and Mom made him buy a bunch of extra headlights and taillights in Belle a while back 'cause they got sick of paying for them. But he doesn't learn. Wanna play a game?"

A truck roared up the lane as we started our second game of Candy Land. The girls didn't look when their parents and brother came inside, but I did. Brock had a goose egg on his forehead, Axel looked ready to spit nails, and Liv marched into the kitchen, her ponytail completely undone.

"Is everybody okay?"

"He hit an antelope." Liv dumped the contents of an ice cube tray into a plastic bag and wrapped it in a dish towel.

Rosalie scowled. "Was he smoking again? Or just driving like a maniac?"

The card I picked up off the stack went flying.

"Get in your room." Axel steered Brock down the hallway.

Liv followed after them. "Back in a minute."

"Rosalie, were you trying to get your brother into more trouble than he's already in? He doesn't really smoke, does he?"

"Whenever he can get away with it." She drew a double orange and took the lead. "He hides his Lucky Strikes outside so Dad and Mom won't find them."

Liv came into the kitchen.

I rose. "How's Brock?"

"He'll be fine. But he won't be driving anytime soon. He's a menace behind the wheel." She glanced at the clock. "It's getting late. Girls, get ready for bed."

Keeva hugged me. "Good night, Miss Newell."

"Good night, Keeva." I hugged her back. "Thanks for the pie, Rosalie. Liv, thanks to you too."

"You don't need to thank me for saddling you with the girls while we chased Brock."

"I didn't mind. We had fun."

I went to my car, pulled out my flashlight, and switched it on. Then I tiptoed past the pickup trucks parked on the gravel patch in front of the house. The headlight covers on the truck Liv had driven to Little Missouri earlier were intact, as were those on the newer model next to it. I paused in front of the third truck. It had seen better days. A chill settled in my bones at the sight of its light covers. Both were cracked. Both were discolored. Both made Brock a prime suspect.

On the drive home I cranked up the heat, but I couldn't get warm. In my bedroom, I put on warm pajamas. I carried two blankets to the living room, spread them on the couch, and crawled under them. Still trembling, I drifted off to sleep.

Chapter 11

An ear-splitting racket woke me. I bolted upright. My fingertips rubbed against nubby upholstery. Oh, right. I was on the couch. Gray light came through the windows. The horrendous noise tore through the silence again. It came from either my bedroom or the spare room.

Someone was in my house! I realized I'd forgotten to lock the door last night. I yanked the granny-square afghan over my head and curled into a ball. If I didn't move, maybe the intruder wouldn't notice me. I listened for footsteps, heavy breathing, a doorknob turning. Nothing. The air under the afghan grew stifling. I poked my nose through a hole where the yarn had unraveled and took a deep breath. Dust and yarn fuzz tickled my nostrils and I sneezed.

So much for not being noticed.

I threw off the afghan, crept to the kitchen, and grabbed the butcher knife. I tiptoed to the bedroom door. The grating noise invaded my house again. I froze.

When the screeching died away, I pressed an ear to the door and held the knife high. The sound crescendoed again and I strained to pinpoint where it came from.

I lowered the knife and stood. The noise was coming from outside, not from my bedroom. I adjusted my grip on the knife, eased into the room, and crawled across the bed on hands and knees. Then I crouched beneath the window, raised my body inch by inch, and looked through the glass.

A spiky silhouette rose above the fence that separated the school property from Merle's farm. The silhouette stretched toward the sky and the rhythmic screech pierced the air again. A beam of sunlight touched the silhouette with color.

Merle's rooster! My body went limp and I sank onto the bed. A rooster had reduced me to a quivering blob. I glanced at the clock. Five-fifteen? I hadn't been awake this early since . . . well . . . since ever.

I didn't want to make a habit of rising at dawn. But with a rooster inches from my window, what choice did I have? I picked up the knife and ran my finger along its edge. Was it sharp and sturdy enough to . . .

No! I would never hurt one of Merle's animals. How could I think such a thing? This was the warped thinking of a woman wrenched awake at an ungodly hour. A little more sleep would cure what ailed me. The rooster crowed again.

Scratch that idea. I returned the knife to its drawer in the kitchen. I needed something to do until church. I went into my classroom and scanned the room for something to keep me busy. My desk. It needed organizing. I opened drawers one by one and emptied them onto the desktop. The last drawer contained a thick Western Dakotas phone book.

I went to the entryway and took a basket of hats and gloves from the top shelf. I dumped them onto the floor and hunted for the mitten I'd buried at the bottom of the basket last night. I picked it up and shook it until the cigarette pack fell out. I took the pack to my desk. The cellophane crinkled as I withdrew the note hidden inside. Then I opened the phone book, flipped to the area code map, and searched for 701. There it was, smack dab in the middle of North Dakota, the only area code for the entire state. I fanned the pages until I found the section for Marmarth. The phone prefix was 279.

The Marmarth listings took up only one page in the phone book. I ran a finger down the first column searching for 279-5556. Nothing. I moved on to the next column and there it was. Third line from the top. It was the phone number for the Marmarth Bar and Grill.

I whooped and hugged the phone book. It was too early to call the number. I marked the page, set the phone book aside, and finished organizing my desk. When that was done I moved the clipboard, the Lucky Strike package and its note, along with Arvid's water-splotched letter into the scarred, oak file cabinet in my classroom. I locked the file cabinet with the key I'd found in my desk. I shut and locked the classroom windows and doors before doing the same in my apartment.

No more ignoring Mom and Uncle Tim's advice. The evidence I was collecting had to be protected. A killer was running loose and another careless oversight could be deadly.

Chapter 12

With my fortress locked tight and my desk tidy, I crossed over into my apartment and fixed breakfast. Then I got ready for church, twisted my hair into a banana clip, put on a white cotton granny skirt with a sleeveless, pink cotton shirt. I pushed my bare feet into worn, beige huaraches, took the clipboard from its hiding place, and walked to church. Pam and her husband, Dan, met me at the entrance.

"Good to see you again." He touched the shoulders of the boy and girl beside him. "Bennan. Cora. You remember Miss Newell?"

They greeted me like an old friend. We chatted until a pickup truck pulled up. Its headlights were in working order. The cab door opened. Tiege popped out, raced down the sidewalk, and collided with me.

Cookie trailed behind him. "Slow down, Tiege. You're at church, not the horse corral."

Dan held the door and we entered the foyer. Tiege ran past us and Cookie shook her head. "From the way he acts, you'd think he hadn't seen a friend in months."

Two men came in after us. The first was the sheriff. The second was dressed in black except for a patch of white at his throat.

The Methodist preachers in Iowa didn't wear clerical collars. I didn't think any Methodist preacher did.

The preacher brushed dust off his jacket and trousers. "I blew a tire between here and Tipperary. If the sheriff hadn't come along, you'da been on your own this morning." He rushed into the sanctuary. "Let's get started, shall we?"

Pam Barkley pointed to the empty space beside Cora. I slid in beside her though there were plenty of empty pews to pick from. If the turnout was always this poor, the pastor was wasting his time. The Sternquists and the sheriff sat in the pew in front of us. Something in Bud's features and the sheriff's, perhaps the set of their shoulders, said they were related. The pastor opened with prayer. We stood for a hymn. Someone tapped my shoulder as the last verse began. I looked up. It was Junior Wentworth, hat in hand. His clothes were neater and cleaner than when he pulled our trailer out of the ditch. More expensive too. He motioned for me to move over and squeezed in beside me. He sang. I didn't. As we sat down, Pam caught sight of Junior and wiggled her eyebrows.

The gossips would have a field day with this.

While the sermon droned on, I composed my phone call to the Marmarth Bar and Grill, rejecting one version after another. Junior bumped my elbow and passed me an open hymnal. I stood and looked around while the others sang. The pews were crowded now, and music filled the sanctuary. When had they all come in?

After the benediction, Pam walked with me to the foyer. She peppered me with questions. Did I know Junior Wentworth? How did we meet? Had he asked me out?

When she ran out of questions and the cluster of people around the pastor dispersed, she introduced me to him. "Jane, this is Jon Petersen. Pastor Petersen, this is the new school teacher, Jane Newell."

"Welcome to Tipperary County." He consulted his wristwatch. "I wish there was more time to talk about what brought you here, but I have to be at Capitol Lutheran in twenty minutes. I've got to go." He gave my hand a quick shake and nodded to Junior, who held the door open for him.

I turned to Pam. "Is he Lutheran or Methodist?"

"Lutheran by training," she replied. "But he pastors this church, Capitol Lutheran south of town, and the Congregational Church in Tipperary. Between the three congregations, we can almost afford a full time pastor." She bent her head close to mine. "Don't look now, but Junior Wentworth is watching you. I think he wants to talk to you."

My insides turned to mush.

"He can wait a little longer. There's someone else you should meet." Pam led me to the sheriff and touched his elbow. "Rick, this is Jane Newell."

His eyes widened. "You're the teacher from Iowa!"

In the periphery of my vision, Junior shrugged and left.

"Why didn't you say that the other day?" the sheriff asked.

I turned my attention to him. "Say what?"

"That you're the new teacher."

"You got in your car so fast I didn't have a chance."

"Guilty as charged." He shifted his weight from one foot to the other. "My little brother won't let me hear the end of it if he finds out that I met his teacher and didn't know it."

Tiege ran over. "Dad and Mom gotta get home to check a sick heifer. Can I ride with you?" He pulled the sheriff toward the exit. "Mom says they won't leave until you say it's okay." The door swung closed behind them.

I turned to Pam. "They're brothers?"

"They are."

"What's his name again?"

We went outside, and I checked the row of parked trucks as we walked along the sidewalk. Not a broken light in the bunch.

"Rick Sternquist. Some people think he's too young and inexperienced to handle Twila Kelly's case."

"Maybe they're right."

"I've known him for years. He's a good man. I think people want someone to blame, and Rick is an easy target as long as Twila's killer is free. Are you keeping your doors locked?" She linked her arm through mine, and we strolled down the street. "You can never be too careful."

Was she in cahoots with my mother?

***

The Barkleys sent me home after Sunday dinner with enough leftovers to last a week. Extra hamburgers, tomatoes from their garden, and thick slices of chocolate cake. The food more than redeemed the hour I'd wasted at church.

Once I'd stored everything in the fridge, I picked up the phone and asked Betty to ring the 701 number from the cigarette pack.

"This is a private call, Betty. Would you please hang up after you connect me?"

She obliged.

The call was picked up on the first ring. "Marmarth Bar and Grill."

"Oh, I'm sorry. I thought this was Twila Kelly's number."

The voice on the line hardened. "Is this some kind of joke?"

"Not at all. Twila said to call this number, and she would give me the address where I should send her birthday present. It's a carton of her favorite cigarettes. Lucky Strikes. Perfect, huh?"

"Ma'am, you got the brand right. And this is where she took calls. But she don't answer anymore. She's dead."

I hung up and paced around the living room. The number was where Twila could be reached, so initials on the note had to be hers. The cigarette pack could be hers, though that was a stretch. Brock was just as likely to have put it in the hidey hole.

I picked up the phone. "Betty, would you call my parents?"

"I'm occupied with other things."

"You can listen in this time."

"I'ww put you straight through."

Mom answered on the first ring.

"Hi, Mom. It's Jane. How was the drive home?"

"Uneventful. Your dad was glad to see me last night. He misses you, Jane."

A lump formed in my throat and my heart ached. "Can I talk to him?"

"He's taking his afternoon nap. You'll have to wait and call Saturday morning when the rates go down again."

I swallowed the lump, but it bounced up again. "I'll do that."

"Did you lock your doors last night?"

"Yes."

"Have you seen that nice Junior Wentworth again?"

"This morning." No need to tell her I'd seen him in church. That was a can of worms I didn't want to open. "But I scared him off."

"That's not funny, Jane." She never had appreciated my humor. "Oh, I think something's burning in the oven. Talk to you on Saturday."

The line went dead.

"Miss Newew, I think you have a very dry sense of humor. Would you wike me to ring with a reminder on Saturday?"

Would you *wike*? What was she saying?

Then I got it. "Oh Betty, I would *like* that very much. Is seven o'clock too early for you?"

"I'ww write it down."

Her kindness dissolved the lump in my throat and

brought tears to my eyes. I groped with the phone and the receiver landed in the cradle on the third try. Then I let the tears flow. I cried for my dad and me, for Twila and Beau, for brokenhearted children of all ages everywhere, until the river of sadness inside me ran dry and I could cry no more.

Chapter 13

Merle's rooster woke me before dawn again Monday morning, establishing the pattern for the entire week. Each day I ate a quick breakfast and walked around town with my clipboard looking for trucks with broken light covers and recording their license plate numbers. Then I returned to the trailer and worked in my classroom.

In the afternoons I tended to business. Tuesday, I ran off worksheets on the school's photocopy machine in Tipperary and got a new driver's license. While I was at the courthouse, I stopped in to see Anna Marie Baumgartner.

"I'm looking at used pickup trucks and want to check for clear titles. Can I do that from their license plate numbers?"

She took me into a room and pointed to a shelf. "Everything's recorded in those ledgers. You can have a look, but it's like searching for a needle in a haystack."

With my job starting in two days, I didn't have time for haystacks. My disappointment must have showed.

"You know," Anna Marie said, "I just got back from a training at the state capital about their new mainframe computer. They enter license plate numbers into it and the computer searches their database. Then it prints out a list of who owns what vehicle. Who holds the title. All sorts of stuff." She worked her gum. "They want us to send lists of numbers so they can run them and work out the kinks. You'd be doing me a favor if I can use what you put together."

I handed her my paper. She unfolded it and ran a finger down the list. "I'll phone them in first thing tomorrow and let you know when they send the results, okay?"

Okay and then some! I danced from the courthouse to my car. At least in my head I was dancing. People going by saw me walking down the sidewalk like a schoolteacher should.

The following day, Velma cleaned the school until it sparkled. She also issued orders about how to maintain the spit shine. "When the playground's muddy, you got to line the cloakroom floor with old newspaper and make them kids park their dirty boots and shoes on it." She jabbed a bony finger at the carpet. "Otherwise, they'll track mud in on the rug and you'll have to clean up the mess. Or better yet, make the kids do it."

"Where am I supposed to get old newspapers?"

"Guess that college you went to didn't teach you much. Just ask the kids to bring what they been collecting all summer. One more thing." She pulled her cigarettes from her pants pocket and shook one out. "If you got plans to use glue or paint or glitter on art projects, don't expect me to clean it up. Stick to crayons and paper is what I got to say." She stomped through the cloakroom and slammed the door on her way out.

I moved so the curtain hid me from view, peeked out the window, and watched her light up. She slipped the pack into her pocket and crossed the playground. Merle had been right. Velma smoked Lucky Strikes. I took the clipboard from the file cabinet and added another column to my chart. After printing "LS" at the top of the column, I wrote Brock, Velma, and Twila's names below.

Both Velma and Brock were connected to the school. Velma had keys to the trailer, and I'd seen Liv's on a hook in their kitchen. Brock could get his hands on them whenever he wanted. That meant that even when the trailer was locked they could get into my classroom. Into my apartment. It was time to add another level of security to the evidence I was gathering.

I took out a new manila folder and wrote "math games" on its tab. I put the evidence I'd gathered inside—the headlight chart, Arvid's letter, the Lucky Strike pack, and Twila's note—inside the folder. I stuck the folder in the drawer containing file after file of math worksheets. I locked the cabinet, took the key into my apartment, and hid it in the freezer under the ice cube trays.

From now on the file cabinet had to be locked at all times. The people I worked with, who I should be able to trust, were the very people I couldn't trust at all.

Chapter 14

When Liv picked me up on Thursday, she gave the once over to my white granny skirt, paired today with a blue blouse and sandals. "I should have warned you about how to dress. We'll be hauling books and supplies all afternoon. It'll be hot and dusty." In her clean but faded Levis, a western shirt gone soft with wear and scuffed boots, she looked up to the task. She'd pulled her dark hair into a tighter than usual ponytail, as if to insure it wouldn't get in the way.

On the drive she told me more about what to expect. Policy meetings in the morning. Burgers and fries at The Nine Pins bowling alley and cafe for lunch. An afternoon lugging boxes of books and supplies to Liv's pickup. When we got to Tipperary the day played out exactly as she had described. By the time we arrived in Little Missouri, our faces were smeared with dirt and sweat.

Liv pointed at my skirt, which was covered with tan grit. "A little bleach in the wash water'll take care of that."

"Who cares about the skirt?" I rested my head on the seat back. "I'm going to bed once we unload the truck."

"Aren't you going to the fair?"

"What fair?"

"The Tipperary County Fair. Nobody told you about it?"

"No. Where's it held?"

"In Little Missouri. A couple blocks west of the school. It starts tonight and runs through Sunday."

"Tomorrow's a contracted workday. And I have so much to do, I'll be working all weekend. I haven't even written lesson plans yet."

"You only need lesson plans for the first couple days. Get them done and show your face at the fair." She sketched out the schedule. Livestock check-in and judging tonight. Exhibit check-in and judging on Friday. Fair parade, rodeo, and dance on Saturday. Cowboy church service, picnic, and street games on Sunday.

"Do I *have* to go?"

"Yes. Little Missouri is a small town. If you don't get involved in things, you'll never get accepted."

"All right, all right. You've convinced me. I'll go."

Liv pulled into the schoolyard and we began hauling boxes. A truck driving down Main Street made a U-turn and parked next to Liv's. Arvid Drent descended from the cab decked out in a brown Stetson and a new western shirt, complete with the boxy creases from the cardboard packaging. His belt buckle was so big I wondered if it collided with his Adam's apple when he swallowed.

He lifted the box from my arms. "Let me take that, Miss Newell. Where does it go?"

"In there." Liv pointed to my classroom.

"Madame, your wish is my command." He clicked the heels of his boots.

My heart melted. "You're a lifesaver."

He adjusted his grip on the box. "I be wanting you to get this done quick, so I can show you around the fair tonight."

His offer was too good to refuse. "That sounds lovely."

"I be working the gate until seven. Could you meet me there when my shift be done?"

"You're on."

He turned and hauled the box to my room.

Liv needled me. "First Junior Wentworth sits beside you in church, and now Arvid's carrying your school books."

"How did you hear about church? Is nothing in this town sacred?" I grabbed a box and flounced to my room.

"Um, that one goes to my room."

I did an about-face and flounced to her classroom. When I came outside, Junior was parking his rusty Ford in the school yard. He got out. "Need a hand?"

"Sure. Could you grab that big box?"

Junior hefted it onto his shoulder and I led him to my classroom. "You can just set it there." I pointed to a bookcase where Arvid stood with his back to the door.

"Gotta warn you." The old man chuckled and turned. "This here new schoolteacher be a slave driver." His grin faded and he hurried outside.

I looked out the window. Arvid was scurrying to his truck. Maybe he was late for his shift at the fair. I went to the landing and waved. "Thank you!"

Junior came out and stood beside me. "What more can I do for you?"

He finished unloading the truck while I unpacked and shelved books and supplies. Then we hauled the cardboard cartons to the burn barrel in the corner between the two school buildings. Junior stuffed the burn barrel full of cardboard. I lit a match and held it to the edge of a box until it caught fire. The wind shifted and sent wisps of smoke in our direction.

Junior moved downwind. "I need a shower."

I rubbed at the ash coating my teeth. "I need a toothbrush."

"Would you like to join me at The Bend for supper?" He checked his watch. "Say about five forty-five?"

"It's a deal. My treat."

"You wanna make me the town laughingstock?"

"No." The fire popped and a spark landed at my feet. I ground it out. "I just want to thank you for your help."

"If you want to thank me, let me pay for supper and take you to the Fair Dance Saturday." He held out a hand. "Deal?"

"It's a deal." We shook on it.

"See you at The Bend." He touched the brim of his hat and walked to his pickup with confident grace.

For the first time in a long time, I agreed with Mom. Junior Wentworth was as nice as she had said. Though I wasn't going to tell her that until I was good and ready. Which, if I had anything to say about it, wouldn't be any time soon.

Chapter 15

Junior was already at The Bend when I arrived. He ordered prime rib, I ordered a cheeseburger and fries, and we talked like old friends. He regaled me with history of the Tipperary County Fair.

"This fair doesn't hold a candle to what you're used to in Iowa except for one thing." He cut into his meat. "Our rodeo is top-notch. We've got local cowboys in the national rankings."

I hid behind my cheeseburger making appreciative noises. I had never attended a rodeo in my life. It was a winning streak I wasn't inclined to break.

"I have to go soon. The cattle judging begins in a half hour." He shoved a massive amount of baked potato into his mouth and chewed.

Resisting the temptation to stare, I dropped a french fry into the puddle of ketchup on my plate. "You're a cattle judge?"

"I am."

"My dad judged cattle when I was a kid."

Each summer Mom pushed Dad's wheelchair into the center of the fairgrounds show ring. My sister, brother, and I retreated to the shade under the bleachers. Not Dad. He sat in the baking sun from morning to night, hatless and grinning from ear to ear. I could hear him explaining why the grand champion in each division deserved the honor.

"This heifer is as sweet any I've ever seen. She's stout across the front and not too long from front to back. Mark my words, her wide hindquarters indicate she'll be prime breeding stock in a year or two."

Once Dad had the microphone, he was loath to relinquish it. He doled out advice to the kids showing their calves.

"Good showmanship is often the only difference between reserve grand and grand champion. Stand straight, control your animal, and look the judge right in the eye."

Sitting in the center ring, Dad was happy and fully alive. But every year, he took longer to bounce back from baking in the hot sun. Every year his eyesight grew worse, until one summer he couldn't see well enough to judge cattle.

I hadn't attended livestock judging since. It was another reminder of what Dad had lost, of what we had all lost.

I dabbed at my nose with a napkin.

Junior stabbed at the last of his prime rib with his fork. "Did I say something to upset you?"

"No, not at all . . . I was just thinking about my dad."

"I'd like to hear more about him sometime." Junior

counted out bills and left them on the table. "But it'll have to wait. I've got to get to the show ring."

I pushed my plate away and checked my watch. Six forty-five. I'd better hustle or Arvid would think he'd been stood up. As I walked to the fairgrounds, a steady stream of pickup trucks passed by. And me without my clipboard. Where were my priorities?

Arvid was waiting at the main gate. He took my elbow and guided me through the brown, crackling grass. He showed off the livestock barn with its paltry collection of cattle and sheep.

"Would you do something for me?" I asked as we left the barn.

"If I be able."

"I'd like to meet Betty Yarborough in person. If she's here, would you introduce us?"

"She won't be here." He spoke with unshakeable certainty.

"How do you know?"

"She doesn't ever leave the switchboard. She says she can't because whenever she trains someone to do it, they leave a right mess for her to sort out. But the real reason be the way people stare when they see her."

"They stare at her? Why?"

"She be born with"—he squinted at the sky—"I can't remember what it be called when the top of the mouth inside isn't right, nor the skin on top either."

"A cleft palette?"

He snapped his fingers. "That's it. And one of them harelips. Her parents took her to Mayo Clinic for surgery. One of the first babies they ever operated on, she was, and it shows."

So that's why she was hard to understand.

Together we walked toward a tall fence and peeked through the slats. The smells of heat and manure rose in waves. Junior stood in the show ring. I leaned against a fence post and imagined Dad sitting beside him, the two of them choosing the winner together.

Arvid rapped his knuckles on the fence. "You can stay if you want. But it be about time for the first round of the horseshoe tournament, and I be scheduled to play. It be on the far side of the exhibit hall."

"I'll go with you."

My knowledge of horseshoes rivaled what I knew about rodeos. Cookie sat on a bench beside the pit and waved me over. She explained how the game worked and I watched Bud and Arvid compete against one another. Arvid's final toss fell short, and the scorekeeper announced that Bud Sternquist would advance to the next round.

Bud went over to Arvid and shook his hand. "You feelin' okay Arvid? I been aimin' to beat you at horse-shoes for years and about give up on it happening in my lifetime."

"Guess I be getting old. If you will excuse me, I be obliged to show Miss Newell the exhibit hall."

We wandered past displays of canned fruits and vegetables, baked goods, garden produce, photographs, sewing, handiwork, flowers, and craft entries.

"I can hardly believe this county has enough people to make all this."

"The winters be long and this is a big county." Arvid's Adam's apple bobbed. "Plenty of room for people to hole up for months, even disappear if they want to."

***

Friday I wrote lesson plans and prepared seatwork. Then I went to Liv's room and we drafted a recess duty schedule. We agreed she would teach gym for both our classes, I would teach music, and we would each teach our own students art.

Liv put down her pencil. "Velma give you her glitter and paint lecture yet?"

"Oh, yes."

"Like I said before, she wasn't so crotchety before Twila died."

"Do you think the sheriff will ever find who killed her?"

"I doubt it. He's too green."

"How'd he get elected?"

"When Rick graduated from the police academy, the old sheriff hired him to be his deputy. The sheriff dropped dead of a heart attack six months before the next election. The county supervisors appointed Rick as interim sheriff and talked him into throwing his hat in the ring. They were pretty desparate because they couldn't find anyone else who wanted the job. He ran unopposed. So here we are, the biggest county in South Dakota saddled with the youngest sheriff in the state."

"Is he that bad?

"More like inexperienced. He strung crime tape across the road and inconvenienced every rancher between here and Marmarth. He knows better than that. After all, he grew up here. And that's not the worst of it, he still hasn't interviewed the Bertholds, even though the whole town knows they're the most likely suspects."

The whole town except for me. I was clueless. "What are you talking about?"

"I suppose nobody wanted to tell you. Not with you teaching both Renny and Beau." Liv frowned, a line appearing between her brown eyes. "I suppose this is gossip but Renny's dad carried a torch for Twila all through high school. Since she moved to Marmarth six months ago, he's been driving that direction once or twice a week. Always after Round the Bend closes, and always when Trudy is gone or busy with the kids."

I picked at a hangnail. "Are you sure?"

"Axel's brother lives in Marmarth, and he saw them hanging onto each other on more than one occasion."

The hangnail began to bleed. I wiped it with a tissue and gathered my planner and pen. "I should get back to my room. There's a lot to do before Monday."

My palms began to sweat as I crossed the playground and entered my apartment. I took the key from its hiding place in the freezer and marched into my classroom. I pulled out my chart and scrawled Glen Berthold's name at the bottom of the list of suspects and then added Trudy's as well.

Another school connection. This investigation was getting messier by the minute. I sank into my chair and picked at my thumb. The hangnail began to bleed again, dripping blood onto my suspect list. I blotted the blood away with a tissue.

I didn't want to unearth any more secrets. Finding the truth wasn't worth hurting my students or my colleagues. I could do more good by helping my students, by becoming the best teacher I could be. I put the paper in its folder, filed the folder in the drawer, and shut the drawer with a bang. I was done investigating.

Chapter 16

The sun rose in a cloudless sky on the day of the fair parade. I woke, eager to talk to Dad. I held off until Betty rang with her reminder. It was a small kindness compared to how she watched over me, but better than nothing.

As usual, Mom picked up on the first ring. "Jane, is that you?"

"Hi, Mom. Is Dad awake? Can I talk to him?"

"Harold, it's Jane. She wants to talk to you." Short pause. "He's wheeling over. Here he is."

"Hello, Janie-Jo. Are you staying out of trouble?"

"I'm not doing anything you wouldn't do, Dad."

"That's what has me worried."

His joke was as familiar as home, and we settled into comfortable banter. When he ran out of one-liners, I launched into a topic guaranteed to hold his interest. I described the Tipperary County Fair in exquisite detail. He didn't interrupt, but snorted at the funny bits.

After several minutes, Mom interrupted. "What

have you been saying to him? He's laughing so hard he's crying."

"It's county fair weekend."

"That explains it. Wait a second. He needs a tissue to wipe his nose."

I hugged the phone and did a happy dance. Dad was laughing and I was the reason. I blew my nose. Twice.

"I'm back, but just to say good-bye. The doorbell's ringing."

"Bye, Mom. Say good-bye to Dad from me too." I blew a kiss into the receiver and hung up. Whatever the rest of the day brought, it was already the best one I'd had in Little Missouri.

I joined the crowd outside the schoolyard fence to watch the fair parade. A light breeze chased away the flies and mosquitos. My jeans, polo shirt, and denim jacket didn't stand out in the crowd, though my tennis shoes marked me as an outsider in a sea of cowboy boots.

Before long, Arvid and Merle took up residence on either side of me, swapping stories of pranks they pulled in country school.

Arvid's Adam's apple bobbed. "One day, I be sharpening my pencil, and Teacher started scolding me. Right then and there, I determined to spite her. So I climbed out the window and played hooky rest of the day."

"You climbed out the window?"

He nodded.

I turned to Merle. "What are you doing after the parade?"

"Oh, just fixin' some non-skid pancakes for me and the escaped convict." He jerked a thumb at Arvid.

"Before you eat, would you bring your screwdriver over to my classroom?"

"What fur?"

"To move the pencil sharpener away from the window."

Arvid's laugh boomed above the noisy crowd.

"Ain't no grass growing under yur feet." Merle chuckled.

I spotted Dan Barkley on the other side of the street talking to Bud and Rick Sternquist. I waved. Bud and Dan waved back. Rick's eyes moved from me to Merle and settled on Arvid. He took a small notebook from his pocket and scribbled in it.

Good grief! If the sheriff suspected two harmless old men like Arvid and Merle, then he was as green as Liv thought. Maybe even greener. I wanted to knock him upside the head and point him toward the Bertholds.

A siren wailed from the south end of town. An older model fire truck, its chrome fixtures and red paint polished and gleaming, rounded the corner and rolled down Main Street. Behind it, Junior Wentworth rode a massive brown horse.

Merle whistled as he approached. "That there's the prettiest bay in the county."

When he was even with us, Junior pulled the reins and bowed in our direction. Then he clicked his tongue and the horse began to move again.

"If I ain't mistaken, you and young Wentworth is getting acquainted." Merle raised an eyebrow.

"As a matter of fact he pulled our trailer out of a ditch the day I came to town."

Merle's eyes twinkled. "And?"

"Yesterday he stopped at the school and helped Liv and me haul in school supplies."

He rubbed his ear. "And?"

"Oh for crying out loud, you probably already know we went to supper at The Bend last night."

"And?"

"He's taking me to the Fair Dance tonight." I crossed my arms. "For your information, my mother thinks he's a very nice young man."

Merle squinted at the sky. "There's them that do, and there's them that don't."

"What's that supposed to mean?" The words came out louder than I'd intended. Several people turned to stare at me. Heat rose from my neck to my ears to the top of my head.

Merle sucked air between his teeth. "You know the ranch on the north side of the highway? Across the bridge?"

"Is it the one with the big tan brick house?"

"That's the Wentworth place. Junior's parents live there when they come out from Spearfish. He runs the ranch and lives in a log affair in the woods closer to the river."

Junior Wentworth came from money? Mom could never, ever find out that in addition to good looks, gumption, and lovely manners, he was well-heeled. I would never hear the end of it.

I looked around. "Where's Arvid?"

Merle shrugged. "Don't know."

Bicycle horns cut our conversation short. Children rode past on bikes festooned with crepe paper streamers. Other kids pulled wagons with balloons and cardboard signs taped to the sides. After the children came tractors pulling hayracks. The members of the Tipperary County High School band sat on the first rack and played *Tumbling Tumbleweeds*. Other floats represented businesses and churches from around the county.

"What's Fly Ranch?" I pointed to a float with several teenage boys surrounding a half-sized replica of a propeller airplane. A man dressed like a priest stood at the front of the plane and waved at one side of the street and then the other. "And who's the guy pretending to be a priest?"

"We-ull. Fly Ranch is about seven miles south of town. It's where delinquent boys get sent for rehabilitation purposes. I don't know how successful they is at getting that done." Merle rubbed his ear. "The priest ain't pretending. That's Father Dan. He's in charge of the ranch and the Catholic churches here and in Tipperary."

Before I could respond, a second fire truck, sirens blaring and lights flashing, signaled the end of the parade. As the crowd scattered, Merle introduced me to a few people passing by. Then we walked across the schoolyard.

He rubbed his bad hip. "If this leg weren't worse than worthless, I'd teach you the two-step tonight. I could surely cut the rug in my day. Have a nice time at the dance. But don't let Junior hold you too close."

I climbed the steps and stood on the stoop watching Merle limp away. I envisioned him, young and strong, twirling around a dance floor with a pretty young woman in his arms.

"I wish we'd known each other then. I'd have danced

every dance with you." I went inside, grabbed a tissue, and wiped away my tears.

***

My fingers trembled as I tucked my red gingham shirt into my navy skirt. Too *Little House on the Prairie* for my taste, but perhaps not for Junior. I heard a knock and answered the door.

It was Junior in his parade marshal clothes. He looked me up and down. "You look nice. Ready to go?"

"Just a minute." I grabbed my key, turned off the inside lights, and flipped on the one above the landing. Then I locked the apartment and slipped the key into my pocket. "Ready. Where's your truck?"

"Right there." He pointed to a gleaming white Suburban parked on the side of the street. He jogged ahead and opened the passenger door.

"What happened to the truck you were driving the other day?"

"That rust bucket is the ranch beater. This one is my personal vehicle."

The interior was luxurious with leather seats and a dashboard gleaming with fancy dials and buttons. I breathed in the scent of it. "It still smells new. When did you get it?"

"A few days ago. A deer leaped out of the ditch and totaled my good pickup truck a couple weeks back."

"It must have been a big one."

"A full-grown buck." He looked sheepish. "And both of us were moving faster than we shoulda been. Don't tell anybody I said that. Okay?"

"Okay." I glanced through the dusk toward the dance hall. "It doesn't look like there's anywhere closer than this to park. We can walk over."

"Fine with me. But people will talk about my outfit being parked near your apartment."

"They'll see us at the dance, they'll see us leave, and Merle will see you drive away shortly thereafter. There won't be a thing to talk about." I raised my eyebrows. "Will there?"

He chuckled. "Not with Merle on guard duty."

"Exactly."

We wove our way around the cowboys gathered outside for a smoke and a swig. At the dance hall, he gestured for me to enter first. The biggest building in town was nothing to write home about. Basketball hoops hung from the ceiling on either end of the half-sized court. A disc jockey stood on the stage at the far end of the room.

My heart sank as couples two-stepped across the maple parquet floor. I wasn't much of a dancer. I was about to make a fool of myself in front of the entire county. The strains of *Slow Dancin'* came over the speaker. Junior took my hand and pulled me onto the dance floor.

I shook him off "I don't know the two-step."

"You'll catch on quick," He put his left hand on the small of my back as his right hand grasped my left one. "Just follow my lead."

Junior was right. After a few trips around the dance floor, the footwork became automatic. We moved in rhythm with the other couples. Pam Barkley waved as she and Dan glided by. The song ended as Bud and Cookie Sternquist did a final twirl. He was so tall and broad and she so small and slight that he lifted her off the ground. He set her down with gentle grace, and they turned as one to face us.

"How about a dance?" Bud held out his hand as *Kiss an Angel Good Morning* began to play.

"Certainly."

He escorted me onto the floor. Junior and Cookie came along too. After a few missteps I was following Bud's lead as easily as I'd followed Junior. When the song ended, Bud gave a little bow and handed me back to Junior. The pattern continued for the rest of the evening. A dance with Junior. A dance with Dan Barkley. A dance with Junior. A dance with Axel McDonald. A dance with Junior.

Junior was my partner when I glanced at the clock behind a basketball hoop. It read ten o'clock. "This'll have to be our last dance. I'm tired and my feet are killing me."

"Fair enough." When we finished, he laced his fingers through mine and walked me to the exit. *Rhinestone Cowboy* blared from the speakers.

The sheriff stood next to the doorway. "Got time for one more?" Without waiting for a reply, he whisked me away from Junior. "My little brother can be a handful. You ready for him?" he asked as we glided across the floor.

"Your parents keep him in line. That makes all the difference. I'm more concerned about Beau Kelly."

Rick's feet faltered. "What do you mean?"

"How is he supposed to learn anything with his mother's killer waltzing around the county?"

He gripped my hand so hard I winced.

"If you want Beau to have any chance of a normal childhood, why are you dancing with me when you could be chasing leads?"

"Thanks for giving your opinion." His tightened his hold on my waist. "Now I've got something to say to you. Folks around here are good people, except for a few who shine up on the outside. Beneath the surface, they're something different all together. So be careful about who you get friendly with."

The nerve of the man! I broke away and found Junior. "Let's get out of here."

Silently he guided me outside and through the crowd. I waited for him to speak first.

"The sheriff gave you an earful while you were dancing. He didn't look any too pleased when you left."

The cool air raised goose bumps on my bare arms and legs. "I don't think he appreciated what I had to say."

"And what did you say?"

"That he should concentrate on finding Twila Kelly's killer and stop going to dances." My ankle twisted on the gravel.

"Careful now." Junior offered his arm. I clung to it until we reached the apartment and climbed the steps. Moths, drawn by the porch light, fluttered around our heads.

"Thank you for a lovely evening." I held out my right hand.

He clasped it and bent down to kiss my cheek. "You're welcome." His kiss slid from my cheek to my mouth. His lips were soft and gentle.

I breathed in the delicious scent of him. That was my undoing. His cologne tickled my nose, and I sneezed.

He straightened. "I don't usually have that effect on women."

"Men don't usually have that effect on me either." I took a tissue from my pocket and wiped my nose.

"I like the effect you have on me." He slid a finger from my ear to my chin. "Can I take you out again?"

"On one condition." I raised an index finger. "Would you wear a different cologne?"

"On one condition." He raised an index finger. "Will you wear what you've got on tonight?" He kissed me again, and I went inside.

Lock the door, Jane. Don't let romance make you stupid.

I shot the bolt, two-stepped into my bedroom, and sashayed in front of the mirror. I would never take *Little House on the Prairie* for granted again.

Chapter 17

The rooster, curse his scrawny feet, roused me early on Sunday. I was fixing my hair when a faint knock sounded at the door. I went to answer and found Merle on the stoop. “I’ll make you breakfast,” I offered.

“Nope.” He pulled at his collar and wiped his forehead with a red bandana. “I only stopped to tell you something. Don’t take this wrong now. The next time you get walked home by a cowboy, you’d be wise to turn the porch light off so the whole town can’t see the two of you saying good night.” He sucked air through his teeth and limped away.

So much for not letting romance make you stupid.

Though it was broad daylight, I did the smart thing and locked the door after shutting it. I was working in my classroom when the apartment phone rang around noon. I hurried to the kitchen and picked up after several rings.

“Jane, what took you so long to get to the phone?”

“Mom?” She wouldn’t be calling the day after we

talked unless something was wrong. "What's going on? Is Dad sick?"

"Good heavens, Jane. You have got to learn to stay calm. Of course, you have good reason to be nervous, what with school starting tomorrow and a murderer on the loose."

This was her strategy to calm me down?

"I just want to soothe your day-before-school-begins jitters. Once you get past the first day you'll be fine."

"Do you really think so?"

"After twenty-five years of teaching, I know so. The first day is always the worst."

"It's nice of you to say that, Mom. Thanks."

"Was Junior Wentworth at the fair?"

"Yes."

"Did you talk to him?"

"A little."

"Is that all you're going to say?"

"There's nothing more to say." Not to Mom anyway.

"Have a good day tomorrow. I'll be thinking about you."

"I'll call Saturday with a full report." About school. Not about Junior. Never about Junior.

We hung up and I fixed a sandwich. As I took my empty plate to the sink, whoops and hollers came from the direction of Round the Bend. I stuck my head out to see what was causing the commotion. Main Street was blocked off from the grocery store to the post office, and a crowd milled about on the street.

The street games! I couldn't afford to miss them if I wanted to be accepted. I put on tennis shoes and hustled to join the crowd. Kids were climbing into gunnysacks and waggling into place in front of The Bend as I approached. Junior Wentworth stood on the sidewalk beside them and fired a starting gun. I reached the sidelines as Tiege Sternquist leaped over the finish line just ahead of Keeva McDonald. He lost his balance, crashed into her, and they landed in a tangle.

Brock ran to Tiege and yanked him upward by his belt. His feet dangled in the air. Axel and Liv rushed over, but Sheriff Sternquist beat them to it. He separated the boys and pushed Tiege in the direction of Bud and Cookie.

Brock charged the sheriff, who deflected the boy's blows and circled his waist. "Axel, can you give me a hand?"

The two men half dragged and half carried Brock behind the post office.

Liv brushed dirt off the seat of Keeva's pants. "There now, you aren't any worse for wear. You go find a partner for the three-legged race."

Cookie sent Tiege off with Keeva and gave Liv a hug, her short, graying hair a stark contrast to Liv's dark ponytail. "I imagine Brock's on edge about boarding in Tipperary for high school. Boys don't like to admit they're scared to leave their mamas. But they are."

"Well, it woulda been nice if Rick had thought about that before he lit into my son just now." Liv walked behind the post office.

The starting gun fired again and the three-legged race began. Keeva and Tiege took an early lead, only to be overtaken by Cora and Bennan Barkley. The crowd cheered, and a new group of children took their places for the next race.

Cookie saw me standing alone and came over. She took me around and introduced me to more people. "Don't worry." She put an arm around my shoulder, her green eyes reassuring and steady. "By the next county fair, you'll know them all."

"You have more faith in me than I do. Tipperary County is so different from where I grew up. Can you explain something?"

"I'll try."

"What did you mean about Brock boarding in Tipperary?"

"Oh that. It's pretty common for kids who live as far out as Brock does to board in town Sunday through Thursday and come home for the weekend. That way they can do sports and other extracurriculars."

"But he's only fourteen. That's pretty young."

"Kids grow up fast out here." Cookie squinted at the sky. "It's almost time for chores. And tomorrow's a school day. I'd best round up my crew and take them home."

Someone tapped my shoulder and I jumped before turning to see who it was. Junior.

"What's bugging you?"

"Nerves. I start my first real job tomorrow and I don't want to blow it."

"Let's take your mind off of it." He took my hand. "Join me for an early supper?"

Not in the middle of the street, Junior! "Thanks, but I'm not hungry." I pulled my hand away.

"Some night this week then?"

"Call me Saturday morning when I've got a week of school under my belt. I promise to say yes."

"I'm going to hold you to it."

"Talk to you on Saturday." I walked and concentrated on happy thoughts that had nothing to do with teaching. Merle's neighborliness. Junior's kiss. Arvid's sweet bashfulness. Mom's encouragement. Dad laughing until he cried. But the knot in my stomach refused to go away.

When I got home, I picked up Agatha Christie's mystery, *The Murder of Roger Ackroyd*, made a nest of pillows in bed, and escaped into the tidy, symmetrical world of Hercule Poirot. I read until my eyelids drooped and my "little gray cells" rebelled.

Merle's rooster woke me in the morning, interrupting the strangest dream. Poirot and I had won the three-legged race, and we celebrated by inviting Junior over to create a grid of symmetrical boxes. In them we entered information about pickup trucks, drivers, and headlights. Our efforts ended when swarms of children invaded my classroom and jimmied the lock on the filing cabinet.

I rolled out of bed, downed a bowl of cereal, and dressed in a glossy blouse, light wool vest, and matching gauchos. Once my knee-high leather boots were zipped, I felt ready for the day, the week, the entire school year.

Bring it on! I fist pumped the air on the short walk to my classroom. *Bring it on*!

My bravado disappeared when a handful of vehicles and the school bus parked on the verge that bordered the schoolyard. My heart beat double time as parents and children streamed across the playground. I counted to ten, inhaled deeply, and went out to greet the crowd of children and parents at the foot of the landing.

"Good morning." My voice quivered.

Take a deep breath and try again.

"Good morning."

There you go.

"Come in."

Pam Barkley entered with Cora and Bennan. Behind her, a tall woman ushered a boy and girl into the cloakroom.

"Miss Newell, this is Mary Borgeson." Pam introduced Mary, and then a fine-boned boy with black eyes and hair as dark as his mother's and a tall, redheaded girl. "And here we have Stig and Elva."

"Pleased to meet you." Mary gave her children their backpacks. "If you need anything, have Betty give me a call." She and Pam hugged their kids and left.

Next, Renny Berthold arrived alone. Trudy waved from her car and drove away.

She's keeping her distance. Interesting.

The children found their desks and began to empty their backpacks. The door opened again, and Iva Kelly entered with Beau. He poked at the linoleum with the toe of his shoe. I put a finger under his chin and met his blank gaze. "Good morning, Beau. You can put your lunch box in your cubby and find your desk."

Before Iva could say anything, Tiege bounded in. His arrival flipped on a hidden switch inside Beau. He slid his backpack from his shoulders and grinned. Iva slipped outside.

"Am I late?" Tiege pulled off his backpack and rummaged through it.

"You're right on time."

"That's good. Dad and me started out early 'cause he said it wouldn't make a good *ippression* to be late on the first day. His pickup wouldn't start, and Rick brung me instead." He dumped his school supplies on the floor. "Where's my lunchbox? I can't find my lunchbox."

The door opened and the sheriff held out a Fonzie lunch box. "Looking for this?"

Relief washed across Tiege's face. "I thought I was going to starve."

"Tiege," I prompted him, "what do you say to your brother?"

He thought a minute. "Did you eat my cookies?"

The day proceeded without a hitch. The kids were so animated, there was no time to be nervous. They listened well and behaved even better. It would take a few weeks for us to get comfortable with one another, but we would get there.

At the end of the day, Elva wrapped her arms around my waist. "Miss Newell, I just love school. And I love you more." She pulled away and looked me over from the top of my head to the toes of my prized leather boots. "But you sure do dress funny." With that, she grabbed her things and left.

So much for becoming Little Missouri's fashion maven.

I kicked off the boots, peeled off my pantyhose, and attacked the mountain of papers on my desk. Two hours later the mountain was gone. I went into the kitchen, fixed tuna salad, and spread a thick layer on bread. I snarfed it down and was about to make a second sandwich when someone tapped on the door. I went to see who it was.

Merle held a bucket of ice cream in one hand and a

box of sugar cones in the other. "I'm thinkin' your first day of school is worth cel-ee-bratin'."

We sat on the landing as dusk fell and the wind gentled. Merle piled ice cream precariously high on our cones. Rivulets of chocolate ran down the side of my cone, and a big, creamy drop landed on my gaucho skirt.

"You want to keep them duds nice, I 'spect." Merle offered me his bandana.

"Everything's washable." Another drop fell on my sleeve. I licked at the melting ice cream. "Besides, I won't be dressing up like this too often. I'd rather be comfortable."

Merle tucked his bandana in the front pocket of his overalls. "You're gonna be a good teacher, Miss Newell. You learn quick."

Merle was right. I'd always been a quick learner. I was already catching on to teaching. I was quick about other things too, and not always for the better. Like abandoning my investigation into Beau's mom's death. The emptiness in Beau's eyes haunted me. Either I could give up the investigation or give up on him. The second was a choice I couldn't bear to make.

Chapter 18

The Borgeson children and their mom arrived early the next day. She carried a cardboard box and set it on a table by the window.

Stig lifted out a Mason jar. "Look what we got!"

"We found them by the road." Elva took out two more jars.

"Monarchs," Mary added. "There were hundreds in a patch a milkweed down in the draw."

Stig stretched out his arms. "They was everywhere. Mom only let us catch these. When we got home, she read the 'cyclopedia about what to feed them."

Elva held up the jar. "Milkweed and sugar water. See?"

"They brought them for show and tell." Mary lifted a book from the box. "I brought the encyclopedia if you want it."

I took it from her. "Guess what we'll study in science this afternoon?"

The day transformed into a butterfly extravaganza,

starting with show and tell. During math the children wrote butterfly story problems. After lunch I set aside *Little House in the Big Woods* and read a picture book about butterflies from our classroom library instead. We discussed the meaning of metamorphosis. I wrote the word on the chalkboard and they practiced pronouncing it. Then they worked in small groups, observing the butterfly jar and taking notes about what they saw.

Mrs. Dremstein, the principal, came in. She sat down at my desk and opened my lesson plan book.

Uh-oh. I had abandoned my lesson plans on the second day of school. All the butterflies we'd been reading about landed in the pit of my stomach.

I went over, and in a low voice, explained what the children were doing. She pursed her lips, nodded, and wrote something on a notepad.

Tiege raised his hand. "Are we having art class?"

I nodded. "After recess."

"Can it be about butterflies? We could make some metahorsaphis pictures about the eggs and the larva and pupa and stuff." He clasped his hands under his chin. "Please, Miss Newell?"

"Yes, and it's metamorphosis, not metahorsaphis."

"Can we stay inside and start art class now?" Renny begged.

"Not on a beautiful afternoon like this!"

The children protested but I shooed them outside.

Mrs. Dremstein pursed her lips again. "You went off your lesson plans on the second day of school?"

My stomach fluttered. "Yes."

"Why?"

"Elva and Stig brought in these monarchs this

morning . . . and things snowballed from there." I sat in Tiege's desk to keep my knees from knocking.

"You capitalized on a teachable moment." Mrs. Dremstein tapped her pen on my desk. "Well done."

I still had a job! The butterflies in my stomach took flight.

"Metahorsophis. Only in Tipperary County." The principal chuckled as she left for Liv's room.

I ushered eight sweaty children inside and passed out scratch paper. They drew and labeled the butterfly stages and begged me to reread the book from earlier as they sketched.

Renny's hand shot up after hearing the description of the life cycle. "Will our butterflies lay eggs that hatch into worms and spin cocoons?"

I turned back a few pages. "The book says that monarchs lay fewer eggs and spin fewer cocoons later in the summer as the weather cools down."

A sliver of hope lit Beau's eyes. "But maybe they will. It's still hot outside."

I wasn't sure how to answer him. "I'd be surprised."

He clenched his hands. "I think they just need us to take care of them. I'll bring sugar water every day."

Soon every child had a job. Stig was in charge of bringing milkweed. Cora and Bennan volunteered to bring a five-gallon jar for the butterflies' temporary home. Renny and Tiege agreed to move it when direct sunlight hit it.

"I could weld some pipes into a cart with wheels to make it easier to push around," Tiege suggested.

I had never met a kid with an imagination like his. One of these days, I would need to nip his wild claims in the bud before the other kids got tired of them. But not on the second day of school.

"Let me think on that." I went to the chalkboard and drew a chart to keep track of the monarch stages. "Elva, would you put a tally mark on this chart behind whatever stage the butterflies are at? I'll do it on the weekends." Then I spoke to everyone. "Would you hand in your drawings? It's time to go home."

I riffled through their sketches while they collected their things in the cloakroom. The drawings were typical for kids their age. Except for one. Beau was my youngest student, yet his attention to detail and use of proportion indicated remarkable talent.

"Mom, guess what we learned about today?" Tiege yelled as he shot out the door and ran to Cookie's truck. "Metahorsophis!"

I went to the landing and hollered at him. "Tiege, it's metamorphosis!"

She stuck her head out the truck window. "Miss Newell, you might as well get used to the fact that in this county, everything's better with a horse in it."

***

The week sped by. Each morning, the kids rushed in to check on the butterflies and were disappointed when the monarchs looked the same as the day before. Each afternoon I felt as though the seven little people in the room had siphoned all my energy into themselves. They tore out of the building ready to go. I wanted to crawl to the couch and take a nap.

But there wasn't time. I had papers to correct, grades

to record, lesson plans to adjust, materials to prepare, and a classroom to tidy, because in the morning, the children would create the chaos all over again.

There wasn't time for investigating either. I counted back to see how many days it had been since I'd gotten my driver's license at the courthouse. More than a week now and Anna Marie hadn't called. I wrote a note for Monday to call her if she hadn't phoned by then.

Beau spent much of Thursday morning staring out the window.

I knelt beside his desk. "A penny for your thoughts."

"What?" His brown eyes were puzzled.

"A penny for your thoughts. It's another way of asking what you're thinking about."

He laid his head on his desk, his face buried in his arms.

I rubbed his back and wracked my brain for a way to dispel his sadness. "What's wrong, Beau?"

His mother was gone. Nothing could be worse for a young child than the loss of a parent. I had been younger than Beau when my father disappeared.

"Where's Daddy?" I asked Mommy.

She didn't say anything, so I asked my older sister. Jeanette.

"He's in the hospital." She began to cry. "He's sick."

I stared at my sister. She never cried. Hospitals, whatever they were, must be bad places. I wanted my daddy to be here so I could crawl on his lap. So he could tell me everything was all right. But he was sick and in that bad place.

I began to cry. "I miss my daddy."

Jeanette put her arms around me and we sobbed together.

"What are you girls carrying on about?" Mom asked.

"We want our daddy," Jeanette wailed. "We don't want him to die."

"Good heavens, where did you get that idea?" Mommy pulled us apart. "He's not going to die. He's sick, and the doctors are finding medicine to help him. He'll be home soon."

Dad came home, just as Mom had said he would. But he didn't jiggle me on his fat belly to make me laugh anymore, because he said the doctors made him get all skinny. And he didn't take Jeanette in the car when he went to talk to farmers, because he said his eyes didn't work right so he couldn't drive any more.

He was still our dad, just not the dad he'd been before he got sick. That dad had been gone for almost twenty years. Jeanette and I still missed him.

My heart ached for Beau, whose life, I knew, would be shadowed by loss forevermore.

"Miss Newell, look at this!" Tiege bounced out of his seat with the gusto of Tigger. He thrust a book about dung beetles at me.

How in the world could I keep this child in his chair? I led him back to his desk, holding his arm a smidgen harder than necessary. Wait a minute! Wasn't there a roll of duct tape in the supply closet?

Jane Newell, do you want to get fired?

The next morning I was on the playground when

Tiege barreled toward me. A kick line of dancers duct taping him to a chair formed in my brain.

"Miss Newell! Miss Newell!" He skidded to a stop, the tips of his boots nearly colliding with my open-toed sandals. He brandished an envelope. "Mom wants you to read this, and I'm supposed to take it home tonight."

Had I bruised his arm? Had he told his parents? I tore open the envelope and removed the paper with shaking fingers. I skimmed the note and my heartbeat slowed. Cookie wanted to know if I could meet them at Sunday services and go to the ranch afterward for dinner.

It took less than two seconds to decide. I wasn't excited about going to church or spending part of the weekend with a child as exhausting as Tiege. Then again, eating someone else's cooking was appealing. I scribbled my acceptance on the back of Cookie's note, sealed it in a new envelope, and watched Tiege zip it into his backpack.

He dashed to his desk, read the assignments listed on the chalkboard, and raised two fists above his head. "I'm ready for that spelling test. One hunnert percent, here I come."

From some deep well of fortitude, I summoned the strength to banish the dancers and their rolls of duct tape.

Chapter 19

I slept in until ten on Saturday. Either Merle's rooster was stewing in a pot, or my first week on the job had tuckered me out. As I made oatmeal, I thought of the hot breakfasts Mom had fed us every morning. I could see her at the stove, barking orders.

"Kids, the oatmeal's ready. Get in here and eat. Now!"

My little brother Jeff scooted into his chair beside Dad and picked up his spoon.

"Janie, get a straw for your dad and pour his coffee. Jeanette, pour milk on his oatmeal."

I stuck a straw in Dad's coffee and set the cup to the right of his bowl, as Mom always insisted. Then I reached for the sugar bowl and sprinkled two spoonfuls on my oatmeal before Jeff tattled.

"Janie, that's enough." Mom took the sugar bowl from my hand. As always, she started to eat last and finished first. Then she carried her bowl to the sink. "You

kids clear the table for your dad. Harold, watch the clock and make sure they leave by eight-fifteen."

Out the door she marched, on her way to a full day at work.

How had she fixed breakfast, taught all day, and cooked supper before supervising homework and putting three kids and Dad to bed? My first week of teaching cast Mom in a new light. She had provided for us and raised us while watching her husband decline. All that, and I had never once thanked her.

I rinsed my bowl and set it in the dish drainer. Then I went to my classroom and tackled the tasks I'd ignored last night in favor of comfy pajamas and a good book. By mid-afternoon everything was in order for the following week.

I went to the landing and looked north on Main Street and then south. No sign of Velma or Liv. Or other casual would-be visitors. I stepped back inside, locked the doors tight, and shut the curtains. Then I took Arvid's letter from the filing cabinet. I switched on the desk lamp and put the paper under the magnifying glass. There was the letter T on one side of the water spot and the letter a after it. I turned the paper over and brought it and the magnifying glass close to my face. Nothing. I held them at arm's length. Still nothing. It was a dead end.

I threw the letter in the trash can, then bopped my forehead with a palm. Velma would be cleaning this weekend, and she was the kind of person who believed pawing through the wastebasket was her civic duty. I fished the letter out of the trash and locked it in the file cabinet again.

My phone rang. Junior had said he would call today. I raced to the kitchen. "Hello?"

"How did your week go, Jane?"

It was only Mom. "I was going to call you."

"So, tell me everything."

"It was hard." Tears sprang to my eyes. "And I'm so tired. Teaching three grades is so much work."

"Oh, dear. I knew that place would be too much for you."

"The week had its high points too." I didn't want her to think I couldn't do the job.

"Really?"

"Everyone's friendly." I mentioned the meals with the Barkleys and the McDonalds and the invitation to the Sternquists. "Keeping Tiege in his seat has led to some weird daydreams about duct tape."

"I know what you mean. My first year teaching, I had this student who talked constantly, and I mean constantly. I took away his recess. He kept talking. I made him stay after school and clean erasers. He kept talking. I sent a note to his parents. The next day he talked all day about how much trouble he'd gotten into."

"Did you give up?" Silly question. Doris Newell never gave up.

"Now why would I give up? The following day I told him to take his chair to the corner in the back of the room so he could talk all day long. Without stopping. For the first hour or so he was as happy as a clam. When recess rolled around he lined up with rest of the kids. 'You go back to your corner,' I told him, 'and keep talking.' He thought I was kidding. But I was not. I made him talk until school ended. From then on he only spoke when called upon." Her voice—the same one that often irritated me to no end—turned soothing. "I know what you're going through, Jane. I really do."

"Are you trying to encourage me or scare me?"

"Encourage you. Your dad and I cooked up something else too. How do gift certificates to the grocery store and beauty salon in Tipperary sound?"

"Can you afford that?"

"Your dad insisted I use some of his civil service pension check. The store owners have the certificates waiting for you."

"I don't know what to say."

"Moving is expensive. We thought you might need a little something to tide you over until your first paycheck."

I held out the receiver and stared at it. Was this my mother? "Thank you."

"And Jane, book a hair appointment soon. You're a professional and need a decent cut. And don't expect much of a present at Christmas. Money only stretches so far."

That was more like it. Mom was still Mom.

I hung up, and the phone rang again.

Oh, good. Junior had gotten through. I lifted the receiver. "This is Jane."

"And this is Liv."

Not Junior. Darn it!

"How's your Saturday treating you?" she asked.

"Pretty good."

"Listen. I apologize for not checking in with you this

week. Between moving cows, school, and going to Tipperary to see how boarding in town is going for Brock, I ran out of time."

"I understand."

"That's nice of you to say, but you shouldn't be riding solo. I want to make it up to you. Axel put together venison sausage pizzas. Would you like to join us?"

Junior, you should have called sooner. "I'd love to. What can I bring?"

"Could you pick up some Coke at the store? Come on out now if you want."

I changed into clean blue jeans and a sweatshirt, grabbed my purse, and locked up. I sped down the landing steps and almost collided with Velma.

She glared at me. "So when the kids isn't here, you act as crazy as them, I see."

"Sorry. I need to get to the store before it closes. Are you here to talk to me or to clean?"

"What in tarnation would I want to talk about? I'm here to clean. Do I got to clear that with you or something?"

"Of course not."

"Then git on your way. It ain't right when folks waltz into the store at closing and keep Burt and Iva from getting home to Beau. Not that you care."

I saw red. "I don't know what you've got against me, Velma Albright. And I don't know what you're saying about me around town. But don't you dare say that I don't care about Beau because I care plenty. If I could find out who ran into his mom, I'll do it in a heartbeat."

Velma's head reared back as if I'd slapped her. The

wrinkles in her face became a dark and silent mask. Her eyes were venomous.

Good. I'd gotten to the old bat. I wheeled around and walked to my car. The store was still open when I got there. I bought a quart bottles of regular and diet Coke as well as 7-Up and drove to the McDonalds.

Keeva opened the door before I could knock. She took me to the kitchen where Axel was pulling pizza pans out of the oven.

"Rosalie, put ice in the glasses and pour the pop." Liv carried a tossed salad to the table and called for everyone to sit down.

The sausage was spicy, lean, and delicious. "I've never had venison before. Who's the hunter?"

"Hunters. Brock and Dad filled their tags last year." Rosalie sprinkled grated cheese on her pizza. "And I get to go with them this year after I finish the hunter safety course."

I pictured her bringing down her first deer with one efficient and perfectly placed shot. Then I spoke to her brother. "Do you like to hunt, Brock?"

He nodded with his mouth full.

"What do you think of boarding in Tipperary?"

"I hate it." He glared at his parents. "I told you both plenty of times that I'd rather drive over in the morning and come home at night. Being in town with people breathing down my neck is making me stir crazy."

Axel wiped his hands on a napkin and set it on his plate. "That discussion is closed until you go two months without bustin' a light or dinging the ranch truck."

Brock's cheeks flamed and his eyes narrowed. Before he could reply, Liv grabbed a pan of table scraps.

"Jane, would you and Keeva take these out to the cats?"

I read the unspoken plea in her eyes. "Sure. Should Rosalie come too?"

"No. She's got clothes to fold in the laundry room."

Rosalie pushed back her chair and left the room.

Keeva carried the pan of scraps to the barn and the cats swarmed around her. She set the pan on the ground and the kitties crowded around it. To give Axel and Liv the time they needed to calm Brock down, I asked Keeva for a tour of the barn. She introduced me to the horses and showed me how to pet their immense, velvety noses. She wanted us to climb on the hay bales, but I nixed the idea. The more my feet stayed on solid ground, the better.

"It's getting late. We should probably go back."

We walked hand in hand to the house, the dim glow of the yard light illuminating the way. When we went inside, Liv nearly collided with me.

"Mommy, what's wrong?" Keeva's hand slid out of mine.

"Please go to your room, sweetie. I need to talk to Miss Newell."

She ran down the hallway without protesting or questioning her mom's request.

Liv sank into a rocking chair and motioned me to the recliner. "Keeva doesn't need to know about this quite yet, but you better hear it now. While you two were outside, Axel replaced the headlight Brock broke this afternoon. When he started the engine to be sure everything was working, he saw that the seat back was tilted funny. He messed with it and found something wedged in the crack between the seat and the seat back." She twined her fingers together and cleared her throat. "It was a Lucky Strike pack stuffed with twenties. They were smeared with blood."

"Did Brock say where it came from?"

She untwined her fingers. "Twila Kelly."

Careful, Jane. Think before you speak.

"You believe him?"

"He broke down as soon as Axel showed them to him." Her fingers trembled. "He swears up and down he didn't kill her."

I waited.

"He claims he found the money a few days ago. He'd hit an antelope in our pasture near where she was killed. It was dark and he tested the lights to see if he needed to switch out any broken ones so we wouldn't find out. The beam reflected off something in the grass and he went to see what it was. He picked up the wallet and pocketed the cash before he saw it was Twila's. His fingerprints were all over it by then and he panicked, certain the sheriff would arrest him. He hiked to the river and threw the wallet in the water."

"But he kept the cash? That doesn't make sense."

"Did you do anything stupid when you were fourteen?"

She had me there. "What are you going to do?"

"Axel already called the sheriff. He and Brock are waiting in his room." She bit her lip. "Can you do me a favor?"

"Anything."

"Would you take Rosalie and Keeva for the night? I don't want them here in case the sheriff . . . until me and Axel know what to tell them."

"Of course I'll take them. How about I say I'm lonely and want to have a sleep over?"

"Thank you." Liv squeezed my hand. "Girls, come out here. Miss Newell has something to ask."

They were delighted to relieve my loneliness.

"Pack your Sunday clothes. We're going to church in the morning."

They ran to their rooms.

"The Sternquists invited me to dinner after church tomorrow. Should I drop off the girls on my way?"

"That'll do."

Rosalie and Keeva came into the living room, their arms filled with suitcases, pillows, and sleeping bags.

"We're ready!" Rosalie said. Keeva hopped up and down.

Liv gave each girl a kiss and a squeeze. "Be good."

"We will!" The girls raced to the Beetle and squeezed into the backseat.

Rosalie helped her sister buckle her seat belt. "That was kind of weird."

"What was?" I started the car.

"Mom usually looks in the suitcase to see if we packed clean underwear."

"Maybe she trusts you to remember now that you're older."

"She never has before."

In the rearview mirror I watched Keeva hug her sister. "This is gonna be the funnest night of my whole life. At least so far. Mommy says it'll only get better when kindeegarten starts."

The girls twittered and chirped on the drive home. I wanted to ask God to keep their world safe and secure.

But prayer was nothing but whistling in the wind. I could do better on my own. I could make our sleepover a good memory for Rosalie and Keeva. It wasn't much, but it was something to cling to when their parents told them about Brock. Once they heard what their brother had done, there would be no turning back.

Chapter 20

The girls checked the butterfly jar while I scrounged in the supply cupboard for kids' games. Rosalie and Keeva voted for *Go Fish* and we played until they grew punchy. Then we made ice cream sundaes, spread their sleeping bags on the floor, and watched a movie on television until Keeva fell asleep. Rosalie made it a little longer. Once she nodded off, I snuck into my room and stretched out in my own bed.

I got up early to make blueberry pancakes. Neither girl stirred when the bacon started to sizzle in the skillet, so I cranked the phone and asked Betty to ring Liv. Then I untangled the phone cord and carried the receiver into the entryway.

"It's Jane." I kept my voice low. "Is it still okay to drop off the girls after church."

"Sure."

"They can go with me to the Sternquists for lunch if you need more time. I don't think Cookie will mind."

"Well, I do mind," she snapped. "Just drop them off after church."

"Should I say anything to the girls?"

"No." Liv breathed in and out, the way people do when they're about to cry. "Betty?"

"Yes, Wiv?"

"This is a private conversation. Would you get off the line? And if anybody else is listening in, please hang up." Her voice broke. "Please?"

"Everybody off the wine. Now!" Betty ordered.

I counted several clicks before Liv spoke again.

"The sheriff has it out for Brock. Don't ask me why. Last night Rick threatened to arrest him. Even took out the handcuffs and waved them around some.

"In the end it was all hot air. He bagged the cash and said he'd send it to the state crime lab in Pierre for testing. He told Brock to stick close around here until the results come back."

"How long will that take?"

"A couple weeks. Maybe more if there's a backlog."

"That's a long time to wait."

"Yeah. But it gives us some breathing room. We can put off telling the girls until there's something to say."

High, excited chatter began in the living room. The girls were awake so I ended our call. When I entered the kitchen Rosalie was ladling pancake batter onto the electric skillet. She put the bowl on the counter and forked bacon onto a plate with practiced efficiency.

Keeva was setting the table. "Where's the syrup?"

I took it from a high shelf in the cupboard and handed it to her. She set it on the table and began to pour juice.

"Time to eat." Rosalie carried two platters to the table, one stacked with pancakes and the other with bacon. "Coffee will be ready soon."

I gestured at the table. "The plan was for me to make breakfast for you girls. Not the other way around."

"Me and Keeva's in charge of making breakfast during calving and lambing." Rosalie filled my coffee cup.

Keeva passed the pancakes. "And during haying, when Mommy runs the baler."

"You girls better be careful or I'll make you come every Sunday to make me breakfast." We ate in comfortable silence. I mopped up the last drops of syrup on my plate with a final forkful of pancakes. "We've got just enough time to get dressed for church."

They got ready in the spare room while I changed in my bedroom. I chose a dark green knit top, plaid blazer, and dressy jeans. They came out in matching western shirts and clean Levis.

We strolled to church, enjoying the sunshine and cool breeze, arriving as the Sternquists pulled in. Tiege jumped out while Bud and Cookie descended more sedately.

Keeva ran to Cookie. "Miss Newell borrowed us last night for a sleepover. She was lonely."

Cookie bent down until they were eye to eye. "Was it fun?"

Keeva beamed. "It was wonderful."

Tiege charged by.

"How do you keep up with him?" I asked.

"That's his father's department." Cookie beamed at Keeva and Rosalie. "Now, if you'll excuse me, I'm going to enjoy some girl time." They went inside as a threesome.

I went up to Bud who was holding the door open. "Do you mind dropping them off at Axel and Liv's on the way to your place?"

"Course not."

We entered the sanctuary and I slid in beside Cookie and the girls. When the service began I replayed my phone conversation with Liv. She hadn't had one good thing to say about the sheriff. Was he a lightning rod for her anger and fear or was he truly that incompetent?

"Hi there."

A whisper tickled my ear and I squeaked.

Junior Wentworth lowered himself onto the seat beside me. "You have got to unwind some."

"And you need to keep your promises."

His response was a blank stare.

If you're not worth his time, then he's not worth yours, Jane. I angled away from him and toward the McDonald girls and Cookie.

After the service Junior touched my elbow. "I'm sorry."

"For what?"

"For whatever I did to offend you."

I held up my palms to stop him. "When you know why you're apologizing, you know where to find me."

Cora and Bennan barged up with Elva and Stig at their heels. They all spoke at once.

"How are the butterflies?"

"Did you feed the monarchs?"

"Have they laid any eggs?"

Once again I turned away from Junior and toward

Keeva and Rosalie. "Girls, can you tell them how the butterflies are doing?"

Pam came over and listened while Keeva and Rosalie gave an update. After they wound down, she said, "The kids talk about those monarchs constantly."

Cookie hurried over. "I almost forgot about the roast in the oven! We've got to get home before it burns to a crisp. Where's Tiege?"

Bud clamped a hand on his son's shoulder. "Got him."

I said good-bye to Pam, gathered the girls, and left with the Sternquists. Bud opened the cab's back door. He held onto Tiege while the girls and I got settled. Then he herded Tiege inside.

"I want to sit next to Miss Newell." He crawled over the girls and plunked down beside me. I'd never been so popular.

Bud stopped at my apartment for the girls' things. Fifteen minutes later Rosalie, Keeva, and I set everything on the McDonald's front stoop.

Liv came out. "Take your stuff inside, girls." She glanced at the Sternquist's truck. "Did you tell them about what's going on?"

"It's not mine to tell. No one mentioned it at church either."

"Was the sheriff there?"

"No."

"Will he be at Bud and Cookie's?"

"I don't know."

"If you see him, don't tell him you were here for supper last night." Her face was hard and protective. "He'll badger you if he finds out."

"Call me if you need anything." I inched backward. "Let me know when you hear from the crime lab."

"Keep your voice down. Me and Axel don't want the girls to know until they have to."

Her fierceness pushed me further away. "Sorry."

"Thanks for watching the girls."

I walked to the truck and waved, but didn't look back.

As I settled in beside Tiege, Cookie turned toward me. "Is Liv okay?"

"No." A wave of despair rose within me. "She's not okay. Not at all."

Chapter 21

Tiege began talking before I could buckle my seatbelt. "Miss Newell, I got some stuff to show you at the ranch."

"You do?" His prattle was preferable to the question in Cookie's eyes. "And what might that be?"

"I ain't telling. But you can try to guess."

We played Tiege's guessing game as Bud drove two miles to their mailbox, turned west down a bumpy lane, and parked in front of a small, white house. It was flanked by a trailer house, and several large outbuildings, all of them hugging the spot where the shortgrass prairie and the dark buttes met.

Tiege pressed his nose against the window. "Rick's here!"

My stomach twisted. The sheriff was the last person I wanted to see.

"Quit your hollering, son." Bud parked in front of the house. "We don't want Miss Newell going deaf."

Tiege opened the door and jumped out. "Do you think he's staying for dinner?"

Please, no.

"Let's find out." Bud chased after his son.

I waited for my panic to pass. "Is your ranch in South Dakota or Montana?"

Cookie led me inside. "Our land is in South Dakota. It goes right up to the Montana border. We lease some pasture land from the Forest Service. That's in Montana."

"How many acres do you farm then?"

Cookie hung her coat on a peg beside the door. "Your East River roots are showing, Jane. People west of the Missouri don't farm. They ranch."

I hung up my jacket next to hers and tried again. "How many acres do you ranch?"

"About eight thousand."

"That's huge!"

Cookie laughed. "It's huge in East River terms, but pretty average by West River standards. Ranches in Tipperary Country run from three or four thousand acres up to ten thousand or so."

My East River brain struggled to keep up, and I retreated to more familiar territory. "Can I help you with dinner?"

She brought her palms together under her chin. "That's an offer a woman in a houseful of men can't refuse."

We went into the kitchen. It was small, the appliances old, counter space almost non-existent. We kept running into each other while we put food on the table. When

Bud, Rick, and Tiege came inside to wash up, the kitchen resembled freeway traffic during rush hour.

Cookie directed me to my seat once the food was ready. "You can sit here." She patted the chair between her and Tiege.

The sheriff took the chair on the far side of his brother. Bud sat between him and Cookie. While Bud prayed, I took in the spread. A relish tray, heaping meat platter, bowls of mashed potatoes, gravy, green beans, Jello salad, a plate of homemade bread, and a butter dish. My mouth watered. I loaded my plate with some of everything as it came around.

Cookie passed the gravy. "Leave room for dessert."

Who could eat all this and have room for dessert?

"What is it, Mom?" Tiege rubbed his stomach.

"Apple dumplings."

"My favorite!"

"Every dessert is your favorite." Bud ruffled his son's hair.

We tended to our full plates. Tiege finished first. "Can I have my apple dumpling now?"

"How about we wait on dessert until later?" Rick pushed away his plate.

Tiege took his to the sink. "That stinks."

Cookie set down her fork. "In the meantime, you can show Miss Newell the stuff you got lined up."

"Cookie, the meal was delicious. Thank you for inviting me." I rose and started to clear the table.

She stopped me. "Bud and me'll finish up. You and Tiege go along."

Tiege took my hand and pulled me outside. He pointed at a low butte on the western horizon. "You ain't gonna believe the view after we hike up there."

We were going on foot? I dug in my heels. "That's quite a ways."

"We can do it."

One of us could handle the hike. And it wasn't me.

"Tiege, that's too far to make her walk."

We turned to see Rick approaching us. "I'll drive you up there."

I eyed the butte. Maybe it wasn't as far as it looked. "I don't mind walking."

"Tiege tends to bite off more than he can chew. And that butte's not as close as it looks." He got in the driver's seat of Bud and Cookie's truck. "Both of you, jump in."

Tiege scooted in beside his brother and I sat beside Tiege.

"Mom and me wrote everything down." He dug a wrinkled piece of paper from his pants pocket.

"Just tell me where we're going." Rick cranked the engine and eased into first gear. "But you're in charge of the gates."

The truck lurched through the dry pasture. Cattle stared and stood their ground, scattering only when the truck's bumper grazed their flanks. On the other hand, the antelope grazing in the distance bolted over a rise with terrorized grace.

My tailbone was begging for mercy when Rick parked at the top of the butte. When we got out the wind threatened to topple me. I put a hand on the hood of the truck to steady myself. Tiege traced the border between South Dakota and Montana with his index finger and pointed out where Arvid lived.

Then he moved on to a tumble-down house to the north. He read from the paper with slow precision. "Dad and Mom bought the Amdahls out about before I was born. All that's left is their Sears and Roebuck house. It was shipped here as a kit in 1925. The Amdahls put it together. Kinda like Lincoln Logs."

"Someday, I'm gonna fix it up and move in." He abandoned his script. "First, I gotta get rid of the owls and snakes that took it over."

"Rattlesnakes?"

"Yeah. We find 'em all over the ranch. You seen a rattler before?"

"No."

"I'll find you one!" He ran off.

"Don't bother." The wind carried my objection in the wrong direction.

My eyes followed the road to the spot where Twila had been killed. "There's the—"

Careful, Jane! You've spent three and a half weeks hiding your investigation. Don't blow it now.

"Wasn't Twila's body found on this road?"

Sheriff Sternquist motioned to the spot I knew quite well.

"Who found her?"

"Frost and Fannie McDonald."

"Axel's parents?"

"The same." His expression was cold.

"Are they suspects?"

"The first persons on the scene are always suspects."

Axel's parents were suspects too? That, coupled with the sheriff's treatment of Brock, could explain Liv's opposition to him.

"Do you seriously suspect an old man and woman who found her together and can back each other up?"

His expression turned glacial. "I'm not at liberty to discuss an ongoing investigation."

"But you were at liberty to badger Brock last night?" I hurled the words into the wind.

His facade thawed and froze again.

Tiege careened around the truck and slammed into his brother. "I seen a rattler on a rock. We gotta kill it." Rick took a spade and a hoe from the truck bed, and they ran off.

I tiptoed toward the truck on the alert. My pulse pounded in my ears while I waited in the cab. When Tiege and the sheriff returned, the pulsing began to slow.

"You gotta see this, Teacher." Tiege opened his palm to reveal a tapered chain of rattles. "It's the biggest I ever seen. Eight of 'em!"

When the sheriff parked in front of his parents' house, Tiege ran inside. He was showing his treasure to Bud and Cookie when I entered.

Bud took a quart canning jar—three-quarters full of . . . something—from a bookshelf and screwed off the lid. "Drop them in here, Son."

"I wanted to show you this right off, but Mom said it was a little much." Tiege handed the jar to me. It was three-quarters full of rattles.

Do not drop the jar! Do not let this seven-year-old know how much this grosses you out.

"Nice." I passed it back.

"Tiege, put that away and wash your hands." Cookie bustled into the kitchen and set a pan of apple dumplings on the table. "Then you can have dessert."

"With ice cream?"

"Yes." Tiege and I washed up while Cookie set bowls

beside the pan of dumplings. The front door squeaked. "That you, Rick? We're having dessert."

"Can you save mine? I want to fix a weak spot in the fence before I leave. Could take a while."

"Will you be able to drop off Miss Newell on your way to town?"

"Don't think so." The door banged shut.

The dumplings were delicious. I scraped the last delectable drop of ice cream and apple syrup into my spoon and peeked at my watch. "Oh my goodness, I had no idea it was this late. I really need to get back."

Bud stood. "Let's get goin' then. You comin', Tiege?"

On the way out I noticed three pictures on the wall. One was Rick's graduation picture. One was Tiege's school picture. The third was of a boy, maybe nine or ten.

"Who's that?"

Tiege stilled. "My brother Larch. He's dead."

Bud filled in the details during the drive. Larch had died the summer after the picture was taken. He'd just finished fifth grade. Rick was between his sophomore and junior years in high school.

"They was practicing calf-tying in our arena for the youth rodeo. Larch was all het up to win it. Cookie had laid down the law to Rick about keeping an eye on Larch, so Rick pulled him off his mare when it went balky and belligerent. Rick wanted to get some sugar for the horse. Told Larch to wait on the fence. Larch was under the mare's feet when he come back." Bud cleared his throat. "He died on the way to the hospital."

"Before I was born. Right, Dad?"

"Right, Tiege." He put an arm around the little boy's shoulder.

"How awful. I am so sorry for your loss."

"We're sorry too." Bud pulled up beside the schoolyard. "Always will be. It was hard on us. Rick most of all." He ruffled Tiege's hair. "But this guy is a gift and a blessing we never saw coming. He keeps us moving forward."

I thanked Bud for a wonderful afternoon. I walked across the playground, pulling my jacket tighter around my shoulders. Everywhere I went I heard about people with secrets to keep and sadness buried deep. The sheriff wasn't immune, nor was I. My students weren't immune either. I couldn't change that. But inside my classroom, I could make a difference. It was my space. These were my kids, and I would shield them from hurt. I would keep them safe. And no one was going to stop me.

CHAPTER 22

My feet hit the floor when the rooster greeted each new day the following week, and I didn't stop moving until I fell into bed each night. My students settled into our routine, checking the butterflies each morning. They were certain they would find eggs on the undersides of the milkweed leaves, only to find them stubbornly unchanged. Hopes dashed, the children went to their desks and attacked their lessons.

Liv stopped by after school Monday. Her forehead was etched with worry lines. "Axel and I want to thank you again for watching the girls."

"They were delightful. You must be proud of them."

"I'll be leaving soon as school's out from now on." Her lips trembled. "We moved Brock home so we can keep an eye on him. Axel drives him over in the mornings, and I pick him up after football practice."

Once Liv left, I unlocked the file cabinet and took out the clipboard. According to the sheriff's way of thinking, Axel's parents belonged on my list. By my way of thinking, they didn't. I compromised and wrote their names in pencil instead of pen at the very bottom of the page. Then I called Anna Marie Baumgartner.

"Are you a mind reader? I just got off the phone with the Pierre office." Her gum snapped. "The mainframe computer went down, whatever that means, and they just got it up and running again. They promised the printout will be in the mail the week after Labor Day at the latest. I sure hope the trucks you're looking at don't get sold before then."

The next two days were so busy, there wasn't time to think of anything but work. I was entering marks in my grade book on Wednesday afternoon when the phone rang.

"Little Missouri School. Miss Newell speaking."

The caller answered with a wet, whistling schlup.

"Merle?"

"A person can't pull nothing over on you, can they, Teacher?"

My stomach growled. "What's up?" Patience, Jane. The tuna melt you have planned for supper will be there when you're done talking.

"We-ull, I'm fixing to make some non-skid pancakes for supper and wondered if you'd be so kind as to join me?"

The tuna could wait. "How soon?"

"We-ull, these is some fancy yeast waffles that the recipe book says need to rise for sixty minutes. Bring your Kodak whenever you please. Me and Snippy'll be ready."

"I'll be there." I hung up, and the phone rang again. What did Merle want now?

"Little Missouri School. Miss Newell speaking."

"Well now, don't you sound professional?"

Not Merle. Junior.

"I'd trust my children with you any day."

"You have children?"

"Not that I know of." He paused. "That came out wrong."

"It certainly did."

"Mind if I change the subject?"

"Go right ahead."

"I want to apologize for not calling you like I said I would."

I waited. He wasn't getting off the hook until he'd dangled there awhile.

"Jane?"

"Hmm?"

"I'd like to take you out to supper by way of apology."

"When?"

"Tonight."

"I already have plans for tonight." A double dangle! "You can call this weekend to ask me out."

"Why not now?"

"You kept me waiting. I want you to know what it feels like. Talk to you soon." I hung up before he could reply.

Triple dangle for the win!

***

I arrived at Merle's with my camera—not a Kodak—in hand. The grass around Merle's house caught at the hem of my skirt. A cocklebur clung to my nylons and a run appeared. Why hadn't I changed into my grubbies?

Merle met me outside a small, unpainted outbuilding. "This here's the barn. Watch yur step in them fancy shoes." He tugged on a door sagging on rusty hinges. "Maybe it'd be better if Snippy come to you."

He shuffled into the gloom and brought out a milk cow by a rope loped around its neck. "This here's Snippy. She's part Jersey. The best milk cow I ever had. And I had a lot of them. I'm mighty grateful yur taking her picture."

I scooted a few steps to my left to capture Merle and his girl in the best light. I snapped a couple shots and promised to bring him the pictures once the film was developed.

"But we ain't took the good pictures yet." He turned Snippy until her head faced the barn door and her backside faced me. Then he pointed at her udder, so full and heavy her teats nearly dragged on the ground. "Now you just squat down and get some Kodaks of her business end. Make it quick. I want to show you my garden and have enough time to eat before she needs milking."

I framed Snippy's . . . ahem . . . business end in the view finder and took several shots.

Merle took Snippy to the barn before walking to the high fence that reached far above my head. He popped the latch on the gate and doffed his hat. "After you."

I stepped into a fairyland. Old-fashioned yellow climbing roses and hollyhocks graced the fence surrounding the quarter acre plot. Long rows of green beans, potatoes, and sweet corn marched from one end of the garden to the other. Tomato plants spilled over the tops of five-foot-tall cages. One corner was crowded with broccoli, cabbage, and cauliflower. Not a single weed marred the hard-packed soil between the rows. A dozen or more chickens ran about snaring insects and swallowing them whole.

I drank in the green vegetation and dark earth, satisfying a thirst for color the brown landscape outside the garden fence couldn't quench. The sprinkler running full tilt in the far half of the plot accounted for the vibrant green, but not for the dirt, which was almost as black as Iowa's rich topsoil.

"What did you do to the—" I yelped and jumped away as a chicken stretched her long neck and plucked a grasshopper from my skirt.

Merle shooed the bird away. "Go on now. Sorry 'bout that." His eyes moved from the beans to the tomatoes to the cabbages, and then back to me. "You like it?"

"It's lovely, but why is the soil so black and rich in here?"

He turned off the water "Soon as the frost's out in the spring, I till rotted sawdust and Snippy's cured manure into the soil."

"Is there anything Snippy can't do?"

"I don't believe there is. Now we got to eat supper. Snip don't like waiting to be milked."

After supper, our stomachs full of non-skid pancakes, bacon, and applesauce, we stood outside and chatted until the mosquitoes found us.

"Better get on your way, Teacher." He eyed the clear sky. "You best get something ready for them kids to do during recess. It's gonna rain all day tomorrow."

The thunder began after breakfast while I loaded

clothes into the washer. I sniffed at a discolored spot near the hem of my skirt from the night before. Chicken poop?

Disgusting! I pinched the waistband of the skirt between my thumb and forefinger and dropped it in the washing machine and started a heavy-duty cycle. Rain began to pound on the roof, and I carried a stack of board games from the supply closet into the classroom. Merle was right. We would need them.

After school, the phone rang. The caller's words gushed out. "This is Lacey Jo from the Dyed and Gone to Heaven Beauty Salon in Tipperary. You got a real nice gift certificate here from . . . Harold Noelle, is it?"

"Newell."

"If you say so." The torrent of words continued. "Would you like to book an appointment for this Saturday morning before the Labor Day rodeo parade here in Tipperary?"

There was a Labor Day parade and rodeo too? I booked a nine o'clock appointment.

"We're on Main Street across from the hardware store. The gals at the grocery store say you should get there early to pick up their gift certificate 'cause they'll close for the parade too."

So much for sleeping in on Saturday.

The kids spoke of nothing but the Labor Day festivities on Friday. Renny was riding on Round the Bend's float in the parade. Several children said they would be in the greased pig contest. Cora intended to ask the rodeo queen contestants for autographs. Beau said nothing.

During recess duty at noon, I noticed several children

from Liv's class playing chase. One girl lurched along the sidewalk and a boy pretending to drive a car rammed into her.

"You hit me!" She screamed and fell to the ground in a heap.

The boy swore at her, using a few words new to me. "What are you doing walking on the road at night?" He grasped an imaginary steering wheel and peeled off.

A second girl pretended to drive up. When she saw the body, she became hysterical. "She's dead! It's a hit and run! She's dead! Call the cops!"

I charged over and broke up the game. The children scattered and I went back to patrolling the playground. Beau sat alone on the teeter-totter. He had pulled his jacket over his head and shut himself off from the world. I sat beside him and put an arm around his trembling shoulders. I waited with him until his trembling ceased.

Some of the same children lingered on the playground after school. After I sent them home, Velma Albright ambushed me. "Did you hear what them kids was saying?"

"I did, and I put a stop to it."

"What more you gonna do about it?"

"They're Liv's students. We'll decide before school next Tuesday."

"If you don't, you best stay away from me. I got no patience with people like you." She stomped off.

I stared after her. Velma wore her anger like armor. Was concern for Beau the cause of her rage? Or fear of being found out for hitting her niece and leaving her to die?

The apartment phone rang and I hurried inside. "Jane Newell here."

"My neighbor boy wore you down yet?" Arvid's voice traveled down the line.

"Not yet. I'm tougher than I look."

"I 'spect so. Say, if you ain't busy, would you like to go with me to supper in Tipperary after the rodeo shuts down?"

"I would love to!"

We made plans to meet at the #3 Steak House in Tipperary at six o'clock Monday evening.

"He's got a crush on you," Betty singsonged after our call ended. "Before wong, you'ww have every unmarried man in the county on your doorstep!"

"When that happens, will you be my social secretary?"

"I'd be dewighted."

I grinned and put the receiver in the cradle. I was ready to enjoy a relaxing Labor Day weekend. I couldn't have been more wrong.

Chapter 23

Saturday began well. I parked in front of the Tipperary Super Value at eight-thirty and made short work of Dad and Mom's grocery store gift certificate. The stock boy tucked my meat and produce around the jug of frozen ice in the cooler in the backseat. He arranged the rest of the groceries in the trunk as pickup trucks chugged up and down the street.

I waited for a break in the traffic and crossed the street. The full impact of the Dyed and Gone to Heaven beauty salon hit as I stood outside its entrance. Had the crowd of friends I ran with in college seen the hot pink and magenta exterior paint, they would have had a field day. They were living their dreams in Chicago and Minneapolis, Kansas City and Phoenix. I was stranded in cowboy country, practically penniless and in dire need of a haircut. I took a deep breath and walked into the salon.

"Hello, dear." A tiny woman, not a day under seventy, greeted me. True to the shop's name, her bouffant hairdo was dyed and almost reached to heaven. "Are you Jane Newell?"

"Yes."

"You're right on time," she sniffed. "That's more than I can say about most people your age. Right this way."

I clutched at my ponytail and imagined this woman snipping and teasing it into a style ten years out of date. If I didn't go home for Thanksgiving, no one would know. It would be grown out by Christmas.

"You sit there." She motioned to a hair station next to an ancient permanent wave machine. "I'll get Lacey Jo. She's in the back."

She disappeared through a doorway at the back of the room. "That teacher from Little Missouri's here!"

A young woman came out with an armload of trendy shampoos and conditioners. Her blond hair was cut in a Dorothy Hamill wedge. She wore a cotton jumpsuit in a style I'd admired in Simplicity's summer pattern book. Her silver platform sandals twinkled with every step she took. She set the bottles on the seat of the permanent wave machine.

"I'm Lacey Jo and this is my grandma, Clarice." She fluffed my hair. "She sold her shop to me after I graduated from beauty school in the spring, and she's been showing me how her ladies like their hair styled."

"Grandma, Miss Newell is a new customer. You don't got to stay around for her. Scoot outta here and get on over to the parade. You won't hurt my feelings."

Clarice glanced out the window. "You sure you don't mind?"

"Not at all. Now go have fun."

Clarice picked up her purse. "I believe I will."

Lacey Jo was silent until her grandmother was out of sight. "Finally! That's the first time she's left me alone here for a week. She knows I'm ditching the permanent wave machine. And the Dippity-Do. And a bunch of other stuff too. Now, what do you want done today?" Lacey Jo turned my head this way and that.

Without waiting for a reply, she turned on the faucet and tested the water temperature. "Little Missouri's getting quite the name for itself, compliments of Brock McDonald. He's been running wild since the day he started high school." She squeezed shampoo into her palm and massaged my scalp. "He acts like there ain't no tomorrow, so he's doing it all today. And he's way too young for what he's doing."

She rinsed my hair, dried it with a towel, and combed it out. "The sheriff's real tight-lipped, though. He's aged ten years since Twila Kelly died. Some people think the job's too much for him. But he deserves a chance, don't you think?" She picked up her scissors. "Scuttlebutt was that he's eyeing somebody from around Little Missouri.

"My money is on that Trudy Berthold. She set her cap on Glen in high school and has been jealous of Twila since he asked her to senior prom. Me and Junior left The Bend at closing time a few weeks after Twila moved to Marmarth. Junior no more than pulled the door shut before Trudy lit into Glen. She swore a blue streak and was throwing bottles at him left and right from the sound of things. If I was the sheriff, she'd be my top suspect."

Lacey Jo made a few snips and whistled at a gleaming white Suburban reflected in the mirror. "Would you look at that new outfit? Why didn't he tell me about it on our last date?" She turned my chair toward the window. We both stared.

"That's Junior Wentworth, isn't it?"

"You know him?" She gripped the scissors like a knife.

Mentioning our date to a woman holding sharp scissors didn't seem wise. "He was the fair parade marshal."

"Oh, that's right." She traded the scissors for a blow dryer.

Disaster averted.

"We date some. He's fun." She picked up a bottle, squeezed something into her hand, and worked it into my hair. "He's a hard one to figure out, but he's definitely worth the effort." She twirled my chair toward the mirror. "What do you think?"

My eyes widened. My hair had never looked this good. "How did you do that?"

She explained how to work her magic at home. I bought the products she suggested and there was still enough left on the gift certificate for another cut. I threw my purchases in the back of the Beetle. Then I joined the crowd a few blocks away as the city police car led the parade, lights flashing and sirens blaring.

This parade was a carbon copy of last week's with one exception. The parade marshal was Arvid Drent. He went by, not on a horse, but perched on a canary yellow Mustang convertible. He waved to the crowd without enthusiasm but became animated when he threw candy to the children.

"Arvid!" I hollered. He turned and his face flamed red. "Are you sure you have time in your busy schedule for supper Monday night?"

"Six o'clock sharp." He gestured toward the restaurant across the street. "Right there."

I gave a thumbs-up. Arvid winked as the convertible rolled by. Without warning the color drained from his cheeks and the light left his eyes. He turned away.

"Congratulations." A familiar voice came from behind me. "You may be the first woman Arvid's ever invited to dinner."

The sheriff? I turned around. It was him. "Shouldn't you be leading the parade?"

"The deputy drew that straw. I got crowd control." His gaze swept along the rows of people across the street and stopped at Brock McDonald and his parents.

"Excuse me." The sheriff trotted over to them. Axel's hand tightened on Brock's shoulder. Liv moved so her body blocked her daughters' view.

A woman behind me started to talk. "Do you suppose the sheriff's blowing the whistle on Brock?" It was Lacey Jo.

I turned to see if she was talking to me, but she was facing Junior Wentworth. They were a stunning pair. Her petite flair and his cowboy elegance were an intriguing contrast. But they were standing very close to one another. Good thing I wasn't the one holding scissors now.

"Could be." Junior tipped his hat at me. "That boy's been cutting a wide swath for a year or more, and the law's bound to catch up with him. But that's none of our concern, now is it?"

"Guess not," Lacey Jo agreed. "But your new Suburban is. Did you get it here in town?"

"Sure did."

"Ooo, when are you taking me for a ride in it?"

"Miss Newell!" Renny waved from his perch beside Glen on The Bend's float, more excited than he ever was at school.

I waved back. "You're looking mighty fine, buddy. Are those new boots?"

He pulled up a pant leg and wiggled his foot. Just then the float lurched and Renny pitched forward. His dad caught him before he could fall.

"Both feet on the ground." Glen thumped his son's head. "Use some common sense for once."

Renny stared at his feet.

I stared at Glen and moved him to the top of my suspect list. A father who humiliated his son like that in public would have no qualms about leaving the scene after hitting the woman he'd been fooling around with for months.

The parade ended and I hurried to the Beetle. I was eager to get home, shut out the world, and dive into a book. When I got to my apartment I checked on the monarchs first. They hadn't changed a bit. It had been almost two weeks since my students had adopted them and still no eggs.

Come on, you sluggards. I tapped on the glass. My students are depending on you.

I read for a couple hours and then called my parents. "Thanks for the gift certificates."

"You used them already?"

"I went to the grocery store and beauty salon this morning. I love what Lacey Jo did with my hair."

"Have that nosey neighbor of yours take a picture and send it to us."

"I will."

"Jane, we miss you."

"I miss you too."

"And I worry about you. You're so far away. And with that murderer roaming around, you're not safe. Are you still locking your doors at night?"

"Yes."

"Maybe you should get a gun."

"Mom, I'm not Annie Oakley. I'm your daughter. The one who got caught in revolving doors as a preschooler. The one who carried her father's urinal to the bathroom and spilled its contents on the pastor who stopped to visit. The one who stabbed herself with a utility knife in college. A world with me carrying a gun would not be a safe place."

"Pepper spray, then. I'll send you a can of pepper spray."

"Fine, Mom. Good-bye."

After our call ended I shuddered. The minute the pepper spray arrived, it would go in the trash. In my hands, pepper spray would be a deadly weapon. I would aim for an attacker and spray myself instead. I was just that dangerous.

Chapter 24

I slept late Sunday, got the classroom ready for the week, and cracked open a new Agatha Christie novel and read until my eyes crossed. My stomach began making noises so I made a sandwich and ate it in front of the television. Flipping between television channels I caught the tail end of a news story about the police investigation into Twila's death.

A reporter stood at the scene of the accident, the camera panning the road and the ditches on either side as he spoke. "The investigation appears to be at a standstill, and the Tipperary County sheriff declined our request for an interview." The image on the screen switched to a school playground—the Little Missouri school playground.

I gasped and inhaled the food in my mouth. By the time my coughing fit ended, the reporter was wrapping up the story.

". . . a little boy goes to bed each night without his mother. From Little Missouri in western Tipperary

County, this is Roger Holmstead for KOTA Channel 3 News."

I wasn't going to stand for him invading Beau's privacy. Not at all. I wrote a note to call Mr. Holmstead at the television station on Tuesday. Then I hauled out my clipboard and wandered around town searching for more trucks. It was a waste of time. The only ones in sight sped by too fast to check light covers and write down license plates.

The Labor Day traffic continued into Monday, but no one stopped by. The privacy was glorious until it ended when the phone rang around four.

"This is Jane."

"You be changing your mind about going to a restaurant with an old codger?"

"Absolutely not," I assured Arvid. "I'm more concerned that the county's biggest celebrity won't want to be seen with an ordinary, everyday schoolteacher."

"Miss Newell, I be telling you how the parade marshal gets chosen. There's this committee that's got a paper with every Tipperary County citizen listed by birthdate from oldest to youngest. Every year they start at the top and choose the oldest geezer who's still breathing and won't blow away during the parade. This year, that geezer be me."

"Why do I think you're selling yourself short?"

A muffled pounding came through the receiver.

"What's that noise, Arvid? Is something wrong?"

"Sorry. I gotta go. Somebody's at the door, and my cats be going bee-zerk. See you tonight."

Someone bellowed in the second before he hung up. "Arvid! Open the--"

The receiver hit the cradle with a bang that hurt my ear.

I didn't like what I'd just heard. "Betty, did you recognize that voice?"

"I know it, but can't quite pwace it. If it comes to me, should I caww you?"

"Please do."

I made a cup of tea and picked up my book again but I couldn't concentrate. So I set up my ironing board, got out the iron, and turned on the television. I sprayed a wrinkled shirt with water and attacked it with the hot iron. After conquering the wrinkles, I dressed for supper in blue jeans, a button-down shirt, and the brown blazer Mom had made from wool she'd salvaged from an old coat. I wore my hair down, delighted by how easy the new cut was to scrunch and shape.

Merle was walking toward the barn, milk bucket in hand, when I walked to my car. "Where you off to?"

"Supper in Tipperary." I settled into the driver's seat. "See you later!" A half hour later I pulled into the #3 parking lot and checked the time. I was a little late. Arvid's pickup wasn't there yet.

I went inside, took a table near the door, and ordered a Coke. Twenty minutes later I beckoned to the waitress. Her blond ponytail made her look about fifteen. "Has Arvid Drent called to say he'd be late?"

"Let me check with the boss." She turned on the heel of one pink cowgirl boot and was back in seconds. "Nobody's called, but the boss said you can use the phone if you need it."

"Thank you—" I glanced at her name badge "—Dakota." She led me to the counter where the phone and phone book sat beside the cash register. I located Arvid's number and dialed.

The phone rang and rang. I hung up.

"Maybe he's on his way." Dakota gestured to my table. "You sit down and I'll bring you another Coke and an appetizer. You like onion rings?"

"Yes, thanks."

Soon she was back with my soft drink. "I called a couple of Arvid's neighbors in case they'd seen him. Sheriff Sternquist was at his folks' and said he'd check on him. He'll call soon as he can. You mind sticking around until we hear back?"

"That's fine." My stomach rumbled.

"I'll get your onion rings."

They were heavenly. I snarfed them down and was on my second Coke when the phone rang.

She snatched the receiver, listened, and waved me over. "Sheriff Sternquist wants to talk to you."

"Miss Newell?"

His tone of voice made my stomach churn. "What's wrong?"

"I'd rather not talk about it on the phone. Can you stay there and wait for Dad?"

"What is it? What's wrong?"

"Dad is on his way. Now let me speak to Dakota again."

I gave her the phone.

She listened and nodded. "Got it." She replaced the receiver, guided me to my chair, and picked up my plate and glass. "You're looking a little peaked. I'll bring you something easier on the stomach."

I swallowed the bile rising in my throat. Dakota

brought crackers and tea and sat down beside me. She pointed to customers, doling out bits of history and family news. I tried to pay attention, but couldn't. The drumbeat of questions in my head was too insistent.

Where was Arvid? What had happened to him? What did the sheriff know? Why had he sent Bud to tell me?

Dakota encouraged me to nibble crackers and sip the tea until I drained the little pot. "I'll get you more hot water and a new tea bag. Maybe you should visit the ladies' room?"

I did as she suggested and bumped into Junior Wentworth on the way back to my table.

"Sorry. I gotta watch where I'm going." He grasped my shoulders and studied my face. "You're upset. Jane, what's wrong?"

The door opened and Bud Sternquist rushed over. He took my hand. "Will you excuse us, Junior?"

Once we were seated, Dakota brought coffee for Bud and hot water for me.

I pushed mine away. "What happened to Arvid?"

"He's gone."

"Of course he's gone. He's meeting me here for supper. What I don't know is why he's running late."

"It's more than that, Jane."

An anvil pressed into my chest. "Is he dead?"

"We don't know. Me and Rick didn't find a body. He and the deputy are still looking."

The weight lifted. No body meant Arvid was still alive. "Maybe he had a flat tire. Or he's checking the livestock. Or . . ."

Bud shook his head. "His front door was wide open. He never left it open for fear his cats would get out. Them cats are his family. And his truck's sitting outside the house with the keys in the ignition."

"But that can't be. He called this afternoon all excited about tonight."

Bud grew alert. "What time was that?"

"Around four."

"Was anything about the call unusual?"

I described the banging and shouting that had ended our conversation.

"You didn't recognize the other voice?"

"It was muffled."

"Rick's gonna want to talk to you."

"Why?"

"Somebody turned Arvid's house upside down. Don't look like anything was taken, so the sheriff suspects foul play."

"Foul play? What does that mean?"

Bud passed me a few napkins. "Could be kidnapping, I suppose . . . or . . ."

Tears filled my eyes. "Who in the world would want to kidnap Arvid?"

"I been asking—" he cleared his throat "—I been asking the same question ever since we got to Arvid's place. We gotta remember that me and Rick didn't find a thing. No footprints. No blood. No vehicles missing. No tire tracks. So far as we know, he's not dead. Just gone."

"Gone?" I swiped at my tears. "Gone where?"

"Rick's trying to figure that out. He's got neighbors checking every road in the county while he and the deputy search the ranch."

"I can help with the search." I stood. The movement set my stomach churning and I sank down again.

"Never seen a person turn green so fast." Bud pushed my head between my knees. "Breathe deep and slow."

An eternity later the nausea passed. I raised my head. Bud handed me a glass of water, Dakota rubbed my back, and a stranger held an ice pack on the back of my neck. Junior asked if he should call for an ambulance.

I sat up. "No. I'll be fine."

"Your color's better, but you shouldn't be driving." Bud turned to Junior. "Could you take her home?"

"Anything to help."

"But what about my Beetle?" My teeth began to chatter. My hand shook and the water in my glass sloshed.

Bud took the glass from me. "I'll take care of it if you trust me with the key."

"It's in my purse."

Before long I was swathed in blankets and buckled into Junior's Suburban. On the ride home I rested my head on the seat back. Arvid's face appeared in the darkness behind my eyelids. Tears coursed down my face. A sob escaped from between my lips.

The Suburban slowed and Junior took my hand. "I'm so sorry, Jane."

With his touch, my fear and grief coalesced into words. Out tumbled Bud's account of what he and the sheriff had discovered at Arvid's ranch. Out came news of the search at the ranch and along county roads. Out burst the realization that I might have been the last person to have heard him speak—along with Betty Yarborough—and how we both heard someone pounding on the door and shouting Arvid's name.

Junior swerved into the other lane and then back again. "This time of night the deer are nearly invisible in the ditches." Junior jerked a thumb over his shoulder. "Did you see that doe?"

I pressed my forehead on the window glass. "No."

"You said Arvid's truck was at the ranch?"

"With the keys in the ignition."

"And there weren't any footprints?"

"I don't think so."

Junior was silent until we crossed the Little Missouri. "Can I use your phone to call my hired hands when I drop you off? They can bring my tracking dogs real quick while we get you settled. Then I can go straight to Arvid's."

"That would be wonderful. Thank you."

"We keep track of our own out here." He sped down Main Street and parked in a flurry of dust. "Nobody wants Arvid wandering around in the cold and dark, least of all me. Stay right there."

He hopped out, jogged around to the passenger side, and helped me out. The wind freshened and thunder rumbled in the distance as he bore my weight until we were inside. Then he helped me to the couch and made his call.

Afterward he sat beside me on the couch and massaged the back of my neck. "Do you want someone to stay with you tonight?"

The idea of gathering linens for an overnight visitor and making small talk was exhausting. "I'll be fine." Thunder boomed, closer now, and raindrops splattered on the roof.

"You sure?"

"I'm sure. Could you close the windows on the way out?"

The rain lulled me to sleep. I dreamed I was out in the storm, searching for Arvid, shouting his name. Once I thought I heard him begging me to let him in. Or it could have been the thunder imitating his deep, rumbling voice.

Sun streaming in the living room windows woke me the next morning. I sat up and blinked. I had spent the night on the couch. The events of the previous evening rushed over me and I bent double. Arvid had disappeared without a trace.

I held my tears at bay. My students would arrive soon and I didn't want to greet them with red, swollen eyes. I stumbled to the bathroom and doused my head with cold water. Then I dressed, ate a piece of dry toast, and walked to my classroom one slow step at a time. It was the only way to survive the awful day.

Chapter 25

Too soon, the morning breeze carried the chatter of young voices through the open windows. I watched Sheriff Sternquist dodge the children playing tag and climb the landing stairs. His shirt was rumpled, his pants and boots were muddy, and his eyes were dark and sunken.

"Wish I'd gotten here sooner." He got straight to the point. "You need to tell me about your phone call with Arvid."

I gestured at the children running in circles around him. "This is neither the time nor the place. School starts in ten minutes."

"When's your first break?"

"Country schoolteachers don't have breaks. You can stop by at three-thirty after the children leave. Now if you'll excuse me, I need to talk to Liv." I rushed across the playground to her room.

Her pale face and puffy eyes shocked me. She said she and Axel had saddled up and searched for Arvid all night in the rain and dark. "We wanted to find him so bad. I keep waiting for them to find something that connects Brock to Arvid's disappearance. Jane, what if they do?"

I hugged her. "They haven't found anything yet, have they?"

"No."

"And you can account for where Brock's been all week."

"We can."

"Then don't listen to the what-ifs. They'll drive you crazy."

I brought up my conversation with Velma. "She's on the warpath about about a game your students were playing." I recounted what I'd seen and done and Velma's reaction.

"You did the right thing. Velma's a bully, and since Twila's death, she's been bullying anybody she thinks she can push around. You better be ready to push back next time."

"Do we need to talk to any parents? Or to the Kellys? Or talk to the principal?"

"No! We say too much and everybody'll get riled up. They'll turn this school year into a Hatfield and McCoy affair." She glanced outside at the children milling about. "It's past time for school to start. I'll ring the bell."

I entered my classroom with no clue of what to say about Arvid. As it turned out, my students knew way more than I did. Those whose parents were part of the search passed along what they'd heard. It took an hour to talk through their excitement and worry. After the rhythm of the school day spun a cocoon of familiarity around them, they got to work.

Only Beau couldn't settle down. He made several trips to the pencil sharpener and stared out the window. By afternoon he'd sharpened his pencil right down to the eraser.

I called Iva during second recess. "Did he see the news report over the weekend? Or do you think Arvid's disappearance is upsetting him?"

"We've been keeping him away from television, so it's not that. He didn't know Arvid, so it's not that either. I think what's bothering him the most is the last time he talked to his mama. You should have seen his face light up when she said she was coming for him the next day. When she didn't show up, me and Burt thought she'd lied to him again. Beau said no, she was coming. Said she promised. When we had to tell him Twila was dead, the life went out of his eyes."

Her words clouded my vision as I watched the children playing outside. Beau sat on the landing steps, looking on. I used to watch the other kids play too, unable to muster the energy to join the fun while my world crumbled as my father's health declined.

"Are you still there, Miss Newell?"

"Ye . . . yes, Iva. What can I do?"

"You're doing plenty. Beau trusts you. And he is so excited about them butterflies, he's out the door every morning. He doesn't have so many nightmares either."

"He's been having nightmares?"

"Uh-huh. They started after his mama died, but like I said, they've died down some since school started. I figure either he likes being there, or you're wearing him out. Maybe some of both 'cause he hasn't had one bad dream since the first day of school."

The recess bell rang. I said goodbye and went to bring in the children lined up at the door. I replayed the conversation with Iva while my students mixed baking soda and vinegar to create a chemical reaction during science class.

The experiment failed to engage Beau. His eyes veered away whenever I tried to meet his gaze. When he slipped his arms into his backpack, his shoulders slumped. He didn't look up or say goodbye before shuffling down the landing stairs like an old man.

As I watched him go, Rick Sternquist parked on Main Street in front of the playground and got out. He waved and walked past the swing sets, stopping at the bottom of the landing. "Is this a better time to talk to you?"

I gestured for him to come in and we sat at the table in the front of the classroom.

He folded into a student chair and pulled a notebook and pen from his pocket. "What time did Arvid call you yesterday?"

"Around four."

"What did he say?"

"He wanted to confirm supper in Tipperary that evening."

"Did you notice anything strange?"

I described the pounding that interrupted our conversation.

The sheriff paused to write in his notebook. "Then what?"

I repeated Arvid's last words and described the shouting in the background.

The sheriff asked me to repeat what the visitor had said. "And you didn't recognize the voice?"

"Just that it was a man's voice and not a woman's. That's not much help, is it?"

"Well, it eliminates half the population. That's a start. If you think of anything else, have Betty ring me up." He paused. "Do you think she was listening in?"

"I know she was. After Arvid's phone went dead she said the voice was familiar, but she couldn't place it."

"That's the best tip I've had all day."

"She won't get in trouble with the phone company, will she?"

He stood. "She and Gus *are* the phone company. If anybody can identify that voice, it's Betty." He went to the door. "I don't think there's anything to worry about. But to be on the safe side, don't tell anyone about the phone call. I'll warn Betty and Gus too."

His progress across the playground was as slow and painful as Beau's had been. When Rick reached his truck, he tipped his hat. His face was tired and empty. When I realized what his expression lacked, I shuddered and looked away.

Hope. It was devoid of hope.

Chapter 26

The search for Arvid continued throughout the week. Its lack of progress was the centerpiece of each morning's show-and-tell.

"Dad and the other Forest Service rangers found a dead . . . campfire in the Long Pines," Bennan announced on Friday.

Cora interrupted him. "And then they found two hippies camping in the forest. They said they were walking across 'merica, but Dad didn't believe them."

"Until the sheriff in Miles City said they were in his jail when Arvid disappeared," Bennan finished.

Elva reported that the sheriff had asked her parents to ride their horses around Arvid's ranch in big circles. "Mom found some denim on the barbed wire and a fresh grave in a ravine." That created a stir until she went on. "The sheriff said the denim was really old and all that was in the grave was a dead dog."

"Mom says it was Arvid's blue heeler, Wrangler. She seen the collar and tag with her name on it," Stig added.

Renny Berthold chimed in. "Somebody at the bar said Arvid probably run off with a woman who wanted his money."

Tiege fell out of his chair. "Or maybe he's a ghost. Last night I looked out the window and seen a shadow wandering in the pasture."

Beau buried his head in his arms and kept his face hidden.

When I spoke there was a hard edge to my voice. "From now on you can discuss Arvid Drent at home, but not at school." I walked to Beau's desk and rested a hand on his back. "Time for reading class. Take out your books, please."

After school I called Iva again and assured her that talk of Arvid's disappearance would be off limits during show-and-tell from now on. Next I asked Betty to connect me to the Motor Vehicle Department at the courthouse in Tipperary.

"Hi Anna Marie. This is Jane Newell. Any word from Pierre?"

"As a matter of fact, it arrived today. The courthouse closes in a few minutes, but I'll put it in a new envelope and mail it Monday. You might get it later that day and for sure by Tuesday."

"That's great."

Except it wasn't. Beau was hurting and I needed—no, he needed—the information now. My investigation was spinning its wheels, but my day job never stopped. I sat at my desk, picked up a red pen, and attacked the mound of papers waiting to be corrected. What a way to usher in the weekend.

On Saturday I called Mom.

"What's new, Jane?"

Arvid's disappearance for one thing, but I knew better than to bring it up. What else could I talk about? "I still love my haircut."

"Have you taken a picture yet?"

"I'll ask Merle to take one when I stop by for milk and eggs."

"Do you want to talk to your dad?"

The floor vibrated and the low rumble of engines distracted me. I glanced out the window. A steady stream of Forest Service trucks and law enforcement vehicles from neighboring counties was flowing north out of town. A KOTA television news van pulled into the school playground and Roger Holmstead got out.

The nerve of that man! "Someone's coming to the door, Mom. I have to go." I hung up and stormed outside.

"You must be Jane Newell?"

I glowered at him. "You promised to leave Beau alone."

"I come in peace." He held up his hands, palms outward. "And I intend to keep that promise. The sheriff organized another search for Arvid Drent and we're here to do a story about that. Twila may be mentioned, but not Beau. You have my word." He held out a hand. "Can we shake on it?"

"Talk's cheap. I'll reconsider after you prove you can keep it." I went inside and slammed the door.

Throughout the weekend I wheeled my television from room to room while I cleaned, cooked, and did laundry. Roger's story aired during the Sunday evening news. He stuck to Arvid's disappearance as promised, made a passing reference to Twila, and left Beau out of it. If we ever met again, I owed the man a handshake.

On Monday Renny waved his hand for show-and-tell. "We watched Channel 3 news. It was weird to hear them talk about Little Missouri and see The Bend on the screen."

Before I could reprimand Renny for bringing up the forbidden subject, Tiege waved his hand wildly. I raised an eyebrow."Yes?"

"Did you forget?"

"Forget what?"

He pointed to the laminated paper cupcake bearing his name on the calendar slot for the day.

I feigned surprise. "It's your birthday?"

Not just his head, but his whole body bobbed.

"Then come up so we can sing happy birthday to you."

"Maybe we can sing it again when Mom brings the cupcakes."

The kid was such an opportunist.

Cookie brought the cupcakes for Tiege to hand out a few minutes before school ended. The children were eating their treats when Beau jumped up, ran to the sink, and vomited. Cookie took the kids to the playground to finish their cupcakes while I cleaned up Beau and called Iva. She picked him up five minutes later.

As soon as the other children were gone, I drove to the post office and checked my box. Empty, darn it.

"Miss Newell?" Dale Cunningham stood at his counter holding a manila envelope. "I've been watching for you. This was too big for your box."

I took it from him. "Mr. Cunningham, I've been waiting for this! I could kiss you!"

"Oh. Well." He retreated to the mail bins and picked up a handful of letters."That's against regulations."

I drove home, rushed into the apartment, and ripped the envelope open. Then I pulled out my clipboard and the math games folder. I matched names from the printout to license numbers on my chart. Within minutes I had identified the townspeople who belonged to the trucks with broken and discolored light covers. Glen Berthold. Trudy Berthold. Velma Albright. I massaged my temples and stared at their names.

Think about what this means, Jane!

For one thing, it did nothing to remove Brock as a suspect. The evidence against him was too damning. But it did cement the Bertholds' and Velma's places on the suspect list. Circumstantial evidence pointed to Velma, but what motive would she have had to hit her niece and run from the scene? Gossip around town gave Glen and Trudy the strongest motives, if the gossip could be trusted. But circumstantial evidence against them was scant.

I arranged Arvid's letter and the Lucky Strike package, along with the note I'd found in it, on the table. I picked up Arvid's letter, closed my eyes, and ran my fingers over it. Then I opened my eyes and, still holding the letter, said the name of each suspect out loud. I repeated the process with each item in front of me.

At the end of the exercise, I reordered the names from the person I considered to be the strongest suspect to the weakest. Behind each name I listed the evidence against them:

Brock: headlight, LS smoker, Twila's money, LS pack and note

Velma: headlight, LS smoker, defensive

Glen: headlight, relationship with Twila

Trudy: headlight, relationship to Glen

My pencil hovered over the paper when I came to Arvid's name. The case against him was weak, but his disappearance could be connected to Twila's accident. He had to stay on the list. At least for now.

Arvid: letter found at the dump, disappearance

Underneath my updated list, I added a few questions.

Why would Brock or Velma leave the scene?

Do Glen or Trudy smoke Lucky Strikes?

What am I missing?

I put down my pencil, gathered the papers and evidence into a neat pile, and hid everything in the file cabinet. It locked with a satisfying click. I was finally getting somewhere.

I tapped a finger to my lips. Now that Glen and Trudy were suspects, supper at The Bend was in order. I was two-stepping across the playground when my purse slipped from my arm and threw me off balance. My wallet fell to the ground and reality hit like a cold rain. My bank balance was closer to zero than ten, and I had no cash. There was no eating out until my first paycheck arrived. Or until my fairy godmother showered me with cold, hard cash. I scanned the sky. Not a fairy wing in sight. Go figure.

Chapter 27

After school the next day, someone knocked as I recorded second-grade math test scores.

"Come in."

The door creaked open. "Am I interrupting?"

Junior Wentworth's voice made my heart go pitter-pat. Even so, I held up an index finger. "Hang on a minute."

He made not one peep while I recorded the score in my grade book and tidied my desk. I swiveled in his direction. "Thanks for waiting."

"It's almost five-thirty. How long you been at that?" Junior motioned to my desk.

"Almost two hours." I raised and lowered my shoulders. "That explains why I'm so stiff."

"And to think me and all my friends thought teachers had it easy when we was kids." He shifted his weight from one leg to the other. "Listen. I'm here to apologize for not calling you about that date we were supposed to have."

"It took you long enough."

"You got supper plans?"

"Hard-boiled eggs and toast if I can find the energy to cook. Otherwise, a peanut butter sandwich."

"Well then, would you be put off if I asked you to join me at The Bend on mighty short notice?"

I twirled my index finger. "Turn around."

"What?"

"Turn around. Slowly."

He obliged.

"Now stop." I studied his back.

Hmm. No wings. Fairy godmothers weren't what they used to be, but I couldn't afford to be picky. "I would love to have supper with you."

He grinned. "Grab a jacket. It's nippy out."

I took my coat from its hook and we stepped outside. "Mmm. The air smells delicious. Do you mind if we walk?"

"Fine by me."

When we arrived at the cafe, I chose a booth where I could observe Trudy without being obvious.

After she took our orders, Junior rested his arms on the table. "I want you to know that even though I haven't stopped by, I've been thinking about you steady since the day Arvid disappeared. You doing okay?"

"I'm fine when I don't dwell on it." I stared at the booth's faded formica table top. "But between the sheriff questioning me and talking to news reporters, I can't get away from it."

Junior's eyes narrowed. "Reporters?"

"Oh, just that Holmstead guy from Channel 3." I filled him in on the details.

Trudy brought our drinks. I asked for a straw to take

a better look at her fingers. No nicotine stains, doggone it.

Junior whistled soft and low. "Jane Newell, there is more to you than meets the eye."

Trudy brought our food and I dug in. Junior had finished his beer and held up the bottle. She took it and brushed against me when she returned with a fresh one. I inhaled deeply. Her clothes reeked of cigarette smoke, but so did the whole cafe.

"You said the sheriff questioned you. What about?"

"He wanted to know about my phone call with Arvid before he disappeared." I put a fry into my mouth and chewed. Heaven!

Junior stabbed a piece of steak with his fork. "It's about time he did more than organize weekend search parties."

"You know the sheriff thinks Brock had something to do with Twila's death. Liv thinks he's looking for evidence to connect Brock to Arvid's disappearance."

"That sounds like a far stretch, doesn't it?"

"To you and me, yes. To a mother going through hell about her son, no."

Junior mopped up the meat juices on his plate with a dinner roll. "The relationship between mothers and sons tends to be complicated."

"Are you speaking from experience?"

He pulled on his beer and swallowed. "You better believe it."

We finished our meals and Trudy brought the check. Junior passed her a wad of bills without looking at it. "Use the extra on a pack of Luckies."

"You're a smoker? I didn't taste it on your breath after

the fair dance when we . . . " I fanned my hot face with a napkin. "When we . . . you know."

"I do know." He twirled a toothpick between his fingers. "The Luckies are for Glen and Trudy, not for me. That's how I guarantee good service."

Junior helped me with my jacket before we walked out into the dusky, chilly air. When we reached his car, he bent and brushed his lips against mine. "Can we do this again sometime?"

"That would be nice. Though perhaps not so last minute?"

"I hear you, and I promise to mend my ways." He cocked his head toward my apartment. "I'll wait right here until you're inside."

I walked to the door, comforted by his thoughtfulness and anticipating having supper with him again. I waved in his direction as I slipped inside. Junior blinked his lights three times, like a fairy godmother should, and drove away.

***

Liv burst into my classroom the next morning. "You know how I said the sheriff was looking for a way to connect Brock to Arvid's disappearance?"

I nodded, sickened by the look on her face.

"He showed up on our doorstep last night and asked to look at Brock's room. I would have thrown him out on his ear, but Axel invited him in. After I told the sheriff to come back with a search warrant, Brock came trotting down the hall saying he had nothing to hide. Before

I could put a stop to things, the sheriff was in Brock's room looking for who knows what."

"Did he find anything?"

"No."

I relaxed. "That's good."

"No, it's not, and don't you try to convince me otherwise. Rick Sternquist won't quit sniffing around until he pins Twila's death and Arvid's disappearance on Brock. You just wait and see." She left, slamming the door so hard, the floor shook beneath my feet.

The week went from bad to worse. The stomach flu picked off one child after another. On Friday Elva added the eighteenth tally to the butterfly category on the chalkboard. The children filed out, subdued and silent, when I dismissed them for the weekend.

I sat down to the piles of papers on my desk, but my head ached and my eyes wouldn't focus. My stomach lurched and I sprinted for the bathroom.

The next twenty-four hours consisted of vomiting into the toilet and watching television from the couch. I'd never been sick without anyone around to care for me before. I thought of how Mom always covered the living room couch with a clean sheet when I had to miss school.

"You hold still, Sweetie." She tucked the blankets so tight I felt like a sausage in a wool casing. "Your dad will keep you company. I'll come home at noon to see how you're doing."

Dad rolled his wheelchair next to the couch. I dozed in and out of sleep while Captain Kangaroo played on the television. Dad's snorts of laughter during I Love

Lucy reruns woke me, but I fell asleep again when the game shows came on.

"Janie." Dad poked me awake. "Your mother said to be sure you get plenty of liquids. Drink this." He held a half-filled glass of water in his shaky hand.

I drank it and snuggled back into the blankets as he wheeled the glass back to the kitchen.

The warmth of the memory wrapped around me and I grew drowsy. I wanted Dad at my side now. I wanted Mom to make a bed for me on the couch and tuck me in before she went to work. My eyes closed and a thought, soft as a feather, carried me to sleep.

Your dad's illness gave you this memory. Embrace it.

By Saturday evening I was tired of television, but encouraged when soda crackers and 7-Up stayed down. Sunday morning my sleuthing itch returned. I curled up on the couch to review my notes about Twila's accident and to move Glen and Trudy ahead of Velma on the suspect list.

I pulled at my bottom lip. Should I move them ahead of Brock too? No. There was a lot of evidence against him, enough for the sheriff to search his room.

The phone rang. I shuffled to the kitchen and picked up the receiver. "This is Jane."

"And this is Mom."

I burst into tears.

"What's the matter?"

"I've been sick all weekend."

I wanted to tell her how hard it was to be sick with my parents far away, how I longed to come home. I wanted to tell her about Arvid's disappearance. I bit my tongue to hold back the words that, once said, would destroy my resolve to stay in Little Missouri.

"Stomach flu. I'm on the mend. Just hungry and weepy, you know how it is."

"Try a poached egg on toast covered with warm milk."

Ah, the taste of childhood. "I'll make some after we hang up."

"We still haven't gotten a picture of your haircut."

"I haven't seen Merle lately."

"What about that nice Junior Wentworth?"

"Trust me, Mom. One look at me right now, and any nice young man in Tipperary County would run for cover."

After she said goodbye I took the last egg from the carton. Merle hadn't stopped by in days. Where was he? Had he fallen and broken a hip? Or had he disappeared like Arvid? What if he needed me?

I put the egg in the carton and raced to my bedroom for a jacket. My headache and dizziness returned with the sudden movement. I swayed and fell onto the bed.

Look at me! I pounded the mattress with my fist. I was no good to Merle. Or Beau. Or Arvid, if he was still alive. I curled into a ball and pulled up the afghan. I watched until the evening light faded to match the darkness in my heart, and I fell asleep.

Chapter 28

I woke with an empty stomach and a clear head. I made Mom's concoction for breakfast and my energy returned. I dressed for work and took soda crackers and tea into the classroom, nibbling and sipping until Beau came in early.

"Can I check the butterflies?"

I swallowed a mouthful of tea. "Sure."

"Miss Newell!" He hopped up and down, pointing at the jar. "I seed some eggs. Come look!"

I hurried over.

"Right there." He pressed on the glass with a grubby finger. "Can I go out and tell the other kids? Can they come in early too?"

"You certainly can."

He ran outside, animated and alive.

I knelt and pressed my hand against the jar, close to the glistening, white eggs. "Please hatch," I whispered. "Beau needs you to hatch."

Beau led the children inside and they crouched

around the jar. He pointed at a cluster of milkweed leaves. "Can you see them?"

"Right there!" cried Cora.

Tiege dropped to his knees and twisted around until he was looking up. "There's one egg on every leaf, just like the book said!"

The room reverberated with excitement. All morning the children made up excuses to crouch beside the butterfly jar to examine the undersides of the leaves. In the afternoon I called Liv and asked if two eighth graders could carry the jar outside.

"I guess so." She sounded worn out. "Send them back soon as the job's done so they don't miss social studies class."

Once the jar was outside I unscrewed the lid and freed the adult monarchs. They glided across the playground, over the fence, and disappeared in the grassy, empty lot across the street.

My students and I walked inside. Elva went to the chalkboard, put a tally behind "egg stage," and returned to her seat.

Renny raised his hand. "How many days are they eggs?"

"Five to ten." Elva pointed to the chart on the chalkboard.

Cora counted off boxes on the calendar. "Today is September 19, so they could hatch between September twenty-four and twenty-nine.

"Probably closer to twenty-nine," Tiege frowned. "The book says the stages take longer when the weather gets cooler."

After work I was too exhausted to go to Merle's

for eggs and called instead. My heart pounded while I waited for him to pick up. Was he there? Would he answer? He said hello with his whistly schlup.

"You're all right!"

"Course I'm all right. Why wouldn't I be?"

"I haven't seen you lately. I thought you might be . . . oh, never mind. Can I stop by for milk and eggs in a day or two?"

"Call first." He hung up with a clunk.

Seriously? He wanted me to call first? Like his social calendar was all that busy.

***

The next afternoon, Liv drove us to Tipperary for another teachers' meeting. "I hope you don't mind stopping at the sheriff's office afterwards to see if the test results are back from the state lab. And we'll need to get Brock after football practice."

Fine by me. Whatever the results were, I wanted to be with her when she got them.

I stayed in her truck while she went into the courthouse. She returned and slammed the door. "The state lab's got a backlog. It'll be at least another week. Who was it said 'waiting is hell'?"

"Shakespeare, I think. In one of the sonnets."

"He got that about right."

We collected Brock at the football field. Not only were Liv and Brock silent all the way to Little Missouri, but she tuned into a country-western radio station—as all stations in the area were—and cranked up the volume. The forty-five minutes on the road were the longest of my life.

I called Merle, as requested, when school dismissed Wednesday. He said to come right over. As I walked over, a stiff west wind tried to blow away my empty egg cartons and my camera. I gripped them harder and knocked on Merle's door. Nothing. I knocked harder, dislodging flaked paint from the door frame. The wind sent flecks swirling around my face and into my nose and mouth.

"Coming!"

I waited, spitting paint flecks until the door creaked open. "Don't git in such a hurry. An old man's bones need a chance to limber up." He took the egg cartons and milk jug. "Come in and git outta the wind."

He filled the milk jug and laid a full carton of eggs on an overturned five-gallon bucket. Then he pointed at the camera. "You got them pictures of Snippy back yet?"

"Not yet. I need to take a few more pictures to finish the roll. Could spare a minute to take a picture of me for my parents?"

"Glad to."

"Do you want to take it in the kitchen? I can sit at the table."

Merle scratched his neck. "The light ain't no good in there. We'd best take it outside."

"In this wind?"

"We can do it in the garden. It's always still in there." Merle limped out the door.

It was his house, so I followed him without arguing. When we entered the walled garden, an oasis of calm and sunshine greeted us.

"Now you stand in front of the rambler rose, and I'll snap you a Kodak." When he was finished he pointed to the lever that advanced the film. "My daughter in Belle, she always winds the film real slow and careful after the last picture to get an extry one at the end of the roll. Like this." He showed me how to do it and opened the gate.

The wind outside almost knocked me over. Grit blew into my face. My eyes watered and blinked. The crack of wood against wood made me jump. The barn door flapped and banged against the wall. Then it slammed shut. I snapped the bonus exposure as the wind flung the barn door open again.

I scurried to the mudroom where Merle waited for me.

"Stay here a minute. Don't move." He shuffled into the kitchen.

I held out my last three quarters to pay for the milk and eggs when he returned, but he waved it away.

"I been a poor neighbor lately." He handed me a tan envelope and two dollar bills. "Keep your money."

"What's this for?"

"It's one of them mailers for your roll of film and the cash to put in it. I give you enough for an extry set of prints."

I slid the envelope in my pocket. "I'll mail it tomorrow."

I kept my word. Dale Cunningham's greeting when I handed him the mailer was the cheeriest moment of the week. Thursday and Friday Liv didn't stop to talk before school, and she left right after dismissal time. No one called with unwanted invitations to church. Junior didn't call either. My only company outside of my young charges was Velma. She was as vile as ever—maybe even worse—when she stomped in to clean the school on Friday.

I attempted small talk. "Such a shame about Arvid."

Her shoulders stiffened.

"Did you know him well?"

She turned on me. "You been here less than two months. That don't make you part of this town. Keep your nose outta my business and everbody else's too, for that matter." She switched on the vacuum and yanked it back and forth in angry swipes.

The intensity of her anger caught me off guard. With her banging around, how was I supposed to eat supper? I retreated to my apartment and hunted for spare change in kitchen drawers and under couch cushions. Not a cent. I opened the door to my bedroom closet and searched the pockets of all my clothes. In the pocket of my winter coat, I hit the jackpot. A five-dollar bill!

I tucked the bill in my purse, locked my apartment, and fled. Velma could grouse to her malevolent heart's content while I ate at The Bend. The weekend was looking up!

Chapter 29

Main Street was deserted and the cafe was empty, strangely so for a Friday night. At least I had the pick of the booths. I selected one that offered a view of the seating area and the kitchen. Perfect for keeping an eye on the Bertholds.

Trudy took my order and left. A few minutes later she plunked down my food with a silent scowl. It disappeared when the door opened and Junior Wentworth entered.

His eyes met mine. “When you weren’t at your place I figured you were here. Mind if I join you?”

“I’d like that.”

He sat across from me and hollered to Trudy. “Bring me whatever’s good, so long as it’s a steak and baked potato.”

“You want a beer with that?”

“You’re too good to me, Trudy.”

She trotted to the kitchen and returned with a frosty bottle.

He pointed at my plate. "Go ahead and start eating. I'll catch up with you."

"Why'd you stop at my apartment?" I picked up my cheeseburger and took the first juicy bite.

"You were so shook up about Arvid last week, I decided then and there to check up on you every week or so until this town gets back to normal."

Tears sprang to my eyes like they always did when people were nice to me. I set my sandwich down. "Will it ever get back to normal with Arvid missing? What if he's dead?"

"There's no reason to think he is. The sheriff didn't find any sign of a struggle. And if Arvid is dead, where's his body?"

Junior's food arrived and he went to work, cutting meat off the bone and trimming the fat. "Old bachelor ranchers like Arvid are an independent bunch. They go off on trail rides and hunting trips without telling a soul."

"Do you really think that's the case?"

"It happens all the time." He split open his baked potato and slathered it with sour cream. "In fact, I'm surprised Rick Sternquist's making such a big deal of it. I think he's trying to distract people who are getting tired waiting for him to solve Twila Kelly's case."

I hadn't thought of that before, but it made sense.

Junior asked if I'd heard anything new about Brock McDonald. I told him about the backlog at the lab in Pierre and about the sheriff searching Brock's room.

"Why did Axel and Liv let him do it?"

"Brock insisted."

"That was stupid."

"Thankfully, the sheriff didn't find a thing."

"That should make the McDonalds rest easier." Junior wiped his hands on a napkin.

"Not really. Liv is even more convinced the sheriff is after Brock."

Junior asked for his check and mine. I protested, but he gave Trudy a handful of bills. She stuffed them in her pocket and we walked to the door.

Junior held it open. "You got plans for the rest of the evening?"

"No."

"Would you like to meet my parents?"

I glanced at Trudy. She was listening. With interest. Junior and I would be the talk of the town by morning. But I didn't care. A look inside that beautiful ranch house was worth a month of gossip.

"I would love to."

We strolled to the Suburban and got in. I ran a hand over the upholstery. "I could get used to leather seats."

"I didn't shed any tears when Tipperary Motors towed away what I was driving before. The Suburban is a big step up." He buckled his seatbelt.

I did the same. "Tell me about your family."

"My parents split their time between their house in Spearfish and the one at the ranch. We pretend that Dad's in charge, but I run things."

"Do you have any brothers or sisters?"

"I'm an only child. Or I should say, I'm my parents' only living child." He turned the key in the ignition and eased onto Main Street. "My mom had several miscarriages. When I was six, she carried a baby to term, but my sister was stillborn."

"That had to be hard."

"It was. Dad was able to move on, but Mom . . . That's a different story." He tightened his grip on the steering wheel. "Let's just say it's impossible to compete with a dead sister. As a woman, she'll be all over you."

Was he jealous?

Junior lifted my hand and kissed my palm. "Fixing up the guest room for grandkids before you know it."

No. It was just my imagination running wild again.

"She can join everyone else in town. I'm pretty sure Trudy called Pastor Petersen and reserved the church right after you paid for both our meals." We laughed. "But I'd still like to meet her. I haven't buried a loved one, but I do know what it is to lose someone."

I stared out the window and told him about my dad. "He played college football. Now he can't walk and has to carry a urinal in a little black bag where ever he goes. I grew up cutting his meat and lighting his pipe."

Junior switched on the blinker and turned into the driveway. "Your dad and I have a couple things in common. I played college football at the University of Nebraska."

"You're a Husker?"

He flinched as though I'd hit a nerve. "Not just a Husker. I was on my way to being a top draft pick until I blew out my knee at the end of my senior year. One tackle flushed my future down the toilet, and I came back here."

His story was similar to Dad's. But unlike my father, Junior sounded bitter. I didn't like it. But I didn't want to think about it either, so I took in the scenery. A grove of cottonwoods hugged the back of the house. Tall pole lights dotted the yard, giving the outbuildings a yellow cast. About fifty yards to the east, light poured from the windows of a log house twice the size of the brick home. He parked in his parents' driveway and switched off the engine.

"Wow. Your parents have a beautiful home."

"Watch your step." He pointed to the cement stair that went from the driveway to a sidewalk leading to the house.

In ten short strides I traversed more hard surfaces than could be found in the entire town of Little Missouri. Right then and there, I fell a little bit in love with Junior. Or at least with his cement.

"Dad and Mom keep things up pretty good." His pride was obvious. "Their house is a little too fancy for me, so I built my own place back there." He pointed to the log house.

"It's huge. You live there alone?"

"Yes and no. There's a wing in the back for the ranch hands. And I got a hunting guide business going. The bedrooms in the main wing'll be full up with antelope hunters when the season opens."

"When's that?"

"Second weekend in October." He rang the doorbell.

The man had cement and a doorbell? If he asked me to marry him tonight, I would have to say yes.

A tall man opened the front door. His hair was more white than black, but his erect frame was the same size and build as Junior's. His western shirt looked custom-made, with its plaids matched to perfection. His dress trousers were of wool flannel. And his gleaming boots were covered with exquisite hand tooling. Like father, like son.

In a blink his expression shifted from surprise to geniality. "Junior, come in. And this is . . ." He cocked an eyebrow.

"Jane Newell. The new schoolteacher from Iowa. Jane, this is my dad. He's the senior Richard Wentworth."

"So that's why everyone calls you Junior."

The older Richard Wentworth closed the door and took my hand. His voice was as sweet as honey on toast. "Correct. We called him Rich, but Merle Laird started calling him Junior and it stuck. You can call me Richard, not Mr. Wentworth."

I stopped myself from curtseying just in time.

He steered me through the foyer into the living room. "Corinne, we have company." He positioned me in front of an overstuffed leather chair. A small woman rose from its depths, the smell of permanent wave solution wafting up from her white, tightly-curled hair.

"I'm so glad to meet you, Mrs. Wentworth. I'm Jane Newell." I took her bony hand.

"Call me Corinne." Her crow's-feet crinkled. "So you're the new schoolteacher?"

"That's me. Your jacket is beautiful." I admired the woven pattern of rich swirls. "Is it tapestry?"

"It is." She stroked the sleeve. "Hard to handle. But it worked up beautifully."

"You made it yourself? What amazing attention to detail."

"Do you sew?"

"Yes, but nothing like that."

She purred at the compliment. "Would you like some hot chocolate?"

"Mom, we barged in on you with no warning. You don't have to--"

"No trouble at all." She rubbed her hands together. "It's an excuse to fire up the Amana Radarange Richard bought me. I'll be back in a jiffy."

I looked at Junior's father. "What's a Radarange?"

"It's a small oven than uses microwaves to heat food. The salesman called it space age technology. I call it expensive." He winked at his son. "But if it keeps your mother happy, it's worth the price."

Richard's condescension irritated me. I switched up the conversation. "How long has your family been on the ranch?"

I'd picked the right topic. Richard Senior—or perhaps I should refer to him as Richard the First in light of his lordly manner—launched into family history. "My parents were some of the original settlers in this country." He was describing the sod house he'd lived in as a child when Corinne carried in a tray laden with mugs of hot chocolate. "No electricity in those days." He lifted a mug from the tray. "And no Radarange. My mother worked hard every day of her life."

Corinne set down the tray and handed a mug to Junior first and then to me.

I took a sip. "It's delicious!"

Corinne picked up her mug. "Would you like to see my sewing room?"

"I'd love to." Anything to get away from Richard the First.

We were headed down the hall when Junior offered

to add a splash of brandy to his father's mug. I pretended not to hear Richard the First's reply. "Anything to improve this stuff. She's never been much of a bartender, has she?"

"Here we are." Corinne flipped a switch and light flooded the room.

I turned in a circle. "Oh, my!"

Her sewing room was a far cry from our setup at home. Mom's sewing machine was a top-of-the-line 1960s Singer. She'd gotten it dirt cheap because it was a demonstration model, and crammed it in one corner of my brother's bedroom. She'd confiscated two drawers of his dresser and half of his closet for her sewing supplies and materials. She spread her fabric on the living room floor to lay out patterns and cut the pieces.

Corrine had a cutting table in the center of the room. A Singer, the same model as Mom's, sat against the large picture window that stretched across the outer wall. Next to the machine was an ironing board and an electric steam iron. A dress form stood in one corner. Shelves stacked with fabric lined one wall. Antique oak cabinets with oddly shaped drawers lined another. They looked like the notions cabinets from the old dry goods store where Mom had shopped when I was a kid. "Where did you get this?" I ran my hand over the smooth oak surface.

"It's from a store in Little Missouri that went out of business years ago. I couldn't resist." She pulled open a drawer. "Feel free to explore."

I peeked inside. It was filled with spools of thread arranged by color in neat rows. Another drawer held bobbins. A third housed hanks of lace. One contained buckles—some were made of plastic celluloid, one was wooden and looked like it had been whittled by the light of a campfire, and several were silver.

I held up a small one. It sparkled in the light. "What's this?"

Corinne traced the design on the oval with a finger. "This is from Junior's first belt. His father had it engraved with our brand. Junior wore it until the buckle cut through the leather and fell off. He cried and cried until I promised to keep it in this drawer forever."

"And this?" I picked up a silver buckle engraved with stylized butterflies. "Was this Junior's too?"

"No." Her forehead wrinkled. "I don't remember seeing it before. Richard probably picked it up at an auction and put it in here. It wouldn't be the first time."

I slid my fingertips along the underside and felt a rough patch. I turned the buckle over and squinted at the faint scratches. "Do you think this is the artist's signature?"

Junior came in. "It's getting late, Jane. Is Mom holding you hostage?"

"If anything, I was the one holding her hostage." I dropped the buckle into the drawer and slid it shut.

Corinne walked me down the hall. "Why don't you come some Saturday and spend the day? Maybe during the opening of antelope season? I spend the entire weekend sewing while Richard and Junior hunt. You can bring whatever you're working on, and we'll sew all day."

"It's a date."

She and Richard the First said goodbye in the foyer. He held my hand a few seconds longer than was necessary.

"Sorry about Dad," Junior apologized once we were outside. "The older he gets, the more imperious he acts."

I wasn't going to argue with him. "Your mother is delightful. We're making plans to spend a Saturday sewing together."

"Of course you are. You're about the same age my sister would be if she'd lived."

We reached the steps that went down to the driveway. I misjudged the depth of the first one and stumbled. Junior steadied me and drew me close.

"You best be careful. If Mom sees us like this she'll start ordering wedding dress patterns."

Only two things about that idea bothered me. The first was having to tell my mother. The second was becoming Richard the First's daughter-in-law.

Arm in arm, we walked into the cottonwood grove. When we reached the shadows, we kissed. When we pulled away from one another, breathless and happy, I said, "Your parents will get suspicious if we don't leave soon."

Junior took me by the hand and led me to the Suburban. We were quiet on the drive until he pulled up outside the school. "Want me to come in with you?"

"What I want and what's wise are two different things."

"Can I at least walk you to the door?"

"Do I look crazy?" I fumbled for the handle. "We both know you'll kiss me again and the whole town will be watching."

Junior grabbed my wrist. "I don't care what they see."

"But I do." I tugged at my arm but he didn't let go. "That's the difference between us."

"What?" His fingers pressed into my flesh.

"Your family's been ranching here for decades. I've only been here a few weeks, and I'd like to keep my job. I'm assuming you'd like me to stick around too." I yanked my arm away.

When I reached the apartment landing I waved for him to go, went inside, and turned on the light. My arm hurt and I rolled up my sleeve. Dark spots were forming where Junior had held my wrist. I rubbed at them, but they didn't go away.

I was certain he hadn't meant for it to happen. I pulled my sleeve back down to hide the bruises, then pushed it back up and traced them with a trembling finger. It had to have been an accident. Junior wouldn't do something like that on purpose.

Or would he?

Chapter 30

Saturday and Sunday were cold and too rainy for investigating, so I sewed instead. Monday I put on the long-sleeved shirt I'd made, tugging its cuffs over my bruises as I entered the classroom.

I checked the butterfly jar, certain the cool weather had stalled the eggs from hatching. Instead, the milkweed plants were crawling with caterpillars. They weren't luminous and lovely as the eggs had been. Nor did they possess the willowy delicacy of butterflies. They were more like awkward teenagers wearing horizontal stripes of black, yellow, and white that did nothing for their pudgy figures.

The sight of the caterpillars cheered the children, but by Friday they had tired of watching them devour milkweed. About an hour before dismissal time I told the children to put away their books. Then I took a stack of papers and a box of paper clips from the shelf. "We're going to celebrate the end of September with an art project."

I gave each child a small piece of paper.

"It's all black." Stig and Bennan spoke in unison.

Then I taped one sheet to the blackboard. "It is black on the surface. But when you scratch the surface, you'll get a surprise." I straightened a paper clip and demonstrated. The children oohed and aahed as a rainbow of colors appeared.

"The small square is for practice." I circulated through the room, dropping paper clips into their hands. "When you've got the hang of it, you can have a bigger sheet for your final project."

Tiege gestured for me to bend down. He held up his paper clip and murmured in my ear. "I could weld holders for these so we don't lose them."

So he was starting up that business again. I spoke softly so the other children didn't hear. "Thanks for the offer, but we have plenty of paper clips."

Stig asked if we could listen to music. When I said yes, he fired up the record player and put on an ancient album of cowboy songs. One by one, the children completed their practice sheets asked for more "magic paper."

Beau was animated in a way I'd never seen before when he asked for his second sheet. "Miss Newell, there's a whole world underneath the black stuff. And I'm the one who diggers it out." He brandished his paper clip.

"What did you digger out?"

"My mom." His hand traced the stick figure he'd created.

Oh, little boy! Does she ever leave your thoughts?

I gave him a new sheet. "And what do you think you'll dig out of this one?"

His face went flat. “The guy who killed her.”

“What in the world?” Tiege ran to the window, and the other children followed like Merle’s chickens chasing grasshoppers.

The view outside the window left me speechless. Several enormous white cattle were wandering around the playground. Not just cattle, I concluded upon further inspection. Bulls. Big bulls. Not one of my college professors had lectured about what to do when bulls wandered onto school property. But since they had pointy horns sharp enough to skewer small children like marshmallows, dismissing the students was out of the question.

Renny spoke up. “That’s the Wentworth brand. Their bulls get out all the time. Maybe you should call Junior and tell him they’re at school.”

The phone rang as I reached for it.

It was Liv. “Junior is sending some hired men. Keep the kids inside until they’re gone.”

The men arrived with livestock trailers around dismissal time. By then several parents were parked along the street. Bud Sternquist and Mary Borgeson got out and helped the ranch hands wrangle the bulls. A half hour later the massive beasts were gone. So were the kids, their parents, and Liv. The only things left behind were the cow pies littering the playground.

And me.

I hauled out the rattlesnake spade and scooped the cow pies into a pile on the property line between the school and Merle’s place. He would know what to do with them. I leaned the dirty spade on the landing and went inside. Then I sat at my kitchen table and laid my head on my arms. Until now, Junior Wentworth had been a bright light in my new life in Little Missouri. But this business with the bulls was disconcerting, Not to mention the bruises on my wrists.

He had pulled my trailer out of the ditch, and he had driven me home after Arvid had disappeared. He raised cattle like my father had. He'd sent ranch hands after the bulls right after Liv called. The bruises were nothing more than I used to get tussling with Jeff. Junior had been an excellent fairy godmother, too. He'd granted me a wish not long ago. The least I could do was give him a second chance.

Chapter 31

Saturday morning I finished lesson plans right before noon. There was just enough time to go the post office to see if my photographs had arrived. I found my jacket and went outside. A heavy stamp and a snort snapped me to attention. A red-eyed bull stood at the bottom of the landing, his horns pointing at me. I backed inside, shut the door, and grabbed the phone.

Junior picked up. "Jane, I am so sorry about the bulls getting out yesterday."

I snarled at him. "Sorry doesn't cut it."

"I promise it won't happen again. And I'd like to take you out to lunch to make it up to you."

"Will that be before or after you remove the bulls that are on the playground right now?"

Dead silence.

"Oh. My men will be right there."

"And you too?" I waited. "Well?"

"All right. Me too. And I promise to walk every inch of the fence line, find where they're gettin' out, and fix it myself. I truly am sorry, Jane." He paused. "Now, would you let me take you out sometime and make it up to you?" The last sentence was more plea than question.

"Only if you also get rid of what your bulls are depositing on the playground. Your ranch hands left that dirty work to me yesterday."

"I'm on my way."

I hung up and scrounged in the cupboard for the peanut butter and made a PBJ. Not just any PBJ. I opened the last jar of Aunt Wanda's plum jelly. I was cleaning the kitchen after lunch when Junior knocked.

I cracked open the door. "Yes?"

"We finished up." He wiped his forehead with a mud-stained sleeve. "The bulls are on the way back to the ranch. We'll check the fence and get it mended today."

I pointed at the rattlesnake spade on the landing. "Come back when the playground doesn't look and smell like a barnyard."

He carried the spade to the nearest cow pie and got down to business. I was scouring the sink when there was another knock. He can't be finished yet.

I opened the door. "Did you clean off the spade?"

Sheriff Sternquist held up an envelope. "What spade?"

"Oh . . ." I blinked. "You're not . . ."

"Junior Wentworth?"

"Uh-huh."

"Thought that was his new outfit." The sheriff looked at the Suburban beyond the playground fence. Then he handed me the envelope. "I was at the school in Tipperary this morning and the principal asked me to drop this off."

"What is it?"

"Your paycheck."

I tore open the flap and stared at it. "Thank you!"

"Don't thank me. Thank Mrs. Dremstein. She heard I was coming this direction and wouldn't quit pestering me even when I said I was coming on official business. Kept saying a teacher's first paycheck deserved special delivery."

"She was right. I really appre—" Before I could finish, Junior Wentworth came around the corner, filthy spade in hand.

The sheriff raised his eyebrows. "Your bulls out again?"

Junior ignored him. "Jane, where's the outside water spigot?"

"Halfway down the back of the building." I pointed a thumb over my shoulder.

He turned and walked away.

A muscle twitched in the sheriff's jaw. He watched until Junior was out of sight and then turned to me. "One of these days his carelessness is going to hurt someone. I sure hope it isn't one of your students. Or you." He ran down the steps and walked away.

I rubbed the fading bruises on my wrist. When Junior left, I closed the playground gate and latched it shut. Then I hurried inside and made sure all the doors were locked. In this country, there was no such thing as being too careful.

Chapter 32

I was checking the window locks when Liv called.

"You got a minute?"

"I do."

"You know that report we talked about?"

"Yes." I held my breath.

"Well, it come. I don't think it's what we was hoping for."

I pulled out a chair and sat down.

Liv's voice broke. "Betty, please hang up. And anybody else that's on the line. Please." She waited until the telltale clicks petered out. "I don't know for sure what the report says. The sheriff is coming to explain it."

So that was his official business. "Maybe he wants to tell you the good news in person instead of on a party line."

"If the news was good, do you think he would be bringing a warrant to search our barn when he gets here?"

Oh, no!

"Do you want me to come out?"

"Don't bother."

"Will you call when the sheriff leaves?"

She hung up.

I imagined what the sheriff would find in the McDonald's barn. Every scenario I came up with ended badly. To distract myself, I wheeled the television into my bedroom and reorganized my closet. When the phone rang at nine thirty, I sprinted for it.

"Liv?"

"They found two blood types on the money. One was Twila's. The other was Brock's."

"Don't you want to clear the phone line?"

Her voice was expressionless. "It'll be in all the papers and on TV soon enough. The sheriff arrested Brock for Twila's murder and took him to Sturgis."

I leaned on the counter and steadied myself. "What about . . ."

I caught myself. No need to broadcast the sheriff's suspicions about Brock's part in Arvid's disappearance to the entire party line. "What about the other thing we talked about?"

"Sheriff Sternquist wouldn't say much. Only that we should go to Sturgis and get Brock a lawyer. He said Mrs. Dremstein's got a substitute lined up for as long as . . ." Her voice trailed off into nothingness.

"Are you still there, Liv?"

She whimpered. "I can't believe this is happening."

"Don't give school another thought. I'll call Mrs. Dremstein, and we'll take care of everything."

I hung up without telling Liv what else I had to do.

Traitor.

That's what I would be in Liv's eyes after I turned over what I'd uncovered to the sheriff. Maybe it would force the sheriff to investigate Glen and Trudy—even Velma—and let Brock go. But even if it didn't, even if it strengthened the case against Brock, I had to do it. My first loyalty was to Beau. I had vowed to find the person who had killed his mother. If that person was Brock, so be it.

Traitor.

I hurried to Liv's room and located her teacher's manuals and lesson plans. I organized everything for her substitute. Then I went back to my apartment and folded laundry during the ten o'clock news. I ironed during *Saturday Night Live*. When my eyes refused to stay open, I went to bed and fell into a fitful sleep.

On Sunday I vacuumed, dusted, and put up new bulletin boards. By evening I had run out of things to do. My stomach rumbled and I padded to the fridge. No milk, one egg, a few strips of bacon, and some cheese in the fridge. I heard a knock and went to the entryway.

Junior Wentworth stood on the landing. He raised one hand in a gesture of contrition. The other held a large white paper bag. "I come bearing gifts," he shouted. "A peace offering."

I pulled at the door. Chilly air rushed in.

He thrust the bag at me. "This is by way of apology for the bulls getting out. I won't come in."

I peeked inside and inhaled. "Cheeseburger and fries. How'd you know?"

"It seems to be your usual order." He thrust his hands

into his pockets. "Can I take you out to supper this Friday?"

"I don't know when I'll feel like going out again."

"The bulls upset you that much?"

"You haven't heard then?"

"Heard what?"

"Brock's been arrested."

He blew out a long breath. "I didn't see that comin'."

"Neither did I."

"You want to talk about it?"

"I want to be alone. Thanks for this." I held up the white paper bag and shut the door. He gazed through the window like a puppy waiting outside in the cold, so I opened the door again. "Yes, I'll go out with you on Friday."

"I'll pick you up around seven." He descended the landing steps whistling.

I wolfed down the cheeseburger and fries and glanced at the clock. It wasn't too late to get eggs and milk from Merle. I scrounged in my purse for spare change and set off. The cold night air was a shock, and I went back for a coat.

I knocked on Merle's door and waited. And waited. And waited. It was only six thirty. He hadn't gone to bed already, had he? No. Light spilled from the kitchen into the mudroom. I knocked harder and zipped my coat.

I was about to give up when Merle stepped into the mudroom and slammed the kitchen door behind him.

"Help a hungry schoolteacher?" I held up an egg carton and the milk jug.

He let me in, took the empties, and silently plunked

them onto the counter. He filled my jug straight from the cream separator.

"Where you been hiding, stranger?" I stacked my coins on the windowsill.

He screwed the lid on the jug. He placed the jug and a carton of eggs in my hands. Then he turned away without saying good night.

Had I done something to offend him? I glanced over my shoulder as he entered the kitchen. I saw a shadow and movement in the doorway between the kitchen and the rest of the house. Merle mumbled something, but he wasn't talking to me.

He had company. Company he didn't want me to know about. Who had told me that Merle had buried three wives and was trolling for a new one? Did he have a new girlfriend?

I hurried home, put everything related to my investigation in a large manila envelope, and sealed it shut. With a black marker, I wrote the sheriff's name on it in bold letters and locked it in the cabinet. It was ready to drop off at his office the next time I was in Tipperary. Now, to move onto a different investigation. I moved furniture around in the spare bedroom so I could see Merle's house from the window. Once everything was ready, I turned out the lights, got into bed, and pounded my pillow into shape. I closed my eyes, but couldn't sleep.

Traitor.

I didn't try to defend myself. The truth always wins.

Chapter 33

The next morning I was waiting in Liv's room for her substitute when Cookie Sternquist walked in. Her forehead was creased with worry.

I didn't bother with pleasantries. "What are you doing here?"

"I'm filling in for Liv."

"You have a teaching degree?"

"Heavens, no. But I'm a warm body with a diploma from a ranch management correspondence course. And I like kids. Around here that made me plenty qualified to sub for Liv after Keeva was born. That was a sight more joyous reason to be here than Brock's arrest."

"What has Rick told you?"

"Not a thing."

"Then who?"

"Mrs. Dremstein. She said Brock had been arrested, and the McDonalds were keeping Rosalie home. They'll send her back tomorrow, but I should plan on being here through the end of the week and maybe longer."

Cookie hung her coat on a hook in the cloak room, put her lunch box in a cubby, and stowed her purse in the bottom drawer of Liv's desk. Then she sat down and opened Liv's lesson plan book. "Have you talked to Liv?"

"She's not good, and that's an understatement."

"She's gonna need you, Jane. I'm here for her too. But when it comes right down to it, my son arrested her son. That means that other than Axel, you're the one she'll turn to first. So you best be ready."

"I don't know what to do." I fought back tears.

Cookie rose and gave me a hug. "Do you know how to keep your mouth shut and stand up for a friend?"

I nodded.

"Then you know what to do."

"What do we tell the children?"

"Mrs. Dremstein's coming this afternoon. We'll take our cues from her."

The morning passed in typical fashion, and Mrs. Dremstein called during lunch. She wanted me to gather all the students and parents, except Beau and his grandparents, in my classroom at two o'clock. We were ready when she arrived a few minutes after the Kellys took Beau home.

Mrs. Dremstein told the children what had happened. "Our job is to help Rosalie and Mrs. McDonald and Beau through a very hard time." She offered suggestions about what to say and how to act when they returned.

One of Liv's students asked when Mrs. McDonald would be back.

"I don't know, but Mrs. Sternquist will be here until she does."

After the parents and children left, I asked Mrs. Dremstein if she had heard from Liv.

"Not yet. The sheriff said someone phoned in an anonymous tip earlier in the week. That resulted in a search warrant and Brock's arrest." She picked up her briefcase and turned to Cookie. "Do you know anything more?"

"Rick's pretty tight-lipped. But to get the judge to issue a search warrant without Rick having to appear before him in person, the tip must have been a doozy."

That evening I stared into the darkness outside the spare bedroom window as the events of the day replayed in my head. There was no movement in Merle's house, except for his slow walk to and from the barn at chore time. At ten, I called it quits and went to bed.

Tuesday night I corrected papers and recorded grades while keeping an eye on Merle's house. Wednesday night was much the same, with a brief interruption when Junior called to confirm supper at The Bend on Friday night.

After work on Thursday I walked to the post office. The sun hurrying toward the western horizon still had enough power to warm my back on the way. I pulled several letters from my box along with a small package. I turned it over. The photos!

Now I could mail Mom the picture and she could find something new to nag about. I tore open the package on the way home and shook the pictures into my hand. They were a record of my weeks in Little Missouri.

There were photos of Mom and Uncle Tim hauling furniture into the apartment, of me signing my contract, and of Mom and me on the apartment landing before we said our final goodbyes. The next picture was one Liv had taken of me and my students by the swing set on the first day of school.

"You gotta be in the picture with your first class in Little Missouri." Her smile had been lovely when she handed back the camera. Would she ever smile like that again?

At last I found the pictures of Merle and Snippy from the front and from her business end, along with the one of me after my haircut.

I went inside for a stamp and an envelope. I wrote a note to my parents and folded it around the photo. It felt too thick. I pulled it out again and saw that the photo was stuck to another picture. I peeled them apart and found the bonus shot I'd taken in front of Merle's barn. Not worth keeping. I tossed it in the wastebasket.

I put the note and picture in an envelope and sealed the flap. Then I sorted through the other photos again and kicked myself. Why hadn't I sent my parents some shots of Snippy? Dad would have gotten a kick out of her business end.

I studied Snippy's magnificent udder. Its sides bulged and drooped, so heavy the swollen teats nearly brushed the dirt. There was something in the background didn't look right. I examined it for several seconds and grabbed the wastebasket. With thumb and forefinger, I picked up the snapshot I'd thrown away, brushed away damp coffee grounds, and set it next to the one of Snippy.

In the photo with Snippy, the interior of the barn

appeared empty. In the second photo, there was something in the corner that hadn't been there before. When I realized what it was I grabbed the photos and marched out the door.

By golly, Merle! In about thirty seconds you're going to wish you'd never asked for a Kodak of Snippy's business end!

Chapter 34

When I got to Merle's house I didn't stop to knock. I barged into the mudroom and entered the kitchen. Merle gimped my direction and blocked the doorway.

"You always sashay into people's houses like that?"

I threw the photos on the table. "You have some explaining to do."

"You brung the Kodaks!" He picked up the picture of Snippy's udder and beamed. "This one gets tacked on the wall."

I tapped the one I'd rescued from my wastebasket. "What about this one?"

"What is it?"

"My question exactly." I held the photos next to each other and pointed at the one without Snippy. "What's that in the corner of the barn?"

He held the snapshot close to his face. Then he rocked back on his heels and sucked air between his teeth. "I reckon it's the sacks from the load of feed I hauled up from Belle a few weeks back."

"Oh yeah? What about the brown Stetson on top of the feed sacks?"

"We-ull." He rubbed his ear. "I reckon it's mine."

"I've only seen one person wear a hat like that."

"Me?"

"Arvid."

He pulled out a chair and sank down. "Shoulda knowed better than to friendly up to a schoolteacher. You's too smart for your own good. Or anybody else's for that matter."

"So I'm right?"

Merle made his lips into a thin line and crossed his arms.

A deep, rich voice came from the shadows in the next room. "You be right."

I pushed past Merle and ran into the darkness. "You're alive!" I threw my arms around Arvid.

"That I be." He patted my back. "That I be." Then he extricated himself from my embrace and fumbled in his shirt pocket. He pulled out a handkerchief and wiped his forehead.

Merle rose. "How 'bout we go on through into the living room where the two a you can fall all over each other without Peeping Toms looking through the curtains?"

A beam of light from the kitchen lit a path past dusty furniture, piles of newspapers, and stacks of magazines. Line after sagging line of yarn was strung from one wall to the other. I ducked to avoid the yellowing Christmas cards hanging on them as we entered the living room.

Thick curtains covered the narrow windows in the west and north walls. One ineffective bulb dangled from a pockmarked fixture in the ceiling. A couch, buried under a mound of quilts and cats, stretched across one wall. A wooden rocking chair and a recliner covered with cracked, worn Naugahyde graced either side of a wood stove.

"Have a seat." Merle gestured at the couch.

I chose the rocking chair instead. The more distance between me and the cats, the better. Merle took the recliner, which left the couch and the kitties for Arvid.

I folded my arms. "What's going on?"

Arvid started to speak, but Merle overrode him. "Now you look here, Miss Schoolteacher. You pushed your way into this house and now you're gonna in-quee-sition my guest? Who do you think you are?"

"Who do I think I am? Who do you think you are, hiding Arvid when the whole county's been trying to locate him for a month? Are you aware that in addition to arresting Brock for Twila's murder, the sheriff now believes he's behind Arvid's disappearance?"

Merle rose faster than I'd ever seen him move. "Git out of my place. Just git out." He pointed to the door.

Arvid stood. "No. I want Miss Newell to stay."

The two men stared at one another, their eyes hard and cold. A message I couldn't read passed between them, intense and electric. The hair on my arms prickled, even after Merle sighed and sat down.

"You got no right to be mad at Merle. I be the one making bad decisions right and left. Until everthing caught up with me." Arvid rested his elbows on his knees. "I come here the night I disappeared, begging Merle for help. He's hiding me until I can get out of the country."

"Out of the *country*?"

"To Can-ee-da. Only one state away."

I closed my eyes and envisioned Beau's mom, dead on the road. Unless Arvid had killed her, he had no reason to leave the country. I opened my eyes and met his gaze. "Does this have something to do with Twila Kelly?"

Arvid blanched. Merle stiffened.

"Did you run her over, Arvid?"

Merle relaxed. Relief flooded Arvid's face. "No, I did not. I promise you that."

"Then why go to Canada?"

He bowed his head and stroked the tabby on his lap. The cat's purring almost drowned his words. "We had some dry summers a few years back. I got myself in a heap a debt trying to save the ranch my pa and ma homesteaded. I was born there and wanted to die there too. Now the fella who made the loan be calling in the note. I'm gonna lose the place anyways."

"That's terrible. But it doesn't explain why you have to go to Canada."

"I saw him doing something he don't want anybody to know about, and I come up with a scheme to hold onto the ranch. Right off I knew it was wrong to blackmail him. When he worked out who I was, I saw how stupid my scheme be. And dangerous. He's one vicious bastard and he's out for blood.

"If I ask the sheriff for help I'll have to admit to blackmail. I can't go to jail. I can't be cooped up like that. And I'll lose everything I got—the land, the buildings, the house. He'll even take the money from my mattress and what was buried in the yard."

"You're kidding, right?"

He smiled for the first time all evening.

"You're not kidding."

"No, ma'am. My pa didn't believe in banks, and he done all right. He filled tin cans with silver dollars and gold pieces. Buried 'em under the chicken coop when they was full. Paper money don't tolerate the ground so good, so the bills went in the mattress."

"How much?"

"Only ten thousand in paper. A while back I dug up one of the cans and took a couple coins to a collector in Rapid City. He got mighty excited and said if there be a hunnert of them, I could sell 'em off slow and retire. So I dug up the rest of them, and that's what I'm gonna do. Take my buried treasure to Can-ee-da and retire."

"Why not sell the coins in the States, repay the debt, and stay where you are?"

"Selling the coins'll take a long shake, and the man who holds the loan says he got to have the money now." A sharp edge crept into Arvid's voice. "I thought through everthing, and this is the way it's got to be. The whole county, outside a you and Merle, thinks I be dead, and it's got to stay that way."

"So you're determined to leave the country?"

"Yes."

I stared into the watery depths of eyes I had never expected to see again. They were filled with a steely, immovable resolve. I thought of Brock and my heart pulled in two directions. If Twila's death and Arvid's situation were connected, surely Arvid would be willing to come to Brock's defense. The only conclusion to draw was that they weren't related at all.

I drew in a deep breath and exhaled slowly. "What can I do to help?"

The two men sketched out their plan while we ate supper in the living room. Antelope season would begin the second Saturday of October, a little more than a week away. The county would be swarming with hunters.

"Nobody'll pay any attention to me leaving town." Merle rubbed his ear. "We can mosey our way on the back roads all the way to Can-ee-da. Never thought them runs I made during Pro-hee-bition would come in handy again. I know where to slip over the border. Problem is, it'll take about twenty-four hours to git there and back, so somebody's got to do the chores." Merle raised an eyebrow. "Interested?"

Me? Milk Snippy? Gather eggs? Feed and water the animals? My answer came out of nowhere. "Sure."

"We-ull then." Merle took our plates. "You are now the lifetime recip-ee-ent of free milk and eggs. Come along now for your first lesson in doin' chores."

After returning home two hours later, I lay on my living room floor with a heating pad and babied my sore muscles. Gathering eggs, feeding, and watering the animals were simple tasks. Milking the cow and separating the milk were not. Merle said I would get the hang of it, but I wasn't so sure.

I dragged myself to the bathroom and took three aspirin. Then, I went to bed dead tired. Even so, sleep eluded me. The expression on Arvid's face when I mentioned Twila Kelly hovered in the darkness. I believed he hadn't killed her, but I suspected he knew more than he was letting on. I had to find out what it was before Merle took him to Canada. My gut said that both Beau's future and Brock's depended on it.

Chapter 35

Friday I woke before the rooster. I assumed he'd muted his cock-a-doodle-do out of gratitude because I'd fed and watered him and his harem the previous evening. Then I glanced at my clock and saw it was seven in the morning. Merle's rooster was a good-for-nothing ingrate!

I rushed through my morning routine. There was no time to mix tempera paint for art class. Instead I grabbed construction paper, glitter, and glue. The students arrived a few minutes later and shed their fall jackets and hats in the cloakroom.

"I bringed some more milkweed. I picked it last night." Stig pulled a clump of mashed leaves from his book bag. His black eyes dimmed. "Mom says if them larvae don't spin cocoons pretty soon, the milkweed'll dry up 'cause it frosted hard last night."

"Cora, would you help Stig feed the larvae?"

Cora and Stig's chests puffed with importance and they hurried into the classroom. For the first time in her stellar first grade career, Cora broke a classroom rule. She ran across the room, grabbed my hand, and pulled me toward the jar. "Miss Newell! Come quick! Something's wrong with the larvae. They're hanging upside down."

"They're curling up and dying." Stig tapped the smudged glass. "You gotta do something, Miss Newell."

I knelt beside them. Cora and Stig hugged my neck and I slid my arms around their wiry waists. The other students circled the jar and pressed in close.

"They're not dying." Wonder reduced Tiege's voice to a whisper. "They're making cocoons, like the picture in the book Miss Newell read."

"I think the book used the word chrysalis instead of cocoon, Tiege."

Hands and arms joined around our circle, and we watched entranced as the larvae spun their chrysalises and hid in plain sight. When I checked my watch, a half hour had passed.

"Oh my word! Kids, look at the time."

My words dispelled the butterfly magic. Elva detoured to the chalkboard and drew a first tally on the "cocoon stage" row of our chart. The students went to their desks, but they were distracted and chatty. Their attention continually drifted from their seatwork to the butterfly jar.

Mid-morning I lowered the boom. "Art class is scheduled for two o'clock folks. But only if you complete your work. Some of you may have to finish your assignments while the others make glitter and glue pictures."

The children buckled down. Tiege and Cora attended to their math lesson with the concentration and seriousness of brain surgeons. The first graders actually trembled before their spelling test.

Beau's eyes brimmed with tears. "Miss Newell, I practiced my spelling list every night this week, but the letters always go the wrong way. Will I have to practice them instead of glitter and glue?"

I pointed at the alphabet line above the chalkboard. "Use that to make sure your b's and d's are facing the right direction.

"Isn't that cheating?"

"No. It's being a problem solver."

He crooked a finger and I bent close. "I want to be one of them problem solvers when I grow up. So I can find the person who hitted Mom and runned. When will we learn how to do that?"

"I can't promise you'll ever find out what happened to your mom, Beau. The sheriff hasn't solved that problem yet." I put my hands on his shoulders. "But I do promise to teach you to be the best problem solver you can be."

"And if I find whoever killed Mom, that person will go straight to prison. Right?"

"I hope so."

"Miss Newell?"

"Yes?" I tensed for his next question.

"Can we do the test now, before I forget how to spell the words?"

He aced it.

By two o'clock, every assignment was turned in. The art supplies and the record player came out. By dismissal time, a thin layer of glitter covered the carpet and a thin layer of glue covered the desktops. The children carried their masterpieces to the entryway, shedding glitter faster than barn cats shed fur in spring, and collected their things. They ran down the landing stairs and across the playground, trailing sparkles as they went.

I pulled out the vacuum cleaner and plugged it in, hoping to clean up the worst of the mess before Velma arrived. I wasn't fast enough. The door squeaked open, banged, and there stood Velma, her eyes flashing.

She stomped over to the outlet and yanked the plug. "How long you been waiting to do this to me?"

An unusual calm descended on me. "Believe it or not, Velma, I don't spend my days plotting against you. I spend them thinking about what's best for my students. And today, what was best for them was an hour of fun with glitter and glue as a reward for working hard all week."

"Them kids got to learn to clean up after themselves and be responsible. They don't need no rewards."

"If that was my philosophy, I wouldn't have seen your grandnephew smile today. How often have you seen that happen since his mother died?"

"I told you once before to quit pickin' at that particular scab." Pure malice laced her words. "And I'm telling you again. Leave it be. You stir things up and they'll get worse."

"Fine. I'll leave things be."

I'd expected my concession to turn her expression smug. Instead, she looked like she'd just dodged a bullet. The realization gave me courage. "In return, I expect you to leave me be. I'm sick of you trying to run my classroom. So just come in every Friday and do your job without telling me how to do mine. Do we have a deal?" I held out my hand.

She stared at it for several seconds, as if it were crawling with maggots. When I was about to give up, she placed her hand in mine. “Deal.”

“Do you want to vacuum while I scrub desks or visa versa?”

“Just go.” She plugged in the vacuum. “I’d rather do it all myself.”

I left her to her work and changed into chore clothes. After I milked Snippy and lugged the full buckets to the cream separator, I stopped in to visit Arvid.

He sat on the couch. The change in his appearance since he’d gone into hiding was startling. His tan had faded and his skin was a pale gray. He’d been a thin man when we met. Now he was gaunt. He huddled on the couch under the pile of Merle’s cats. A tic pulsed under his left eye.

“How are you doing, Arvid?”

“Not so good. I be cooped up in here for eight more days. That’s a long stretch.”

I sat in the rocking chair. “Maybe for you. But for me, eight days isn’t enough time to master Merle’s chores.”

“We was wrong to get you involved.”

“No, you weren’t,” I snapped.

He flinched.

“I didn’t mean to bite your head off. I chose to help. I want to help.”

“I know you do.” He sat up straight. “Me and Merle, we be doing what we can to protect you. But we was still wrong to ask you.”

“Don’t you know it’s been my lifelong dream to milk cows and gather eggs?”

My attempt to lighten his mood fell flat. So much for

my future career in stand-up comedy. I stood. "Merle's waiting to supervise chicken duty. See you tomorrow."

After chores, I begged off supper with the old men, having eaten my fill of non-skid pancakes the night before. On the way home I picked chicken feathers out of my hair. The sun was sinking and the chill breeze sent a shiver through me.

Tires crunched on gravel and I glanced up. Junior tooted the Suburban's horn and pulled up next to me. He took in my work clothes. "Where you been?"

I crossed my arms to hide the dried chicken droppings on the front of my sweatshirt. "Why do you ask?"

"I'd just like to know what made you forget about supper."

Our date!

"I'm so sorry. We've been dealing with fallout from Brock's arrest all week and I had a run in with Velma tonight." I bit my lip, fighting back a sudden temptation to tell him about Arvid.

"Say no more. You have a plate full of worries in front of you."

I ran a hand through my hair. "Give me fifteen minutes to clean up?"

"You could show up looking like you do now, and folks'll think you're trying to fit in." He reached an arm out the window and plucked a feather from behind my left ear.

I paused. Half the county would be there tonight. Being seen there with Junior again would set tongues to wagging. As if they weren't already. The least I could do was arrive in clean clothes. "Go save us a booth. I'll meet you there in a bit."

Gossip wasn't the only damage to control tonight. What I'd almost said scared me. I had nearly betrayed Arvid. Not under duress, but of my own free will. I didn't want to be that kind of person. But between my close call with Junior just now and the evidence I planned to give to the sheriff, maybe I already was.

Chapter 36

I arrived at The Bend sporting feather-free hair and clean clothes. I entered the cafe, passing from chilly darkness into brightly lit warmth. Every table and booth was crammed with diners. No sign of Junior, but the Barkleys occupied the booth closest to the kitchen. I detoured in their direction for a quick chat.

Trudy Berthold shouted from behind the cash register. “Renny won’t stop talking about them caterpillars and their cocoons. I never seen him so excited about school before this. Oh, Junior said to tell you he’s in there.” She gestured toward the bar.

Pam Barkley raised her eyebrows.“You’re meeting Junior Wentworth? In the bar?”

“Not too shabby in the money department. I wouldn’t want to meet him in a dark alley, though.” Dan helped Cora take off her jacket.

She climbed onto his lap. “What’s a dark alley, Dad?”

He covered her ears and mouthed, “Little pitchers have big ears.”

I embroidered the truth a bit. "It's just a friendly date. Nothing special. It's just a thank-you for mending the fences and solving the bull problem at school."

Bennan bounced in his seat. "Just like you promised Beau."

I had no idea what he was talking about.

"You know. When he wanted you to teach him how to find who killed his mom. You said you could only teach him to be a problem solver."

Pam put a hand to her chest. "That sweet, sad boy. Does he break your heart, Jane?"

"Every single day. Though you should have seen him today. He was engrossed in watching the caterpillars spin their chrysalises, and acted like a kid without a care in the world. For a few minutes anyway." I glanced toward the haze in the bar. "I'd better join Junior."

"Have fun." Dan winked.

Pam chimed in, "But not too much fun."

Cora's voice rose above the din as I walked into the bar. "What will happen if Miss Newell has too much fun?"

"Jane!" Junior called from a dark corner near the pool table. "Over here."

I choked on a lungful of smoke and clumped across the pitted wood floor to where he sat.

"Are you ready to eat?"

"Thanks, but I'd better go."

"But you said--"

"Can you imagine what the rumor mill will report tomorrow if I sit in the dark with you? In the bar?"

Junior rubbed his chin and looked toward the cafe.

His expression brightened. “Look at that! A table just opened up.”

Soon Junior and I were seated two booths down from the Barkleys. Trudy came, and Junior ordered prime rib for both of us. I tried to object, but he insisted. “You’ve been taking care of everybody else all week. It’s about time somebody took care of you.”

I asked him question after question about antelope season and anything else I could think of. The more he talked, the less I had to worry about spilling Arvid’s secret.

Junior said his place would be full up over the week-end with thirty hunters coming in for hunting season. I asked how his mother was doing.

“Good, I guess.” He paused when Trudy brought our plates heaped with tender beef, baked potatoes, and salad.

“She invited me for a sewing day next Saturday, and I need to call her. It’ll keep my mind off—” I stopped myself. I’d almost mentioned Arvid again.

“Keep your mind off of what?”

I picked up my steak knife and cut my meat into small pieces. Then I described my run-in with Velma.

By the time the story was done, Junior was laughing so hard tears streamed down his cheeks.“That woman is a terror.” He raised his beer bottle and took a swig.

“It wasn’t so much her being a terror, but more like she was terrified. Like she was hiding something.”

“Hiding something?” He gave me his full attention.

“I’d like to think she has some information about what happened to Twila. Mostly because I don’t want it to be Brock." I blinked away tears and blew my nose on a napkin from the dispenser.

"I'm sorry for bringing it up."

Dropping the soggy napkin on my plate, I stood. "I'd like to go home. Alone."

"I understand."

Something flashed in his eyes. I thought it was compassion. "Thanks for supper." Outside, I breathed in the almost frosty air and walked home shivering. The trembling continued as I entered my apartment and locked the door. I built a cocoon of afghans on the couch and brewed some herbal tea. Two cups later the shivering stopped and I fell asleep.

***

The remainder of the weekend was the familiar cycle of schoolwork, cleaning the apartment on Saturday, and talking to Mom on Sunday, with farm chores adding novelty to the mix. After evening chores on Sunday I traipsed into Merle's living room to chat. Arvid was cordial until he heard about my supper with Junior.

"What'd he want?" Arvid's tone was belligerent.

"Me," I joked. "We had a date."

"You best put a stop to that."

First Dan Barkley. Now Arvid. What did they have against Junior?

"Who I go out to eat with is my business, not yours." I rose to leave.

Something in Arvid's expression stopped me. At first, I read his flared nostrils and clenched jaw as anger. But the trembling in his fingers as he stroked the tabby's tail betrayed him. He wasn't angry. He was terrified.

The penny fell into the slot.

"Is it Junior Wentworth? Does he hold the deed to the ranch?"

Arvid closed his eyes and lowered his head.

Chapter 37

The opening of antelope season was all my students could talk about during show-and-tell the next morning.

"Rick says Mom and Dad are kicking me out of the house so the hunters can use my bedroom," Tiege announced. "Rick's coming over to sleep outside in a tent with me."

"We got hunters coming too," Elva confided. "They're hauling their own campers to sleep in. I got to help Mom make breakfast for them."

Stig's head popped up. "And I got to help Dad clean up the old outhouse for them to use. It stinks."

"We got so much extra food at the cafe, the freezer door won't hardly shut. Dad and Mom say the hunters spend a fortune every year. Enough to help pay for Christmas." Renny rubbed his hands together.

"Hunting season's no fun." Bennan looked glum. "Cause Dad'll be grumpy."

Cora explained. "Dad says he spends opening weekend telling greenhorns on Forest Service land to put on their orange vests."

Beau said nothing at all.

I worried about him throughout the school day and while doing Merle's chores. I didn't have the heart to visit with the two old men that night. As Beau withdrew further each day, worry distracted me, and I forgot to check in with Merle and Arvid the next night. Or the night after that. Merle brought me back to earth Thursday night when I brought the milk and eggs in the mudroom.

"What you in such a blasted hurry for? Don't you got time to come in and visit with Arvid? He's leaving in two days."

"I'm sorry, Merle. Between teaching all day and chores every evening, I'm exhausted. All I want to do once the chores are done is go home and go to bed." I didn't mention how I was searching for a way to expose Junior's cruelty without implicating Arvid.

"I shoulda knowed that. With Arvid cooped up in here, me and him gets tunnel vision. I'll take care of these tonight." He took the milk pails out of my hands and set them beside the milk separator. "You go home and get a good night's sleep."

"Tell Arvid I'll see him on Friday for his farewell supper."

Merle nodded and poured a foamy white stream into the separator as I opened the door and hurried home in the dark.

Thursday was another late night. When I got up the weather was bright and brisk, the sky a serene October blue. My students' excitement about hunting season escalated by the hour. The afternoon was a jumble of whispered conversations, excited giggles, and sloppy seatwork. It didn't end until I threatened them once again.

"Are you looking forward to art class later this afternoon?"

"Art class one day and hunting season the next?" Tiege raised his hands over his head. "Life doesn't get any better!"

"It'll only stay good if your schoolwork is done and done well when art class begins."

When two o'clock rolled around every assignment was completed, and I passed out the paper clips.

"Hot dog." Bennan wriggled with joy. "We get to use magic paper again!"

I passed a sheet of paper to each child. "Today you can to turn the sketches you made of the larva's cocoons into magic metamorphosis butterfly drawings."

Cora pointed to the record player and I motioned for her to start the music. The children sketched and scratched while I corrected papers, bringing masterpieces for me to admire every few minutes.

Beau brought up his paper. His drawing was exquisite. It reminded me of something I'd seen before, but what it was escaped me.

I traced a finger over his distinctive, stylized monarchs. "Where did you learn to draw butterflies like that?"

"From my mom." He met my gaze for a short second. "I got a question."

"What is it?"

"Metamorphosis is a big word for how butterflies change, right?"

"Yes. It's such a good word, it can be used to talk about all kinds of changes."

"Like about people?"

"That's right."

"The last time I talked to Mom, she kept talking about butterflies and how she'd changed. She said she had a job and a place for me to live with her in Marmarth. And she promised to bring a present she made."

"Did you ever get it?"

"No." He wadded his picture into a ball and threw it in the trash can. "Probably she never made nothing. She was lying. Just like always." He went to his desk and buried his head in his arms. He remained there, unmoving until dismissal. I pulled his drawing from the trash can and smoothed it out on my desk.

When the other children went to the cloakroom to ready their backpacks and put on their coats, Tiege stopped at Beau's desk and put his lips to his friend's ear. Whatever he whispered to Beau roused him. He gathered his things and the two boys walked out the door together.

Tiege ran to Liv's classroom, but Beau dragged, scuffing his feet on the sidewalk. I watched his slow progress, picked up his drawing, and called the grocery store. When Burt answered, I described Beau's behavior. "I thought you'd want to know in case he has a rough night."

"That's real good of you, Miss Newell."

I glanced at the picture Beau had drawn. "Was your daughter artistic?"

"She sure was. When she was sober she made good money as a silver engraver."

My breath caught as I put the phone receiver in the cradle and covered my face with my hands. I couldn't persuade Arvid not to go to Canada, but I knew how to return to Beau a little of what he'd lost. And how to exonerate Brock. All I had to do was ask Arvid a question tonight and do a little snooping at Corinne's house tomorrow. I knew who had killed Twila and left her for dead. By tomorrow night, if all went well, I would be able to prove it.

Chapter 38

Snippy was a stickler about her six o'clock milking, but I didn't want to wait until after that to talk to Arvid. I changed into ratty chore clothes and showed up at Merle's house an hour early. I banged on the mudroom door and walked in.

"Anybody home?"

Merle and Arvid were at the kitchen table. The shades were pulled down and the curtains drawn.

Merle rose. "Well now, ain't you Janie-on-the-spot this evening? You hungry yet?"

"Starving. Lifting sacks of chicken feed and lugging milk pails for a week has given me quite the appetite."

"Don't I know it?" He arranged bacon strips in the frying pan and spooned batter into the waffle iron.

Arvid pulled out my chair. "I thought you be coming later."

I sat down and fiddled with the lid of the syrup bottle. "That was my original plan. But I'm beat and was hoping for an early supper and going to bed right after chores."

Merle poked at the sizzling bacon with a fork. "Them kids giving you a ride for your money?"

I filled them in on the kids' antics and the butterflies while Merle put butter on the table and added more bacon to the pan.

When the bacon was done, he forked it onto a plate lined with paper toweling. "We-ull, we got to be long gone before dawn. So we'll be hittin' the hay early too." He lifted the waffle iron lid and pulled the golden squares loose with a pair of tongs before placing them on a plate. He shuffled across the worn linoleum and set the food on the table with a thud.

"How's that for grub?" He slid three waffles onto each plate.

Arvid coughed. "You mind waiting for a minute? I'm thinking we should pray first."

Arvid prayed?

He'd never been in church, at least not the times I'd been there. Still, if a prayer would calm an old man preparing to flee the country, I wouldn't stop him. I folded my hands in Iowa-polite disbelief.

He bowed his head. "Well now, Sir. I got no right to ask you for any kind a help. But I ain't asking for me. I be asking for my friends. They is doing good by me because they be good people. I be asking you to keep these two fine people safe. And I be asking you to make right outta what I and others has done wrong. Thank you, Sir."

I waited, then peeked. Arvid's eyes were squeezed shut and his head remained bowed. I waited a little longer and peeked again. This was getting awkward. I glanced at Merle.

Merle was staring at him, one renegade eyebrow cocked and quizzical. "Amen?"

"Amen." Arvid looked up. "Pass the bacon?"

We busied ourselves buttering waffles and pouring syrup. The conversation stayed light, though my heart was as heavy as the food.

Merle stood while Arvid and I were still eating and took a loaf of bread from the bread box. "I got to pack provisions for tomorrow. Enough to get me there and back. And enough to get Arvid through a few days after that."

I laid my fork beside my plate and rose. Arvid looked so miserable, I couldn't bear to confront him yet. It could wait until after chores. "I'll stop in to say goodbye when I'm done with the chickens and Snip."

An hour later the chores were done. I trudged to the house with the milk pails, my heart pounding. However Arvid answered my question, it would free some families and devastate others. But the events yet to come had been set in motion by the person who killed Twila, not by me. Still, I dawdled in the mudroom, sorting eggs until the conversation could be put off no longer. I walked through the kitchen where Merle was washing dishes, ducked under the lines of greeting cards into the next room, and stood in the doorway of the room where Arvid and the cats waited.

"I'm done."

Arvid shoved the cats off of his lap and rose. "So we got to say goodbye then."

"We do. Would you tell me something first?"

"Whatever you want, Miss Newell, after the help you've been."

I looked him straight in the eye. "Who killed Twila Kelly?"

The color drained from his face. He swayed and threw an arm back, groping for the couch. I caught his wrist and eased him onto the sofa. He put his elbows on his knees and hid his face in his hands.

"You know, don't you?"

He nodded.

"Was it Junior Wentworth?"

He took a deep, shuddering breath and nodded again.

There it was. I had been ignoring clues that pointed to Junior for weeks. Every time he was anywhere near Arvid—hauling boxes at school, at the fair parade and in the cattle ring, in the crowd at the Labor Day parade—the old man had gone pale and left as soon as he could. Equally appalling was how easily Junior had manipulated me since Arvid disappeared. When Junior had driven me home from Tipperary on Labor Day, his questions had been designed to find out what I knew. He'd done the same thing during all our dates, asking about what the sheriff had said, what Liv said, and anything else he could weasel out of me.

And boy, had I been weaseled. I'd leaked information and he had acted on it. After each date, something happened that led to new evidence to implicate Brock. If I was a betting woman, I would bet my paycheck Junior was the source of the anonymous tip leading to Brock's arrest. He had played me for a fool for weeks.

Never again! My hands curled into fists. I wasn't going to run from him. I was going run straight at him and bring him down. And if he ever tried to kiss me again, if he so much as touched me I would . . . well, I wasn't sure what I would do, but whatever it was, he would wish I hadn't.

"Do you hate me?" Arvid lifted his head and his Adam's apple bobbed as he wiped his tears with the corner of a quilt.

"I don't hate you. Does Merle know?"

"No."

"Arvid, you have to tell the truth. Brock McDonald was arrested for Twila's murder."

He winced. "God forgive me for being a coward. Would you get Merle? He oughta hear this too."

I fetched Merle. We sat and waited for Arvid to speak. When he did, the words rushed out in a flood.

"My dogs woked me with their barking the night Twila died. An old coyote had been slinking around the sheep pasture for about a week, so I went out to check. No sign of the coyote, but the sheep was antsy. So I settled down by a fence post to watch for a bit and musta fell asleep. The rumble of an engine barreling down the road from the south shook me awake. I was most ways to upright when there was a shout and a thud. The driver stopped, backed up, and parked beside the road. He got out and played his flashlight along the road until it lit on a body. The driver turned it over and shined the light on the face. It was Twila. When he bent down, the pickup truck's taillights lit up his face. It was Junior Wentworth.

"I kep still while he checked her pulse and put an ear to her chest. He must have been certain she was dead, 'cause he climbed right back into his pickup truck and lit out. Next time I seen him, he was driving that shiny outfit he got now.

"Once he drove over the next hill, I went to see if he'd been wrong. Maybe she was still alive and needed an ambulance." He twisted his handkerchief and squeezed it into a tight ball with his fist. "But he'd knocked the life out of her. She was gone."

Merle sucked air through his teeth. "And you didn't call the sheriff?"

Arvid swallowed hard. "My intention was to call him. But on the walk home I come up with a way to save the ranch and I talked myself outta makin' the call."

The rest of the story came out. The next day Arvid mailed Wentworth an anonymous letter describing what he'd seen and demanding a cash payment to be mailed to a post office box as hush money. He sent a letter every day demanding more payments, each one to be sent to a new post office box he'd rented in a different town. Part of the cash went to pay down the ranch debt and part went under the mattress.

The scheme worked without a hitch until the Friday before Labor Day. "Not too long after you come to town," Arvid's eyes grew cloudy. "Wentworth sent me a letter here in Little Missouri. Said he'd been to Meadow and seen me and my pickup truck outside the post office. Wondered why a body had to drive two counties over to get his mail. Said he didn't figure on sending any more payments."

He worked his lips for a minute and stared at the floor. "Said he was keeping tabs on me, living alone like I did, just waiting for the right time when no one was watching so's he could rec-tee-fy the situation."

"He was the person pounding on your door while we were on the phone, wasn't he?" I sank into a chair and put my head between my knees until the waves of nausea subsided. Then I looked at Arvid. "This isn't right. You can't let Junior get away with this."

"He already has." The words fell hard and dead between us. A tear trickled down Arvid's cheek. I stared, willing him to say he was ready to fight. But other than the rapid bobbing of his Adam's apple, he remained motionless.

As the fight left him, a strange thing happened. The western gumption draining from him poured into me. Not enough spunk for me to wear boots or get on a horse, but more than enough to find a way to expose Junior as a bully and a fraud. I didn't know where to start or who to enlist as allies, but I wouldn't drop the matter until everything had been done to make things right.

I touched his knee. "Why didn't you take off then?"

"I packed a bag with the money from under the mattress and what I dug outta the yard and hung it by the back door. But I couldn't make myself go. Tipperary County be all I got. I lived on the ranch all my life."

"Until Labor Day when Junior showed up on your doorstep during our phone call."

"After I hung up on you, I snuck out the back door with the bag and hid in a culvert. I walked to Merle's house once it be dark."

"Arvid, you know that what you did was every bit as wrong as what Junior did."

He took a ragged breath. "I do. That little boy of Twila's never leaves my mind. And now Brock. I can't never get away from it. Call the sheriff if you like and turn me in. I'll plead guilty. I'll pay for what I done." Tears rolled into the wrinkled folds of his weathered cheeks.

The idea was tempting. Arvid's testimony would remove the cloud of suspicion over Brock. But it could also send the old man to jail. And the sheriff could bring charges against Merle for aiding and abetting a crime. Me too, for that matter.

There would be other consequences from Arvid's testimony too. Beau would be caught in a media circus, and he didn't need that. He needed assurance of his mother's love. Proof that she'd kept the promise she'd made during their final phone call. And I knew where that proof, and the evidence needed to free Brock, was hiding.

"Arvid, you said Junior checked Twila's pulse and heartbeat. Did he do anything else?"

The old man leaned the back of his head against the wall and shut his eyes. I waited. He said nothing. Maybe he was asleep. I jostled his shoulder.

His eyes flew open and he sat up. "Yes. He took something outta her pocket."

"Did you see what it was?"

"Just a flash of metal in the taillights. A mirror maybe."

Or a belt buckle.

We sat until Merle broke the silence. "Arvid, you got to do something to get them charges against Brock dropped, or we ain't going to Can-ee-da." He pursed his lips in a perfect imitation of Velma. "Wouldn't hurt if you could point the finger at Junior too."

Arvid pulled off his right boot and reached into his

sock and pulled out a limp, wrinkled envelope. "I kep Junior's letter as my personal insurance policy. In case I ever got the gumption to come back and face him. But I be fooling myself anyway. I ain't never comin' back." He turned the letter over in his hands a few times and bit his lip. "On the way to Can-ee-da I'm thinking I should mail it to the sheriff instead."

I stood and put trembling arms around Arvid's leathery neck. "I'm going to miss you. And I won't forget you. Not ever."

He patted my shoulder and his face turned beet red. "I won't never forget you, Miss Newell. You can count on that."

"Send a card now and then? To my post office box?"

When I got home I pulled out the envelope with Sheriff Sternquist's name on it from the filing cabinet. In the wrong hands, its contents could lead to the conviction of innocent people, one of them still a child. I took the envelope outside to the burn barrel, lit a match, and watched until the flames reduced it to ashes. Then I went inside and put the magnifying glass in my purse. Tomorrow I would use it to confirm the link between Twila and Junior. The man was going down, and I was going to see that it happened. Then Arvid could come home.

Chapter 39

Patches of light frost sparkled in the low spots as I drove to the Wentworth Ranch on Saturday. I stood on Corinne's doorstep clutching my portable sewing machine and a bag of supplies. I was about to ring the bell when the door opened.

"Come in, come in! Let me take that for you." Corinne reached for the bag.

I released it and lugged my machine to her sewing room.

She pointed to a sturdy table next to her sewing machine. "Set up your things right there while I take care of your jacket."

My gaze went straight to the drawer with the buckle.

Stop looking!

I turned my back on the cabinet. For the next few minutes we unwound power cords, plugged this into that, and leveled my machine.

When everything was arranged to our satisfaction, Corinne sat at her machine. "I got my things ready last night. You can use the cutting table if you want."

If she knew I was about to ruin her son's life, she wouldn't be sharing this room with me. She'd throw me out and lock the door.

Stop fretting about Corinne. She can take care of herself. Beau can't.

"Thanks." I avoided her gaze and found the pantsuit pattern Mom had bought before I started student teaching. The outing had been her idea and a rare event because money was always tight. I remembered standing at the pattern counter with her.

"This cut would look good on you." Mom pointed to a page in one of the books. "It'll hide your hips and accentuate your small waist."

"But it's so expensive."

"And worth the price. You'll use this pattern over and over. Besides, I'm buying."

"Mom, I have money."

"I know you do. But I want to celebrate with you."

We wandered around the store admiring the beautiful fabric. Mom stopped and fingered a piece of dark red knit. "This would do up nicely. Let's take it to the counter. After we're done, we'll go out to lunch. My treat."

She'd been right. The pantsuit I'd made using that fabric and pattern hid every wrong curve and enhanced all the right ones. More than that, Mom's kindness and anticipation of my future as a teacher in Iowa had made the day a true celebration. I had repaid her by taking a job twelve hours away and moving to Little Missouri. My eyes filled with tears.

I held the pattern next to several lengths of fabric Mom had insisted on packing when I had moved. "Because you'll need something to occupy your time when the weather turns chilly," she explained.

"Do you have enough of this for a pantsuit?" Corinne reached over and fingered a piece of blue, fine wale corduroy.

"I think so."

She helped unfold the fabric and smooth it flat. I laid out the pieces while she sorted and stacked geometric scraps of material.

"You're a quilter?"

"I am." She spoke through a mouthful of pins. "We finished the quilt for the Methodist Ladies' Aid Society auction last week. These pieces are for the quilt I'll put together this winter."

"What vibrant colors! Is it a gift for someone?"

She gazed out the window and the set of her shoulders hinted at a deep sadness. "No. It's just something to do. Speaking of something to do, would you like some hot chocolate?"

"I would love some. Could you bring the recipe so I can copy it out? I keep forgetting to call and ask you for it."

"I'll write it down while the milk is heating."

When her footsteps faded down the hallway, I took the magnifying glass from my pocket, tiptoed to the antique cabinet, and opened the drawer of buckles. I lifted out the one with the spare, elegant etching of a butterfly. My fingers trembled as I ran them over the cool, smooth metal and turned the buckle over. I peered through the magnifying glass and examined the tiny scratches. The artist had used the same stylized economy of line to sign her creation, and I recognized the name.

Well done, Twila Kelly!

My mind raced as I nestled the buckle into its drawer and slid it shut. What was a buckle made by Twila, one Corinne didn't recognize, doing in her notions cabinet? Had Junior taken it from Twila and hidden it there? Why would he hang onto evidence that linked him to Twila? It didn't make sense, but there were many things about Junior that didn't make sense.

When Corinne returned, I was at my machine.

"Where do you want this?" She held up a recipe card.

"My coat pocket is fine." I picked up my mug and took a sip. "Yum! It's so good."

"I'm glad you like it."

She sat down and we sewed in companionable silence until noon.

"Time for lunch." Corinne stood and stretched.

I got up and draped my half-finished jacket over the back of my chair. "How can I help?"

"Keep me company."

We went to the kitchen where the table was set for two. "I'll get the chicken salad from the refrigerator and you can freshen up in the bathroom." She gestured toward the hallway beyond the kitchen.

I used the facilities and looked at the framed picture hanging beside the sink mirror while washing my hands. It was a photograph of a much younger Corinne with her arm around Junior. They looked not at the camera, but at one another. She beamed at him. He was expressionless.

Corinne's hot chocolate soured in my stomach and I braced my hands on the sink.

You can't sit across the table and eat lunch with a mother you're about to destroy.

I returned to the kitchen and told Corinne my stomach was upset. "I think I should leave before it gets any worse."

If she was disappointed she hid it well. "You sit right there while I pack your things and take them to your car. Or do you need a ride to town?"

"I think I can make it."

She walked me to the foyer and lowered me onto a bench beside the door. Then she padded down the hallway and returned with my things.

Her solicitousness made me more miserable. "I'm so sorry."

We stepped outside and Corinne paused in the sunshine. "What a lovely day. I wish you felt well enough to enjoy it." When we reached the car, she loaded my things into it while I sat in the driver's seat. "We'll schedule another sewing date when you feel better. Richard and I will be at our Spearfish place for a few weeks starting Monday. I'll call when we get back. You know, you can use the sewing room any time you like while we're gone. The key's under the mat." She handed my jacket to me.

I took my keys from the pocket. "I'm so, so sorry."

"You have nothing to apologize about." She shut the car door with great gentleness.

Oh yes I do. And after I ruin your life, you won't be so kind. I wept as I steered the Beetle down her lane.

Junior's Suburban zipped past as I turned onto Main Street. In the rearview mirror I saw him make a speedy U-turn and follow me.

I pulled in beside my apartment and took my sewing

things out of the car. If I hurried, I could get inside before Junior caught up with me.

A car door slammed.

Faster! *Walk faster*!

"Let me take those for you."

"I'm fine."

He caught up with me when I reached the landing. "Aren't you supposed to be out guiding antelope hunters?" I poked my key at the keyhole.

"These city slickers purchased the 'deluxe hunting experience.' " He added air quotes for emphasis. "They spend the weekend fortifying themselves at the bar. First half of the week, they do target practice at the ranch during the day and scouting in deer stands near the national forest at nightfall. Come Thursday morning we break out the ammo and start hunting for real." He hitched up his pants. "How come you're not at Mom's? She said you were going to be there all day."

"I came home early. I'm not feeling well." I aimed for the keyhole again. The key slid into the lock. I yanked at the door and picked up my things.

"I can carry those in."

"I don't want your help." I pointed the key at him.

"Whoa!" He backed away. "What's eating you?"

"People have been trying to warn me about you for weeks, and I'm finally taking their advice."

His eyes narrowed. "What did Mom say to you?"

"She didn't have to say anything. I figured it out all by myself."

I backed into the apartment and pulled the door shut with a click. I shot the bolt and stood sentry until the Suburban was out of sight. Only when I was certain he hadn't doubled back to keep tabs on me did I enter my classroom and flip on the lights. I opened the filing cabinet and yanked out the clipboard. I slid a sheet of graph paper under the clip and drew a timeline, starting with the night Twila died. In quick succession I added my moving date, the Tipperary County Fair, and the Labor Day celebration, leaving space between each. Junior had said he'd gotten the Suburban a few days before the fair because he'd run into a buck a couple weeks earlier. I added both dates to the timeline.

I lifted the clipboard above my head and crowed. Junior had shown me how to prove he'd hit Twila! Then I locked away the clipboard, checked my watch, and grabbed my purse. If I got a move on, there was enough time to drive to Tipperary and meander around the car dealership. Make up a story about being in the market for a different vehicle.

I patted the Beetle's hood and opened the door. "Whatever I may say to the car salesman to wheedle the truth out of him, remember that you're in no danger of becoming a trade-in." I got in, backed onto the street, and revved the engine.

This was gonna be fun.

Chapter 40

The car dealership on Highway 85 bore no resemblance to the ones in Iowa. It was no more than a service station with two gleaming pickup trucks in a tiny showroom beside a service bay. If it hadn't been for the prices painted on the windshields of the used trucks in the side lot, I would have driven on by. A cowboy rushed out and opened the Beetle's door before I took the key from the ignition. A car salesman if ever there was one. I half-expected his blue jeans to be plaid. They weren't.

"Hello there." He offered a hand to help me out. "You looking for something a little more sensible on the roads out here, little lady?"

"Did Junior Wentworth tell you I was coming?" I batted my eyelashes like the proper little lady he thought I was. "He said you gave him a good deal on his new Suburban here. I don't suppose the trade-in value of my Volkswagen is anywhere near what he got for his truck."

"Leave it to Junior to try to pull the wool over your

eyes, little lady. He paid full sticker price for his new outfit."

I opened my eyes wide in mock surprise. "Then where's the truck he used to have?"

"He ran into a deer between here and Little Missouri. We towed it for him, but it was totaled. He told us to get rid of it."

"Before he made an insurance claim?"

"There are so many deer and antelope around here, Tipperary County's collision premiums are the highest in the state. Junior said he didn't want his rates to go up again."

"He deserves a hard time for lying to me. It would be hilarious to take a picture of it sitting in the salvage yard and send it to him. Can you imagine the expression on his face?" I bumped an elbow against the salesman's arm. "Where'd you send the wreck?"

He bumped back. "It would serve him right for lying to a pretty little lady like you, but I'm afraid it's too late. Junior had me haul it to a place in the Hills to be crushed. It's long gone by now." He took my elbow and guided me to the showroom. "But I can put you in a 1978 model pretty darn quick."

I reclaimed my arm and glanced at my watch. "Oh my goodness! I had no idea it was so late. I'll come back another time. Bye."

I sashayed to the Beetle and got in, with a cheerful wave and pert smile to the salesman. As I pulled onto the highway, my little ladylike charade fell away. The slow rumble of anger that began after hearing Junior's truck had been destroyed crescendoed into a howling fury.

"You may think you're home free, Junior Wentworth,

but you are not. You don't know where Arvid is. You don't know that I'm onto you. You don't know the danger you're in after messing with the lives of Arvid and Brock and Beau. Nobody treats my people like that. Nobody. You're one cocky cowboy. You've let down your guard. Which means you won't see me coming for you."

I yelled at Junior for the entire drive home. Inside the apartment I checked and double-checked every lock in the trailer. For good measure, I pulled the curtains and piled pyramids of empty cans in front of the doors in case Junior decided to pay me a visit. Except for doing Merle's chores, I stayed inside all afternoon and evening. Thinking about Merle and Arvid's progress and worrying about what Junior would do if he knew what I was up to drove me batty.

I set up the sewing machine on a card table in front of the TV and sewed into the wee hours of the night. When I grew too tired to see straight, I piled pots and pans in front of my bedroom door, slid the butcher knife under my pillow, and went to sleep.

Merle's rooster roused me on Sunday and I did the chores again. I ate tuna fish and mandarin oranges for breakfast and lunch, adding the empty cans to the pyramids.

Mom called in the afternoon and thanked me for the picture. "Do you have snow tires for your car? With all that gravel, you should get studded snow tires. And chains. Chains would be better if it's a bad winter. Can the man at the gas station help you?"

I didn't want to talk about snow tires. But the secrets I was keeping—Arvid, Twila, Brock, and the truth about Junior Wentworth—left me with limited options.

"Put Dad on the phone. He'll get a kick out of this."

He snorted with laughter when I described Tiege and metahorsaphis.

At some point Mom took the phone back. "What is so funny, Jane?"

I repeated the story.

"Oh my goodness, Jane! By spring, you'll be able to write a book about living out west."

"Mom?" I paused.

"Are you there, Jane? Is something wrong?"

Well, yes, everything was wrong. But I wanted to say something else. "I just want to say thank you."

"For what?"

"For everything. For taking care of Dad. For sending me to college. For helping me move."

Her voice, tender and sweet, reached my ear. "You're welcome."

"I love you, Mom."

"I know you do." She sniffled and ended the call.

I went back to my sewing and discovered several seams I'd put in backward the night before. I grabbed the seam ripper and tore them out. Once the damage was repaired, I sewed steadily for several hours. When the phone rang late in the afternoon, I dashed to pick it up.

Merle delivered his cryptic message. "The letter and the package done been delivered, and the mailman done made it back home." With that, he got off the line.

Betty did not. "What in the Sam Hiww does he mean? That owd coot gets goofier by the day!"

Maybe so. But he's my old coot, and he's home! I hurried over to Merle's. Now that Arvid was out of the country, it was time to tell the sheriff what we knew. And we needed to do it right away.

Chapter 41

Merle was on the phone when I burst into his kitchen. He raised a gnarled finger, and I waited as he bobbed his head in agreement with whomever he was talking to. The bobbing grew more emphatic the longer he listened.

At long last, he spoke. “Me and the teacher’ll be waiting when you git here. If we ain’t, come on out to the barn and give us a hand with the chores.”

He listened a little longer. “That’s right. I got her doing chores. She can milk ol’ Snip with the best of ’em.” He sucked a schleppy breath and hung up.

“Who was that?”

“The sheriff.” He shuffled into the mudroom.

“How did you know?”

“Know what?”

“That I was coming over to persuade you to phone him.”

He rubbed an ear. “Some folks is inclined to call it dee-vine intervention. But I put my money on them hours alone on the road thinking 'bout what Junior and Arvid done wrong and how we might put things right." He took a jacket off a hook on the wall. "Snippy's waitin' for one of us to milk her. Betwixt us, we should finish chores 'bout when the sheriff shows up."

While we ran the cream separator I told him about my tin can booby traps.

"You et tuna and canned oranges for how many meals?"

"Two." I crushed a clod of dirt on the mudroom floor with my toe.

"Then we best fry up some bacon and start some non-skid pancakes before you faint from mal-nu-tree-tion."

We moved into the kitchen. Merle took a pound of bacon from the refrigerator and pointed me toward the stove. I peeled off bacon slices and put them in the cast-iron skillet. He plugged in the waffle iron and cracked two eggs into a bowl. A knock sounded and I went to see who was at the door. When I returned with the sheriff, the two men shook hands.

Merle motioned toward the waffle iron. "Got room for some non-skid pancakes?"

"Always." Rick hung his hat on a wall hook and went to the silverware drawer. "I'll set the table while you and Miss Newell tell me what you know."

"It can wait until you're sitting down." Merle mixed the batter and poured some into the waffle iron. Once the table was set and Rick was nursing a cup of coffee, Merle told Arvid's story. He talked until the waffle batter was gone, the bacon was ready, and we were all seated around the table.

I started to pass the bacon but Rick stopped me. "If

you don't mind, I'd like to pray before this goes any further." He didn't pray out loud, however. Instead he bowed his head, closed his eyes, and after a minute opened them again.

"Ain't you gonna tell us what you was asking the good Lord for?" Merle spread butter and poured syrup on his waffles.

"Patience and the ability to control my temper." Rick speared his waffle with his fork. "I believe what you said, but without Arvid's testimony, there's not enough proof to make a case that will stand up in court, even with Junior's letter."

"I have more evidence." I described the belt buckle I'd seen at Corinne's house the day before.

"No judge will issue a search warrant based on what you told me. Arvid never said he saw Junior take a buckle out of Twila's pocket, only that he saw something shiny."

"But Twila's signature on the belt buckle creates a direct link between her and Junior."

"It would if Corinne could testify that Junior put it there. But from what you said, she doesn't know where it came from." Rick doctored his waffles with butter and syrup. "A search warrant is not a possibility."

"Brock shouldn't have to spend another night in jail when we know he's innocent." I pushed my plate away and stood. "It's not right."

"It ain't right, but that ain't nothing new." Merle pointed his fork at me and then at my plate. "Going hungry won't solve nothing. You sit back down and eat them waffles until me and the sheriff is ready to walk you home."

I sat down with a huff and poked at my food.

"Ain't there nothing we can do for the McDonald boy?"

"The phone call that led to his arrest smelled funny from the get go. I've been working on getting him out ever since. There's still a ways to go, but what you've said gives me an idea of where to start sniffing around." He looked at Merle and me in turn. "You think of anything more, call right away. With what we've got right now, it'll take a miracle to pin Twila's death on Junior, but Brock could be cleared of suspicion sooner than you might expect." Rick patted his stomach. "The non-skid pancakes were delicious as always, Merle. Now let's walk Jane home."

I appreciated their presence and wanted to invite them in for coffee. But then the sheriff would have seen my tin can booby traps. So I waited on the landing until they were out of sight, then went inside. I rebuilt the booby traps and checked every lock in the apartment and my classroom before calling it a night.

I was in bed before I remembered that I'd forgotten to ask Mom if she was still sending pepper spray. Now that I knew the truth about Junior, the idea of carrying it around appealed to me. A snoot full of pepper spray was small payback for what he'd done, but it was something. I rolled over and grinned into the darkness. Seeing him howl in pain would be so worth it.

Chapter 42

A strong north wind in the night blew away the weekend's mild, pleasant weather. The work week dawned with gray clouds clumped like grubby marshmallows glued to the weak blue sky. The furnace turned on with a whoosh and warm air puffed from the heat register. I pulled on wool trousers and a sweater.

The start of the hunting season had taken a toll on my students. They trickled in, grumpy and out of sorts. Many of their parents had been gone because of it, either hunting or working, and their absence had disconcerted the children. They didn't even bother to check on the butterfly jar.

I slipped a forty-five record onto the record player and placed the needle on the vinyl. When my students heard Robert Preston belting out the lyrics to *Go, Chicken Fat, Go!*, they came to attention.

For several minutes we touched our toes, marched around the room, and did calisthenics. By the time the song ended, I was huffing and puffing like the big, bad wolf.

Tiege ran to the record player. "Can we do it again?"

I put my hands on my knees and gasped for air. "Not today." They groaned, but I didn't relent.

The rest of the day was unremarkable until Cookie stopped by after school. "Liv will be back tomorrow."

"Have the charges against Brock been dropped?"

Cookie paused and studied my face. "That's quite a leap from Liv coming back to dropped charges, don't you think?"

"Wishful thinking gone wild, I guess. I just want this to be over for Liv and her family."

"Me too." Cookie crossed her arms.

I picked up a stack of blank report cards. "Do you know anything about these? Conferences are in a few weeks, and I don't know how to fill them out."

"Call Liv tonight and ask her. She might appreciate something other than Brock to talk about." She straightened and moved toward the door. "Will you be at the bazaar at the Methodist Church on Sunday?"

"What bazaar?"

"I didn't tell you about the Methodist Church Bazaar?"

"I don't think so."

"This business with the McDonalds musta driven it out of my brain. Either that or I'm getting old. The bazaar's a big deal around here. You really should go. It's a good meal."

Why hadn't she led with that? "I'll be there."

I called Liv after supper. "I hate to bother you, but can I ask you some questions about report cards? They have me stymied."

"Go ahead."

She answered my questions—and I had a lot of them—with thoroughness. "If you think of more, stop in before school."

"It'll be good to have you back."

"I'm not sure how good it'll be to be there, but it'll be a relief to think about more than Brock all day long."

I worked on the report cards the rest of the evening, stuck them in the back of my grade book, and went to bed. I slept like the dead and woke with a start at five in the morning.

I knew how to implicate Junior and spring Brock from jail! I jumped out of bed, assembled supplies, and laid them out on the couch. Then I reviewed the scheme, troubleshooting every possible obstacle. When I was convinced the plan was flawless, I got ready for school.

When I walked outside I found a warm breeze had chased away yesterday's dingy, marshmallow clouds and cold. Rosalie was sitting on a swing, and I waved to her on my way to her mom's room. When I got there Liv looked tired. And sad. And hopeless.

"How's Brock?"

"He's fourteen years old and in jail. How do you think he's doing?"

"That was thoughtless of me."

What could I do for her? What did she need from me? I gathered her into my arms. Her body tensed and then went limp. She leaned in, and I held her close, smoothing her hair and rocking her like a mother comforting a child.

"Mom, are you all right?" Rosalie stood in the doorway, her eyes wide with concern.

Liv straightened, pulled a tissue from her pocket, and blew her nose. "I'll be okay, sweet pea."

I dabbed at my eyes with a tissue. "What do you need me to do before school starts?"

"Wait to ring the bell for another five minutes?" She blew her nose again.

"Anything else?"

"Don't be nice or I'll fall to pieces."

I murmured into Rosalie's ear before I left. "If she needs anything, come get me."

Rosalie didn't come for me, but after school I hurried across the playground to check on Liv.

Rosalie met me outside. "Mom said to tell you she made it through the day okay."

"Do you agree with her?"

She gazed at the calm blue sky. "She did good."

"And how about you, Rosalie? How are you doing?"

"I liked being at school and not having to think about Brock for a change." She chewed her lower lip. "Does that make me a bad sister?"

"Not at all. You just want life to get back to normal. If I had a younger sister, I'd want her to be like you."

Liv came outside."Let's go, Rosalie." She held up the box she was hauling to her truck. "I'm gonna work on this at home."

Rosalie trotted off. I went into my room, took my schoolwork into the apartment, and spread it on the kitchen table. I worked and watched television, in case the station aired a report about Brock's release. None came.

I threw down my pen and switched off the television. What was taking the sheriff so long?

I fixed a sandwich but couldn't force it down. I corrected and recorded grades until dark. Then I changed into the clothes arranged on the couch—black jeans, black sweatshirt over a black turtleneck, and black canvas tennis shoes.

I fished my keys from my purse and locked the apartment. Then I stood on the landing waiting for my breathing to slow and for my legs to stop quivering. When I could wait no longer I jammed a flashlight into the waistband of my jeans. It was go time!

Chapter 43

I backed the Beetle into the street and ran through the plan in my head. According to Corinne, she and Richard the First were in Spearfish and the key was under the mat. According to Junior, he and his merry band of city slickers were out night scouting. That made tonight the ideal evening to do what had to be done.

My hands shook as I inched down the Wentworth's lane. When I reached the windbreak, I steered the car between the lilac bushes along the lane and the Russian olive trees behind them. Then I made a tight U-turn and parked with the car facing the road.

I cut the engine and eased out of the Beetle. The metallic click of the door latching shut thundered in my ears. I pressed the flashlight switch, covered its glow with trembling fingers, and talked to myself as I crossed the uneven ground.

Only thirty yards to go until the windbreak ends. No distance at all. You can make it.

I took a deep breath and forged ahead. Ouch! I

aimed the flashlight beam. A barbed wire fence? The trees didn't go clear to the house after all. I found a gap between the wires and slipped through carefully to avoid the thorny barbs. I covered the light, crept across the pasture, and slipped between the wires on that side. I crossed to the back door and jiggled the knob. Bother! It was locked. I sidled along the back wall, away from the driveway. Hidden by darkness, I tiptoed toward the front of the house. I held the flashlight between my teeth and dropped to my hands and knees. I crept behind the bushes until my knee bumped against the front porch. From there I army crawled up the steps.

I felt around under the mat and my fingers closed around the key. Now for the dicey part. The yard lights would expose me like a prison escapee in a searchlight when I stood to unlock the door. If even one hunter had stayed behind and was watching from Junior's lodge, I was dead meat.

I slithered to the door and unlocked it. I crept back to the mat and tucked the key into its hiding place. Then I pushed the door open and crawled through.

I was in! I shut the door and turned the bolt. When it clicked, I sprawled on the floor until my heart slowed and my legs quit shaking. Then I switched on the flashlight and made my way to the cabinet in Corinne's sewing room.

I rose and pulled open the drawer where Twila's buckle was hidden, grabbed it, and pushed it deep into my pants pocket. I slid the door shut and left the room. I retraced my steps to the foyer. Then I cut through the living room and kitchen. I trotted down the hallway and swung open the door at its far end. The smells of gasoline and weed killer stung my nose. Only a few more yards and I would be outside! I entered the garage, used the flashlight to locate the back door, and slipped outside. I pushed in the lock button and shut the door.

I'd done it! I had the buckle! In the morning I would hand it over to the sheriff so Brock could be released.

I covered the flashlight beam with my hand, crossed the backyard, and slipped through the fence. I was halfway across the pasture when I heard breathing. Heavy breathing, only a few feet to my right. A man most likely, and a large one. From the sounds of things, he was bigger than Junior. Much bigger.

My spit dried up. My hands went clammy. I tried to think. A guy this big wouldn't move fast. I could outrun him if I surprised him first. I raised the flashlight and shone the beam straight at him. Red-rimmed eyes fringed with lashes so long they almost brushed the horns above them stared back at me.

My stalker was a bull.

Please, God, I prayed, as I ran for the fence, *you know how I hate to run. Keep me from turning an ankle.*

Thudding hooves spurred me on. Sweat burned my eyes. A stitch in my side made running and breathing a chore. But I ran anyway. Faster than ever before. If I could just reach the barbed wire fence . . . ten yards to go. I narrowed my eyes, searching for an escape—there! A gap in the fence. Salvation!

The bull snorted and his pounding hooves faltered. Was he adjusting course to intercept me? Was he giving up the chase? I didn't dare look back to check. I had to keep running if I wanted to stay alive.

I dove through the gap in the fence. My jeans ripped. A spur of wire gouged my calf. Pain shot through my leg. I stifled a scream and rolled away. I rolled until the hooves stopped thundering and the earth quit shaking.

I lay on the ground and gulped air into my lungs. When I could breathe again, I stood. I took a step. Pain surged through my leg. My vision blurred. I dropped to the ground and willed myself to remain conscious. When the wave of pain subsided, I slowly made my way to the Beetle on hands and knees. I crawled into the seat.

I nosed the car out of its hiding place, down the lane, and onto the road. The landscape, bathed in silver moonlight, was otherworldly. My leg throbbed. Blood trickled down my leg and pooled in my shoe. When I arrived home, I crawled inside and wiggled out of my jeans. I examined my wound.

Did it need stitches? Possibly.

Did I need a tetanus shot? Absolutely.

I snatched a wad of tissues and applied pressure to the wound. When the bleeding stopped, I limped to the phone and called Mrs. Dremstein.

"This is Jane Newell. I'm sorry to call this late. But I'm not feeling well and need a substitute tomorrow."

"I'll try Cookie Sternquist first if that's okay with you."

"I'll get everything ready for her."

"The physician's assistant in Tipperary gets there at eight if you think you need an appointment."

"I'll do that." And visit the sheriff afterward about the new evidence in my possession.

"Good night, Miss Newell. Feel better soon."

I replaced the receiver and dragged into the bathroom. I stripped off my clothes, stepped into the shower, and let hot water wash over me as I picked the cocklebeburs out of my hair.

I toweled off and pulled an oversized T-shirt over my head. Then I swathed my leg with a ridiculous length of gauze bandage. I secured it with enough adhesive tape to take a grown man hostage. One of my first grade students could have done a better job.

I took four aspirin and limped to my classroom. When the belt buckle was locked away in the file cabinet and things were ready for Cookie—or ready enough anyway—I returned to my apartment and collapsed on my bed. Just as I was relaxed enough to doze off, the sound of thundering hooves jerked me awake. I put a pillow over my head to block them out.

Chapter 44

My leg buckled when I tried to stand the next morning. I glanced down, half expecting to see a knitting needle impaled in my ankle. It was swollen, but the skin showed no signs of infection. I downed four aspirin and hobbled around, taking twice as long as usual to dress and fix breakfast.

A stop at the sheriff's office was out of the question. He might not ask questions about how the belt buckle came into my possession if I marched in on two good legs, but he would if I limped in.

I called the clinic as soon as it opened. The nurse said the physician's assistant had an opening in forty-five minutes. I collected my purse and half walked, half hopped to the car.

Two hours later I was parked outside my apartment again. My leg was bandaged, properly this time, and my arm ached from the tetanus shot. The white paper bag on the passenger seat contained a bottle of Extra Strength Tylenol with codeine and another of antibiotics, minus one pill each. I had taken the first dose of each before leaving the pharmacy.

The medicine didn't agree with me. My stomach churned as I grabbed the bag and gimped to the door. Saliva gushed into my mouth. I hobbled to the kitchen and upchucked the contents of my stomach in the sink. As I stood there waiting for my stomach to calm down, a hand rubbed my back.

"Wipe your face with this." Cookie tore a couple sheets of paper toweling from the roll on the counter and wet them under the faucet. She found a glass in the cupboard and filled it with water. "Now rinse your mouth and spit."

I followed her instructions, grateful for her fussing.

She felt my forehead. "No fever, so it's probably not the stomach flu." She guided me to the couch.

I sank into the cushions with a sigh. "Shouldn't you be with the kids?"

Cookie tucked a pillow under my head. "Lunch recess. Liv has duty."

I closed my eyes. The next thing I knew Cookie was shaking my shoulder and saying, "Jane, wake up. You're having a nightmare."

"Is lunch over?" I sat up.

"It's long past. You slept the afternoon away. I was putting your room in order when you hollered something about Brock and Junior Wentworth." She handed me the white pharmacy bag and a glass of water. "Do you need to take these?"

"Yes."

"Are you okay, Jane?"

"The PA gave me pain pills for my period. I guess they didn't agree with me."

"You limp when you have your period. Interesting." She brought me a tray with soup, soda crackers, and hot tea. "It's hard to be sick when your family's so far away. Do you need me to substitute again tomorrow?"

"I'm not sure. Can I call you in the morning?"

"No need. Just let me know when I bring Tiege to school tomorrow."

I looked up in alarm. "Is he alone in my room?"

"I know better than that. He and Renny are at The Bend playing pool. Do you need anything more?"

"You've done enough." I sipped at the tea. "Thanks for everything."

"It's what friends are for."

My emotions bounced from gratitude to guilt while I ate the food she had prepared. Gratitude for a good friend like Cookie. Guilt over the secrets I was hiding from her and others. Poppycock. Junior was the source of the secrets I was keeping. I had no reason to feel guilty. But I had every reason to rejoice over a friend like Cookie.

I carried my tray to the kitchen and spent the evening watching television and resting my leg. By the time I went to bed it felt much better. I was almost certain I could teach tomorrow, maybe even arrange to meet with the sheriff after school if he would come to me.

In the morning I swung my legs out of bed and put some weight on the injured one. Not bad! I stood and took a tentative step. Stiff, but not sore, I got ready for the day and was sitting at my desk when Cookie poked her head in before school.

"How are you doing?"

"Much better, thanks to your hot tea and chicken soup."

"Call if you need anything?"

I promised I would. She walked across the playground and gathered my students into a circle. She pointed first at them and then toward my room. What was she up to?

The children treated me like royalty all day. They insisted I stay seated and brought everything to me. When they went outside for first recess, I called the sheriff. He agreed to stop by after school. When my students returned, I was at my desk again.

Cookie stopped in at the end of the day. "How did things go?"

"How did you bribe them?"

"I might have said something about throwing a Schwann's ice cream party for Halloween in a few weeks. Is that okay with you?"

"You plan the games and it's a deal."

"Consider it done." She glanced out the window. "What's Rick doing here?"

"Official business. You don't want to know more. Trust me."

"I do trust you."

I watched the sheriff park and pause to talk to Tiege when they met on the playground. Cookie might trust me, and Tiege certainly did. But would the sheriff trust what I was about to show him? I wasn't so sure about that.

Chapter 45

Rick came in, laid his hat on my desk, and pulled up a chair. "You have something to show me?"

"I do." I unlocked the file cabinet and pulled out the buckle, covering it with both my hands. "Have you received a letter from Canada lately?"

"I have."

"Have you read it?"

"Yes."

"Is it enough to charge Junior?"

"No."

I laid the buckle on the desktop and gave him the magnifying glass. "Flip the buckle over and read what it says on the back."

He brought the magnifying glass close to his face and examined the buckle. When he was done, he set both items on my desk.

"Does that help?"

"Only if you can prove that Junior took the buckle from Twila and hid it wherever it was you found it. And you have to tell me how it came into your possession. Can you do that?"

I avoided his gaze.

"Well, then . . ." He picked up his hat.

Anger surged through me. I hadn't stolen the buckle and outrun a bull only to be stopped by a sheriff who cared more about enforcing laws than protecting people. Unable to contain my anger, I hissed, "I'm sick and tired of you and the rest of the justice system sitting around until someone presents the truth on a silver platter. If that's how you operate, just tell me what's needed to nail Wentworth and I will find it. With or without your help." I shot him a mean teacher stare.

He scooted his chair away a few inches. "Anybody ever mention that your look could make a rattler back down? You gotta remember I want to bring Junior to justice as much as you do. I'm not the snake. He is. And he'll slither away unless we can scare him into doing something stupid. We need to poke him with a stick, so to speak."

"Who are you volunteering to do the poking—me or you?"

"Or maybe Merle?" Rick rubbed at his chin.

I pointed to the phone. "Get him over here."

Merle arrived a few minutes later. I showed him the buckle. He asked how I'd gotten it. I refused to answer.

He sucked air through his teeth. "I suppose it don't have nothing to do with you missing school on Wednesday?"

The sheriff fiddled with his badge. "Or with the pain pills and antibiotics you got from the clinic? Or the fact that you've hardly moved from your chair all day?"

"Does anyone in this county mind their own business?" I crossed my arms. "I'm not saying another word."

Merle stroked the bristles on his ear. "Teacher, the whole town knows Cookie took your class on Wednesday, and a good number saw you driving to Tipperary that morning."

"Mom saw the prescriptions when she checked in on--"

"She was spying on me?"

"More an easy mark than a spy. I asked a few questions and she delivered the goods without a second thought."

"Did you wait for Tiege after school today and pump him too?"

He grimaced. "Guilty as charged."

"But he ain't got all the guilt," Merle objected. "I carry a big share of it for making you part of carting Arvid off to Can-ee-da when I shoulda got the sheriff involved."

"But you . . ."

"And you ain't all innocence either, Miss Schoolteacher. One week you got no buckle, and the next week you do. So we ain't leaving until you tell what you done."

The two men stared at me.

I stared at them, intending to wait them out. However my leg screamed for a pain pill and my bladder was protesting. I caved and told the story straight through.

Merle spoke first after I finished. "There ain't no reason you should be alive after a stunt like that. I ain't heard nothing so stupid since I don't know when."

His words hurt, but the sheriff's wounded me to the core. "What you did has ruined any chance of convicting Junior in Twila's death. His defense attorney will claim that you added Twila's signature. He'll accuse you of tampering with the evidence and get the charges dropped. What in the world were you thinking?"

What had I been thinking?

"What I think is that Junior should suffer for what he did to Twila and to Beau. And I want to get an innocent kid out of jail." I hoisted myself out of the chair. "I need to take my medicine and visit the restroom."

When I returned, Merle was talking nonstop and Rick was scribbling in his notebook. He held up a hand to silence him.

I pointed at the buckle. "Who's in charge of this?"

The sheriff pulled back as if it were poison. "You keep it until Sunday. I have to be able to swear it's never been in my possession."

I locked the buckle into the file cabinet again.

The sheriff stood. "Do you promise to call if anything unusual happens?"

"I promise."

Merle rose too. "Phone me right after him. I'll be here 'fore you hang up. You got that?"

"Got it."

I started correcting papers as the men walked to the cloakroom. When the door squeaked open but didn't click shut, I looked up.

Merle was gone, but the sheriff was staring at me. "Are you scared?"

"No. I'm angry Brock has to spend another weekend in jail." I fiddled with my pen. "And a little scared."

"You can stay with Dad and Mom at the ranch for a while."

"Anything out of the ordinary could make Junior suspicious. I'll keep the building locked. I'll be fine."

"Keep the lights on. Even at night. Got it?"

"Yes."

He tipped his hat and closed the door behind him. I got up and limped from room to room turning on lights and checking locks. I piled tin cans in every doorway, made a bed of blankets on the kitchen floor, and laid my sleeping bag on top of them. I set the phone next to the bed. After that I ate a cold supper and watched television until it was time for more medicine.

Then I laid on my makeshift bed fully clothed, spread the sleeping bag over me, and put my head on the pillow. I closed my eyes but didn't expect to sleep a wink. The sheriff had asked if I was scared. My answer hadn't been a lie. I wasn't scared. I was beyond scared. I was terrified.

Chapter 46

The next morning my leg was only a little stiff. I didn't even limp when I crossed into the classroom and put seatwork at the students' desks. I stopped at the butterfly jar. The cocoons hung still and unchanged.

After school Beau checked the jar. "Are they dead?"

"Let's wait and see what Monday brings." I steered him to the cloakroom. "What do you think?"

He frowned and put on his coat.

Cora pulled on her jacket. "Are you coming to the church bazaar?"

"Yes."

"Will you sit by me?"

Beau lifted his head. His frown deepened.

"Beau, will you be at the bazaar too?"

He struggled with the zipper on his coat. "Yes."

"Then how about I sit between you two?"

He grinned at Cora. "Is that okay with you?"

"Sure. Want to walk to the store with me?"

"Race you!" He shot out the door.

She snatched her bag and followed, screaming, "No fair, Beau! No fair!"

Beau's spark of spirit cheered me. Now I needed to rustle up enough spark to average grades and complete report cards before Sunday's bazaar. I sat down at my desk and pulled out the calculator.

By noon on Saturday the job was done and I was ravenous. I went to the kitchen and took eggs, mustard, and bread from the fridge. I slapped the frying pan on the stove and switched on the burner. Nothing happened. I tried the other burners, but they didn't work either.

I grabbed my coat and purse, then phoned Velma before going to the cafe for lunch. "This is Jane Newell. I hate to bother you on a Saturday, but my stove isn't working."

"You expect me to drop everything I got going on to take care of you?"

"No hurry. I'm going to The Bend for lunch. Just take a look at it when you can."

I double-checked the locks and fought the wind on the way to the cafe. Low-hanging gray clouds scuttled across the sky. The air was chilly enough to fog my breath. Pickup trucks lined both sides of Main Street. No Suburban. Good news!

Every booth and table in the cafe was occupied. Tiege leaped from his seat. "Miss Newell, come eat with us. We got a extra spot." He dragged me to the booth where his parents and the sheriff were seated.

"I would love to." I put an arm around his shoulders and gave him a squeeze. "What brings you to town?"

Cookie answered. "We're setting up for the church bazaar. This morning Bud and Rick moved the pews out and set up tables and chairs." She motioned Trudy over. "We're ready to order, dear."

"How did the four of you move everything by yourselves?" I asked after Trudy left.

Rick chuckled. "We weren't the only ones there. About half the town showed up. People were working in the kitchen, setting up the country store, and arranging the auction display."

"I got all the poles and prizes for the fishing booth." Tiege rolled his eyes. "With magnets and paper clips. I told Mom I could weld some hooks. But she said the little kids might poke their fingers on them."

Neither his parents nor Rick reacted to his little speech. Maybe, like me, they'd discovered the best way to shut down his fanciful claims was to ignore them. Our food came. While we ate, Bud and Cookie said people came from three states to eat great helpings of turkey, beef, and rabbit with gravy made from the meat drippings, real mashed potatoes, garden vegetables, and pies made from scratch. They bought home-canned jellies and jams and handmade craft items donated to the country store. Children swarmed the fishing booth.

Bud chewed on his toothpick. "The quilt auction after the meal is the main moneymaker. The Methodist women make the quilt, and it usually goes for a couple thousand dollars."

I choked on my cheeseburger. "A couple thousand?"

"Oh, yes," Cookie replied. "The entire bazaar brings in four or five thousand every year. Enough to pay for a year's worth of Sunday school materials, vacation Bible school, and repairs on the church."

"I didn't know the county had so many Methodists."

Cookie wiped her fingers on a napkin. "It doesn't. Everybody comes. The Methodists, the Catholics, the Lutherans, the Congregationalists. In this country, we all got to work together."

I picked up my Coke and stirred it with my straw. Cookie's words didn't mesh with some of what I'd witnessed in Little Missouri.

"Hello, Bud. Cookie."

I knocked over my glass. It fell to the floor and shattered, its contents pooling on the floor and the seat Tiege and I were sharing.

Junior Wentworth touched the brim of his hat in the sheriff's direction before he turned to me. "Jane."

I scooted away from him and the puddle of diet Coke and put an arm around Tiege. He shrugged me away and hissed, "I don't want people to think you're my date. I'm too young to get married!"

Bud began to laugh, infecting Cookie and Rick. Tiege and I remained straight-faced. I stared at the pop splattered on Junior's boots until he turned and walked away. Trudy appeared with a rag and a mop. I cleaned the bench and she took care of the floor. When my heartbeat returned to normal, I apologized to Trudy.

"The way you jumped, you must not have seen Junior coming up behind you."

"Something like that." I handed her the rag and sat down again.

Bud and Cookie were assuring Tiege that they were laughing with him and not at him. He wasn't placated until I vowed to never to put my arm around him again and agreed to assist him at the bazaar's fishing booth.

"What time do you want me to be there?"

Cookie considered before answering. "Eleven o'clock."

"Eleven o'clock," Tiege parroted.

"On the dot." I saluted my young boss and waited until I was sure Junior was long gone to pay my tab.

The sheriff jumped up when I headed for the door. "Mind if I join you?"

I wanted to hug him. "Please do."

We went outside and the north wind sliced through my jacket. "Are you done at the church?"

He buttoned his coat. "I'll go back once you're safe in your apartment."

"I appreciate it." I glanced up. "Can I ask you something?"

"Shoot." He bent into the wind.

"Why are you spending your Saturday getting ready for the bazaar?"

"You mean instead of putting the finishing touches on our plan to catch a bad guy?"

I tried to laugh but couldn't.

"I guess to say thank you."

"For what?"

"For life." He eyed the sky, now a clear October blue. "For food and fresh air and a body that works. For the privilege of living next to the buttes." He looked at the Long Pines.

I followed his gaze. The buttes stood dark and somber against the sky. Sun glinted against the rocky outcroppings. The leaves on the cottonwoods glowed rich and golden. Living next to them was a rare privilege. "They are beautiful."

"They constantly remind me of the beauty of their

Creator. A weekend helping with the bazaar seems like a pretty paltry thank you by comparison."

We arrived at my apartment and he paused on the landing. "I want to make sure the doors are locked before you go in."

"There's no need. I checked them before I left."

He tested the latch and nodded his approval. Once I was inside, he tested the lock again. He gave the door a satisfied pat and descended the landing.

I stood at the window and watched a gust of wind lift the hat off his head. He put on a burst of speed and snatched it before it sailed across the schoolyard fence.

Chapter 47

I went to my classroom, pulled out my teachers' manuals, and was just starting lesson plans when I heard footsteps coming from my apartment. Heavy footsteps.

"Hello again, Jane."

I stiffened and the hairs on the back of my neck prickled. I turned to face Junior. "How did you get in?"

"One of the doors to your apartment was unlocked."

"You're lying." I stood and positioned myself so my desk was between us.

"Funny, isn't it? How quick liars are to accuse the innocent?"

"What are you doing here?"

"I wanted to see why you're so thick with the sheriff." He stepped closer.

My throat tightened. How was I going to get rid of him? I glanced at the scissors caddy within reach on a low table. Could I grab a pair in each hand and stab him? I thought so. Except they were safety scissors. Darn.

He took another step closer and clamped a hand around my wrist. "Where is it?"

"Where's what?"

"You know what." He tightened his grip on my wrist.

You won't make me scream, Junior Wentworth! I bit down on my lip.

"I searched your apartment in every place women usually hide their little trinkets. I was sure the buckle would be in your underwear drawer. But it wasn't."

He'd been in my undie drawer? I shuddered. If I got out of this alive, I was going to buy all new lingerie. Even if it meant eating peanut butter sandwiches and water every meal for a month to pay for them.

"Where is it?" He twisted my arm.

I slid my free hand over my desk, feeling for a sharp pen. A craft knife. A straight pin. Anything I could use as a weapon. My fingers closed around a small plastic cylinder. With my thumb, I popped off the lid and threw its contents into Junior's eyes.

Tiny grains of golden glitter hit his eyes, and his lids squeezed shut. His mouth opened, and he inhaled glitter. His hands flew to his face and knocked off his hat. He coughed and choked and sneezed. Glitter spewed in every direction.

The phone rang. I sprinted to answer it. "Jane Newell speaking."

"Jane, it's Velma. I lit your pilot light. It's a disgrace that a woman your age got to ask someone to do that for her. You stay put and I'll be right over to teach you how to do it." She hung up.

I glared at Junior. "Velma Albright's on her way over.

You want to stick around and explain why there's glitter on the floor?"

He picked up his hat and ran for the door, twinkles bathing his shoulders.

"You coward."

He turned back. Flecks of glitter marred his otherwise perfect smile. "Oh honey, nobody steals the mementos I keep to remember my ladies. Someday I'll shove those words down your throat so hard you'll wish you'd never said them." He smoothed his hair and left in a cloud of fairy dust.

My legs shook, and I sat down. I wasn't sure what scared me more—Junior's threat or the anticipation of Velma's reaction when she found the carpet covered with glitter. Again.

I ran into the kitchen and looked under the ice cube tray. The file cabinet key was still there. I took it into my classroom and unlocked the drawer. Then I set the buckle on my desk. Had Twila been one of Junior's "ladies"? Was that why he'd taken it from her? I was still staring at it when Velma arrived, her head wreathed with cigarette smoke.

"I suppose they don't got pilot lights where you come from."

I stepped back and my foot slipped on a hillock of glitter. I landed on the carpet with a thud. Pain radiated up and down my leg as bits of gold scattered every which way.

Velma went ballistic. "You been into the glitter again! I oughta report you to the school board." She stormed off in the direction of the vacuum cleaner.

I wiggled my toes and flexed my knees. Nothing felt

broken. I got to my feet and rubbed my tailbone. While Velma muttered and slammed doors, I concocted a story to pacify her.

The vial of glitter rolled off the desk and I accidentally stepped on it.

That didn't explain why the stuff was scattered to eternity and back.

Mice chewed through the plastic and made the mess.

Velma would check the plastic for chew marks and find none.

I'd been throwing all the glitter into the garbage, as she'd requested, and a lid popped open and spilled everywhere.

That might work if I could sneak the remaining boxes of glitter out of the store room and into the garbage before she reappeared.

I limped to the storeroom and returned with a stack of glitter boxes. But I was too late. Velma was standing stock-still, vacuum cleaner hose in hand, beside the desk. I braced for another scolding. It didn't come.

Instead, the vacuum hose clattered to the floor. Velma's face drained of color. "Where did you get that buckle?"

My mouth opened and closed. If I told the truth—I had stolen it from Corinne Wentworth—Velma wouldn't believe me. So I borrowed Corinne's explanation and lied. "I got it at an auction in the Black Hills."

Velma picked it up. "I know this buckle. I seen it before."

"Where?" I held my breath.

She ran a finger over the butterfly design. "In Marmarth. At my niece Twila's place."

I exhaled. "You saw her in Marmarth?"

"Twila, she was always my girl. From when she was little, she always come to me to talk over her troubles. Not that she took my advice much. While she was in high school, she went off the deep end and stayed there most of her life. Them last few months, before she died, they was different. Something changed in her, and she was trying to get Beau back. I gone up to see her most every month once she moved to Marmarth. She was working on this buckle. She was gonna give it to Beau before they moved into their new home. Kept talking about butterflies and new life and a whole lot of other nonsense every time I seen her. After she got kilt, I searched her apartment and didn't find it. I figured someone else got there first."

Velma could prove Twila had the buckle in Marmarth. She could be the link we needed to prove that Junior had taken the buckle from Twila's body and hidden it. I wanted to bolt into my apartment and call the sheriff, but that might spook Velma. I stuffed down my impatience and bided my time.

I turned the buckle over. "I thought it was Twila's work from her signature. I want to give it to Beau. He said Twila had promised him a gift. Ever since I found this, I've been trying to figure out how to give it to him, but not as a gift from me. As the gift promised to him by his mom."

Velma stood, stiff and indignant. "Miss Newell, I believe an apology is in order."

I poked a toe at the glitter on the floor. "I know. I'm sorry about the . . ."

Tears began trickling down her cheeks. "Not from

you. From me. I been loaded for bear where you was concerned ever since you come to Little Missouri. You being an outsider with your la-dee-da education. I got you all wrong."

"You did?"

"I did. You ain't la-dee-da. You just seemed that way with them clothes you wear and that silly car you got." She wiped at her wet cheeks with a frayed shirt cuff.

I pulled a tissue from the box and handed it to her.

She blew her nose. "There's something else I'd best confess too. I forgot to lock your apartment door after I fixed your pilot light today."

So that was how Junior had gotten in. I lied again. "Oh, well. No harm done."

"Thank you." She raised her arms as if ready for a hug. At the last second she gave my hand a weak squeeze. "I'll get the glitter cleaned up and then show you how to work the pilot light on the stove."

While Velma vacuumed, I went to the phone and asked Betty to call the church. I told her to tell the sheriff to get Merle and bring him to the school as soon as they could get away. I was locking the door Junior had used to get in when Velma entered the kitchen. She demonstrated how to relight the stove pilot and made me practice until I could do it myself.

"That's a good job done. I'll be on my way."

"How about some hot chocolate before you leave?"

"That'd be dandy."

She sat down at the table. I prepared hot chocolate for four using Corinne's recipe, and Velma chatted like we'd been friends for decades. Velma said she was roasting a turkey with dressing for the bazaar. I told her about being conscripted for the fishing booth. A knock at the door put an end to the chitchat.

"Come in." I stirred the milk in the sauce pan.

Velma greeted the sheriff, but her eyes went hard as she gazed over his shoulder and saw Merle. "Look what the cat drug in."

"Have a seat." I gestured at the table with the dripping spoon and set empty mugs in front of them. "Velma, would you tell the sheriff and Merle about the buckle while I finish with this?"

Velma scooted her chair away from Merle's and related what she had told me.

I poured hot chocolate into our mugs. "Is that enough proof, Sheriff?"

Velma's forehead wrinkled. "Proof of what?"

I sat down and we unfolded the tale bit by bit.

"Now you know everything we know." The sheriff placed his cup on the table.

"Not quite." I described my recent encounter with Junior. Their reactions were not what I'd expected.

Velma stood and began clearing away the dirty mugs. "You can use glitter twice a week if you want from now on."

The sheriff banged a fist on the table. "Wentworth didn't admit a thing."

"I'da gived anything but ole Snip to see Junior with glitter between his teeth," Merle snorted.

Velma put her hands on her hips. "I think I know how to give Beau his buckle and put Junior outta action. You maybe can't send him to prison for killing Twila, but something's better than nothing, and I got a little something up my sleeve."

She explained her idea. We unfolded and tweaked it until we'd smoothed out every possible wrinkle. When we were done, Merle and Rick watched Velma wrap the buckle in tissue paper and bury it in her purse.

She marched at the door, turned back, and pointed to me. "You make me a bed on the couch. I'll be back in a jiffy with everthing I need."

"Everything you need for what?"

"Everthing I need to cook for the bazaar. And my overnight bag."

"You're staying here tonight?"

"Do I got to spell it out for you? Junior Wentworth got in here 'cause of me, and it ain't gonna happen again. Not over my dead body." She stomped outside and heaved the door shut.

Merle recovered first. "You're gonna have a slumber party with Velma Albright? Will wonders never cease?" He shuffled across the room and left with a wink.

The sheriff stayed and helped Velma cart in a twenty-five pound turkey, a giant roasting pan, sauce pans, and sack upon sack of dried bread, spices, butter, celery, and onions.

"That's the last of it." She plunked her overnight bag on the couch, dusted her hands together, and went to the stove. "Jane, you git over here and start choppin' vegetables. This turkey ain't gonna stuff itself."

The sheriff straightened his hat. "Tomorrow's a big day, ladies. Don't stay up all night gabbing about boyfriends."

I threw a towel at him, but it went wide and hit the window instead. The sheriff hurried out the door.

"Good thing you throwed a towel and not a sauce pan." Velma turned on the oven. "You got a lousy aim."

Chapter 48

The rooster crowed at seven-thirty on Sunday. I groaned. How would I make small talk with Velma first thing in the morning? I tiptoed to the kitchen and saw a piece of paper on the counter.

It was a note from Velma. One long sentence saying she'd waited clear to six in the morning for me to git up and help haul the stuffed turkey to the church kitchen, but how long was a person supposed to wait, so she done it all herself and she'd see me at the church if I somehow got up in time for the big doings.

The night before, she'd suggested I donate baked goods for the country store at the bazaar. I turned on the oven and while it was heating, tested the locks on all the doors. Then I baked a pan of bars and a batch of cookies. While the goodies cooled, I changed into a burnt orange sweater and jeans. No sense dressing up to sit on the floor in the fishing booth with Tiege.

I piled my hair on my head and secured it with pins. It hadn't been cut since Labor Day weekend and was getting shaggy again. Then I arranged the cookies and bars on plates, covered them with plastic wrap, and carried everything to the car in a cardboard box.

Merle was loading wooden cartons and egg crates into his pickup truck. He hitched over to the Beetle. "You oughta know, I don't partic-ee-lur agree with them Methodists endin' every hymn with amen. But I'm still donating twelve cartons of fresh eggs, sixteen pints of Snippy's fresh cream, and them tomatoes I picked green before it frosted. They been ripening real nice in the house."

He opened the passenger door and I set the box on the seat. Then I straightened and shut the door. "See you there?"

"Shortly." He hooked his thumbs under the straps of his dirty overalls. "Once I change into my Sunday best."

Merle in his Sunday best? I couldn't even imagine.

I got into the Beetle and drove to the church. Pickup trucks lined not only the street where the church sat, but also every street within a two block radius. This was the closest thing to a traffic jam I'd witnessed in Little Missouri. I eased into the long line of vehicles prowling the dusty streets for a place to land. I made a snap decision and double-parked outside the church. I hopped out, hurried to the passenger side, grabbed my box, and charged inside.

Cookie Sternquist stood inside the entrance. "I'll take that."

I thrust it at her. "Thanks. I'm going to park back at the school and walk over. Tell Tiege I'll be back in five minutes."

I was true to my word. Tiege grabbed my hand and

pulled me to the fishing booth tucked in a corner of the sanctuary. Nails had been pounded about six feet from both walls. A blue-green shower curtain covered with psychedelic fish hung from a wire with its ends looped over the nails. Tiege ducked under the curtain, then held it back and gestured for me to step in. He took a bamboo fishing pole from the corner. "Now here's what you got to do."

After completing his crash course in fishing booth operation, I hunted for Cora and Beau. She was at the beverage table assisting Iva. He was at the country store organizing the cash box with Velma. Tiege tagged along, and the children and I got in line with the other workers to eat dinner before the bazaar began. At the table, Cora and Beau sat on either side of me with Tiege across. When the doors opened to the general public at eleven-thirty, Tiege and I were behind the shower curtain, our stomachs full, and our fingers itching to get to work.

We didn't have to wait long. A flood of people, the entire town and half the county, poured through the double doors. Soon the dining tables were crowded with patrons. The minute one person vacated a chair, someone else slid into it.

Parents bought tickets at the country store and handed them to their kids for the fishing booth. Tiege crawled out from under the curtain. "A ticket a turn." He looked over his shoulder and hissed at me. "I take the tickets and throw you the lines."

About a half hour into the madcap fun, one of the paper clip hooks caught in my hair. I untangled it and sent the recipient a green fish decorated with a hunk of frizzy, dark blond curls. I asked Tiege if we could switch places. A good move, as it turned out, because when I crawled through the curtain, Beau was waiting for his turn at the booth. "Do you know where your Aunt Velma is?" I asked.

He pointed to the kitchen. "In there."

"Would you get her for me?"

He balked.

"You'll get your place back in line."

"Promise?"

I crossed my heart. "Promise."

Velma came out of the kitchen and scanned the room. I wiggled my eyebrows and directed her attention to Beau. She sauntered over to Iva at the country store and whispered in her ear. Iva stood and walked toward the bathroom. Velma sat down and saluted me.

"Ticket?" I held out a hand to Beau.

He tore one from the strip peeking out of his shirt pocket, and I gave him a pole. He cast his line over the curtain and held it steady until Tiege yanked the string. Beau brought up a hot pink fish, slid his catch off the paper clip, and dashed off to redeem it.

I spoke to the three girls at the front of the queue. "Hang on just a minute."

"Would you look at that?" Velma's gruff voice rose above the chatter in the crowded room. "I been holding back a special prize for when you brought your fish over." She took it and gave Beau a package wrapped in tissue paper. He tore it away and gazed at the silver buckle.

"It's something your mama showed me before she died. Said she was makin' it for you."

"Mama made this?" Beau chewed his lip.

Velma turned the buckle over and rubbed his finger over her signature. "That's her name. Can you feel it?"

Beau ran a thumb over the rough etching and held the buckle up so it caught the light. "Butterflies. Like she promised." He whipped his belt off, replaced the old buckle with the new one, and put the belt on again. He showed it to Iva when she returned, and Velma repeated her story.

"Can we fish now?"

"Oh." I started and blinked at the girls in front of the fishing booth. "Um, yes." I grabbed three poles, and their lines tangled together. "Blast it! I've made a mess of things."

"We'll help." The girls tugged until the tangle came undone and then gave a loud cheer.

Several people ambled over to see what we were doing. Wentworth was among them.

"Looks like fun. Can I try?" He smiled and a fleck of glitter sparkled beside one canine tooth.

Look who doesn't floss.

Things were proceeding according to plan. "Sure. But you have to buy tickets at the country store."

He sauntered over to Velma, who was stationed at the cash box. Beau leaned against her. I scanned the room for the sheriff. Either he hadn't arrived yet, or he was lost in the crowd. Not good. My body tensed.

Junior slapped a twenty on the table in front of Beau. "Let's see what you've been learning at school. How many tickets can I get for this?"

Beau shrank back. Velma whispered in his ear. He stood tall again. "Eighty." He counted out the tickets and tore them off the roll. "The best prize is gone already. It's mine."

Junior picked up the tickets. "Oh, yeah? What did you get?"

Velma took Beau's hand and they stepped in front of the table.

When Wentworth saw the buckle, he dropped his string of tickets. They coiled at his feet like a paper snake. He flinched as if bitten. A golden twinkle near his earlobe caught the light.

He doesn't scrub behind his ears either.

The sheriff walked to the fishing booth and pulled back the curtain. "The booth is closed until after the auction."

Tiege pointed at the line of kids. "What about them?"

Rick turned to them. "You'll get your places back when the auction is over."

They scattered, and the sheriff gave Tiege a gentle nudge. "Mom's looking for you. Miss Newell and I will clean things up." Tiege left, and the sheriff motioned for me to join him behind the curtain. "You ready?"

"And raring to go."

"Then let's make him mad."

We stepped out from behind the curtain. Junior Wentworth was watching with narrowed eyes. "I think we already have."

Pastor Petersen's voice blasted through a battery-powered megaphone. "It may be after the fact, but I've asked Father Dan to offer a prayer of thanksgiving for the wonderful meal the cooks served us."

People bowed their heads as if having a priest lead the praying at the Methodist Church happened every day, so I did the same. When he was done, Father Dan introduced the auctioneer, Orvil Magnuson, a short, stout man in his mid-fifties. His plaid shirt, blue jeans, silver-buckled belt, and boots didn't stand out in the crowd, but his gray, ten-gallon Stetson and handlebar mustache did. His auctioneering skills were mesmerizing. He blazed through the items heaped on the table, coaxing top-dollar bids for crocheted toilet-paper-roll covers, braided-wheat wall hangings, shell-and-macrame plant holders, and color-crazy granny square afghans. Before anyone in the crowd could lose interest, the only item that remained was the hand sewn quilt.

It was a beauty. A traditional double wedding ring pattern, like the ones my grandma pieced together for each of her eight children before they got married. The quilts Grandma made were a hodgepodge of colors, pieced together from the remnants of the shirts and dresses she had sewn when her children were young. This one was also made of hundreds, maybe thousands, of tiny squares of cloth. Unlike Grandma's quilts, the fabric used in this one had been carefully chosen. The colors were reminiscent of the autumn yellow of the cottonwoods by the river and of the tawny, tall grass prairie stretching to the horizon. The patches formed lovely rings of color against a white muslin background.

Magnuson set the opening bid at two hundred. Sheriff Sternquist raised his hand. For the first few minutes the sheriff, Dan Barkley, and Bram Borgeson waged a friendly bidding war. The price inched up in fifty-dollar increments.

When the quilt hit the thousand-dollar mark, Junior Wentworth edged to the front of the crowd. Orvil tried to coax the men to up the bid another two hundred and fifty dollars.

Junior entered the contest. "I bid fifteen hundred."

The auctioneer didn't miss a beat. "Fideen hunnert, now sebenteen fitty? Sebenteen fitty, anyone?"

Dan shook his head. "Too rich for my blood. I'm out."

Orvil turned to the sheriff. "Sebenteen fitty?"

He hesitated.

Orvil scanned the crowd. "Do I hear sebenteen fitty? Sebenteen fitty, now, do I hear sebenteen fitty?"

Wentworth perused the crowd too. When he saw me his expression turned sour.

The sheriff's voice rang loud and clear. "Seventeen fifty."

Wentworth narrowed his eyes at me and spoke before Orvil could do his job. "Two thousand."

"Two thousand five hundred." The sheriff stared at Wentworth.

"Three thousand."

"Four thousand."

Every eye in the place was on the two men.

"Five thousand." Wentworth's smile glittered gold.

The sheriff raised the bid to six thousand.

Junior swallowed the bait. "Seven thousand."

The sheriff took the megaphone and raised it to his mouth. "Sold to Junior Wentworth. The Little Missouri Methodist Church appreciates your generous support."

Junior flipped open his checkbook, stabbed at it with his pen, and threw the check at Orvil. Then he stormed out of the church.

I wanted to follow him, but the sheriff stopped me. "Wait five minutes and then go home."

When the time was up, I ran half the distance to the door before a strong hand clamped around my wrist.

The man grasping it spoke low and slow. "Walk and don't say anything until we're outside."

Chapter 49

Merle didn't loosen his hold until we were outside in the bright afternoon sunshine. I didn't know what he was up to, but I did know that it wasn't part of our plan. I tried to pull away, but years of milking cows had turned his hands into vise grips.

"Let me go, Merle. I need to go home."

His grip remained firm.

"Please." I tried to twist my arm free. "Please!"

"Nope." He opened the passenger side of his truck cab and cocked his head at the grassy patch where Tiege, Beau, and the Barkley children were playing. "You gonna get in by yourself? Or do I got to heft you in with them kids watching?"

He'd bested me. I climbed into the passenger seat. When he got in and shut his door, I lit into him. "What do you think you're doing?"

He fired up the truck and backed out. "I ain't never seen a man as angry as Junior Wentworth when he left. He drove off like a mean bronc with a burr under its saddle."

Merle shifted into drive and turned down the short road home, sucking in air between his teeth. "Made me think this old cowboy would be wise to get you home safely."

"The sheriff has things under control. We don't need to worry about Junior Wentworth."

"Now that's where you're mistaken, Teacher." Merle's eyebrows furled into a single, angry slash. "You know how Junior operates. You ain't going into your apartment alone. You got that?"

He pulled into his driveway. The second he braked I leaped out, hurried to my landing, and unlocked the door. I rushed to the bathroom to relieve my screaming bladder. I didn't even shut the door before unsnapping my jeans.

Wentworth stepped out from behind the shower curtain. "Looks like I got the best seat in the house."

He isn't supposed to be here yet. I froze in the act of unzipping my fly. *Stay calm. Play for time.*

"Oh, don't stop now." He leaned against the wall with wolfish self-assurance.

That was his first mistake. I shot through the bathroom door, ran into the kitchen, and pulled the knife drawer open. Junior's fingers wrapped around my arm. He yanked so hard my shoulder popped. My body slammed into his, and I felt the hard, cold smoothness of a gun against my cheek.

At least I assumed that's what it was—my elementary education degree hadn't covered gun safety or taking down bad guys, but I had watched every episode of *Gunsmoke* as a kid.

Junior's hot breath burned my skin. "You ready to tell me how you got the buckle?"

I heard the click of a gun hammer. At which point I wet my pants for the first time since kindergarten.

An instant later the apartment door opened. Relief washed over me. But when Merle walked in instead of the sheriff, fear squeezed all hope from my soul. Our plan had gone horribly wrong.

He grimaced when he saw Junior pressing my body against his and the gun jammed into my cheek. Without a hint of urgency or concern, the old man pulled out a chair and sat down.

"Gotta rest these old bones more than I used to. Junior, how 'bout you sit down and let Miss Newell be?"

Junior shoved me in front of his body so mine shielded his. He moved the gun to the hollow of my neck. "How about you quit talking and put your hands where I can see them?"

"Be glad to." Merle rested his hands on the table and sucked air between his teeth. "You know Junior, you is about to do the stupidest thing you done since the night Twila Kelly died."

Junior's body went rigid and he squeezed my arm until I cried out in pain. "What are you talking about?"

"You know." Merle stared at Junior until the younger man loosened the pressure on my arm the tiniest bit. "Miss Newell and the sheriff know too. And so do Arvid Drent."

"You just proved you're the crazy old man everyone says you are. Arvid Drent is dead." Junior clamped his arm around my torso.

I gasped for air, but couldn't breathe. I couldn't kick. I couldn't do anything but pray for the sheriff to show up. Where was he?

"No." Merle shook his head. "Arvid Drent is alive and well. Same as he was the night he seen you hit Twila Kelly. Same as when he seen you put that silver buckle in your pocket and leave her for dead."

Wentworth's voice didn't betray him, but the trembling of his body against mine did. "If he saw something, why didn't he call the sheriff?"

"Because Twila was already dead, and he couldn't do nothin' bout that. On the other hand, he figured to use the sit-ee-ation to blackmail you and save his ranch. Not sayin' that was right. But it's what he done. Me and Teacher here, we snuck him outta the country to where you ain't gonna find him. We don't even know where he is now."

Merle rubbed the top of his head. "He saw how you treat women and knowed you was a sneaky devil. So before he lit out, he wrote down everthing he seen the night Twila died. He give my lawyer and his lawyer and the lawyer for Tipperary County Schools sealed copies.

"Know what he told all them lawyers? He told them if anything unusual happened to Miss Newell or me—say one of us disappears or we gets hurt bad or if, God forbid, one of us dies—they is to take them letters to the Tipperary County Courthouse for the sheriff to unseal and read out loud once the news reporters git there." Merle folded his hands. "Ain't that the cleverest thing you ever heard?"

"Wentworth!" The sheriff's voice came from behind Junior and me. "My rifle is pointing at the back of your head, so put down the gun and let go of Miss Newell."

The air went out of Wentworth. His arm went slack and he slumped against the table.

The sheriff circled around into our line of vision and motioned for Wentworth to lay down his gun. When he did, I dropped into the nearest chair. The sheriff kept the rifle trained on Junior while Merle removed the bullets from Junior's gun. I tried to sort out what Merle said before the sheriff arrived. A sealed confession from Arvid? Copies left with lawyers? Newspaper reporters? The shy, old bachelor had done all that to protect us? And Merle had known all along.

My eyes flitted from the sheriff to Merle and back again. Hope bubbled inside me. Surely the sheriff had enough to arrest Junior and free Brock now.

I started to speak, but Merle shooed me away like one of his chickens. "You go get yurself put back together."

The cold, wet denim sticking to my legs, clammy socks, and the stench of my own urine rose to greet me as I stood. Heat crept up my neck and onto my cheeks.

"No need to feel shameful. I 'member when a balky mare bucked off this here cowboy at a rodeo, and the one and only Junior Wentworth filled his pants." He winked. "While you is gitting all tidy, he'll clean the floor. Outta apprec-ee-ation for me not breathin' a word to anyone about how he messed himself back then."

I squelched by, gathered clean clothes in the bedroom, and sloshed into the bathroom. I stripped off my clothes, got into the shower and sobbed until the hot water ran out. Then I dried off and splashed my face with cold water at the sink, because that's what my mother always said to do after a good cry. Then I squared my shoulders and opened the bathroom door.

Chapter 50

I joined the three men in the kitchen. Except there was only one. The sheriff and Wentworth were gone.

Merle sat at the table. " 'Bout time you come out. You missed the afternoon's main attraction."

What could have topped me being held at gunpoint in my own kitchen?

"Rick arrested Junior and slapped on the handcuffs faster than Tipperary bucked off every cowboy who tried to ride him."

"So the sheriff thinks there is enough evidence to convict Wentworth of Twila's murder?"

He rubbed his ear. "Now Teacher, don't you go jumpin' to conclusions. The sheriff arrested him for what the three of us seen with our own eyes. Assaulting you and nothing more."

The bubble of hope inside me burst. "What about Brock?"

Merle brightened. "Ain't you heard? Charges against

him have been dropped and he is out of jail. Compliments of his little sisters."

"When? How?"

"We-ull, Rosalie and Keeva kep' asking Axel and Liv to talk to the sheriff. Badgered 'em 'til they brought them girls to Tipperary after school one day last week. Rosalie marched into Rick's office and opened her 4-H Record Book to a page 'bout some sorta hay bale playhouse she been making for Keeva in the barn. She used her parents' Super 8 camera to show each step of how and when it was built. Gave the date and time whenever she turned the durned film camera on. She showed Rick the movie too. It proves clear as day that she and Keeva finished the project 'fore the tip come in that made the sheriff rustle up a search warrant for the barn. Turned out, the bales where the ev-ee-dence was found was in the last wall they built. Keeva's movie showed the tip come in before they built it. So whoever phoned in the tip planted the ev-ee-dence after the call was made."

"The sheriff hauled the record book and the movie down to Sturgis. When the judge got back from vacation some place or the other, he sprung Brock quicker than a coyote can kill a jackrabbit. And he says Rosalie oughta git a purple ribbon for her 4-H Record Book. But that's beyond the jur-ee-diction of the law."

I charged at the old man and beat his chest with my fists. "You and the sheriff knew about Brock's release yesterday and didn't bother to mention it?"

He caught my flailing hands and held them in his.

"He killed Twila, and the only charge against him is for assaulting me? That's not right." I yanked my hands free of his and rubbed the spot where Junior had held the gun to my neck. "Every time I look into Beau's eyes, I know that however hard I try and however hard his grandparents try, we can never fill the emptiness inside him. But the most we can do to Wentworth is give him a slap on the wrist."

Merle stared at the tabletop for a long minute before speaking. "Long as I live, the sight of Wentworth will stick in my craw. But gittin' older, I have come to some ree-lizations about life. One of them is that we all got emptiness in us. We all got a place in us that nobody and nothing can fill up. Junior Wentworth ain't the cause of my emptiness, and he ain't the cause of yours or Beau's neither."

"Then who is?" Heat ran through me, and I slammed my hands on the table. "If you're going to invoke the benevolence of some happy, clappy God, save your breath and go away. I can't believe in anyone or anything who takes parents away from their children." The words lodged in my throat.

"Course you can't believe in anything like that." He rose and put a hand on my shoulder. "Course you can't."

His kindness was my undoing. I leaned into him and cried. He waited until my sobs faded to nothing. Then he took a napkin and wiped my eyes.

When I was done, he limped to the door and put his hand on the knob. "Just so you know, I never been inclined to believe in any such thing either. Even so, the older I get, the more I wish there was a way to fill empty hearts with what they need."

He sucked air through his teeth. "What's a lonely old man with too many regrets and a heart full of holes know 'bout how to accomplish that?" He pushed the door open and walked away.

I sat at the table until the room went dark. Then I rose and began checking locks. That's when it hit me. Twila's killer was in jail and I was safe. I could leave the doors wide open if I wanted. Even so, I made sure they were locked, though I did shut off the lights. As I prepared for bed, the question I'd ignored the night I'd stolen Twila's buckle came back to haunt me.

When you were waiting for the sheriff to show up, who were you praying to?

Chapter 51

The next day I stuck my head out the door and discovered the weather had turned unseasonably warm. I changed out of my wool pants and sweater into a cotton jumper and blouse. A banging on my classroom door sent me scurrying to see who was there.

Liv burst in with Rosalie in tow. "Have you heard? The charges against Brock have been dropped. He's home!"

I acted surprised. She embraced me in a bear hug. We laughed and cried. We praised Rosalie up one side and down the other for the fine work she'd done on her record book. We might have carried on all day if not for Rosalie pointing out the time.

"It's almost time to ring the bell." She ran outside to join the other children.

"One day that girl will rule the world."

Liv laughed. "You might be right."

The children arrived, antsy with anticipation of the upcoming Friday off because of parent-teacher conferences and next week's Halloween party. They could talk of nothing other than their costumes.

"Mom's making me a Tigger costume," Tiege said. "without springs because she says I already got plenty of invisible ones already."

Renny and Stig announced they would be wearing a two person horse costume, though they couldn't agree on who would be the head and who would be the . . . ahem . . . business end.

Elva was in a huff. "Mom said she would make me a rodeo queen costume with a rhinestone-studded shirt, a satin sash, and a tiara. But she's up to her ears canning tomatoes and wants me to be an old lady in old gramma clothes."

"My costume is all made." Cora put her lunch box in her cubby. "It's pink with a twirly skirt and sparklies everywhere. Even my shoes are covered with glitter."

My alarm over Velma's reaction to Cora's sparkle storm ended the moment Beau opened his mouth. "Gramma says I can be a cowboy." His words tumbled out. "Grampa's makin' me a new leather belt for my buckle. And real leather chaps. And boots with spurs that jingle."

Don't you cry over his little-boy swagger, Jane Newell! You ought to know that even the smallest cowboy—wearing a pint-sized belt with a silver buckle, tiny chaps, and spurs that jingle—isn't going to appreciate being blubbered over by his teacher.

"Thanks for telling me, Beau. Otherwise I might not recognize you on Halloween and mark you absent."

He whooped and made a beeline to the butterfly jar. Tiege was on his heels. "You could make a mustache to really trick her." The boys giggled, but went still when they reached the jar.

Were the butterflies dead? Why hadn't I checked the jar this morning and gotten rid of their shriveled cocoons. I crossed the room and put a hand on the shoulder of each boy, ready to do damage control.

I closed my eyes, unable to watch Beau's spark snuff out again. His hand grasped mine. The early morning chatter ceased. Soft footfalls came nearer and my students pressed around us. The room was silent as a grave.

"Miss Newell." Cora's voice trembled.

"They have wings." Renny's words were almost a prayer.

What? My eyes flew open. The monarchs, in black and orange splendor, flitted from one side of the jar to the other.

"Look here." Stig crouched and pointed to the lowest milkweed leaf. "This one's just coming out."

We knelt and drank in the magic. A monarch encased in a transparent chrysalis butted its tiny head against the floor of its self-made prison. The movement slowly cracked its clear shell. The butterfly emerged, first its head, then its wings. In a twinkling, it flipped around and clung to the empty chrysalis with trembling legs. Its wings unfurled and quivered. They flapped, gently at first. Then harder and harder until, with a mighty and delicate motion, the monarch was airborne.

I wanted the moment to last forever. I wanted to absorb the beauty of the butterflies. I wanted to watch their transformation reveal the hope of better things to come. But this was school, and we had work to do. The children groaned when I sent them to their desks. They rallied when I said we would have a butterfly release party in the afternoon.

During the morning recess, I called the children's parents and invited them to the party. The sheriff phoned at lunchtime to ask if I would come to the courthouse after school to press charges against Junior. I agreed, but refused to allow the disconcerting news to break the spell wrought by the butterflies.

My students' parents arrived a few minutes before the butterfly release. Dan Barkley and Glen Berthold gently carried the jar out to the playground. My students formed a circle around the jar and their parents formed a ring around them.

I asked Beau to open the jar. He unscrewed the lid and stepped back. We waited and watched until one butterfly after another smelled freedom and winged up and out of the jar. When the last butterfly took flight and disappeared above the treetops, the children and their parents went home.

If I had believed in holy moments, this surely would have been one.

Chapter 52

I didn't have time to savor the loveliness of the moment once everyone was gone. Instead, I hopped into the car and floored the gas pedal. The sooner I could put the business of pressing charges against Junior behind me, the better. Clutching my purse with both hands to stop their shaking, I entered the sheriff's office. He ran through the process of filing assault charges and what to expect in the days and weeks to come. Then he asked me to recount what Junior had done. As I described discovering him in my bathroom, the terror of his assault engulfed me. The flash of pain as he wrenched my wrist. The cold gun against my flesh. His hot breath in my ear. My starved lungs gasping for air. The sharp odor of my own urine. My shame and helplessness. I began to tremble.

"Do you want to take a break?" Rick asked. "Maybe try this again tomorrow?"

"Just give me a minute." I closed my eyes and listened

to the ticking of the clock. "I'm not leaving until you have what you need."

He brought me a glass of water. I took a few sips and began to speak again. His pen flew across the paper. When we were finished, I signed the form and handed it to Rick.

Once I was in the Beetle, I beat a tattoo on the steering wheel with my fists. Junior wouldn't have an easy time charming his way out of those charges. But just in case he tried, I had another card up my sleeve. I pulled it out when I got home.

I rang Betty and asked her to put me through to Roger Holmstead at the KOTA television station. When he came on the line, I asked, "Would you like a juicy story?"

"Always," he replied.

The next night, his report about Junior's assault led the evening news. The day after that, several other women in South Dakota and Nebraska filed charges against him. Little Missouri was once again at the center of a media circus for a few days. But Roger Holmstead made sure Beau remained out of the spotlight.

I barely had time to fret about parent-teacher conferences before they began on Friday. To my relief, there were no complaints. In fact, the parents were pleased with their children's progress.

Iva Kelly was effusive with her thanks. "Beau sleeps with his belt buckle under his pillow. He's still grieving for his mama. Me and Burt is too. But now we got some hope he'll be okay one day."

The final conference was with Bud and Cookie. I

brought up Tiege's rambunctiousness as diplomatically as possible.

Bud laughed. "However you want to discipline him, we're behind you one hundred percent. Even if you need to tan his behind a time or two."

Cookie gave his hand a light pat. "Good heavens, Bud. Miss Newell don't need that kind of advice. She's got more ideas about how to keep these kids in line than you or I can imagine." She rose and picked up the construction paper folder containing Tiege's report card and work samples. "Jane, it's been too long since you been to the ranch. How about you come out this Sunday for dinner? We been cooking up a little surprise for you. I better not say any more or I'll break my promise."

I could glean nothing from their expressions. "I'd love to come. Thanks."

Bud stood and zipped his coat. "Can we pick you up for church?"

"That would be fine."

I had just agreed to go to church without hemming and hawing. What was wrong with me?

"Good. You better wear warm clothes and warm shoes. This time of year, the days can be sunny enough for rattlesnakes, windy enough to blow a person plumb into Montana, or cold enough to make your teeth chatter."

After they left, I went into the apartment. The phone rang while I was putting grounds into the the coffee maker. "Jane Newell speaking."

"This is Corinne."

I dropped the spoon and coffee grounds flew in all directions.

"Is this a bad time?"

There would never be a good time to talk to Junior's mother.

"No . . . I just dropped something."

"Um." Corinne hesitated. "I'm not sure how to tell you this, and you may not believe what I have to say." She asked Betty to clear the party line and get off the call too.

"Jane, I want you to know that I'm not angry with you for pressing charges against Junior. In some ways, it's a relief." She cleared her throat. "There's been something very wrong with him since he was a child. I wanted to take him to a psychiatrist, but Richard wouldn't hear of it. Even when Junior shoved me into a wall and broke my arm, his father said it was my fault because of my breakdown after our daughter was stillborn.

"Who was I to argue? Richard's accusation was true. I had neglected our son. Out of guilt, I went along with my husband. I made excuses for the way Junior treated women. God forgive me, I covered for him more than once.

"If I were a stronger person, I would file charges against him myself. I would tell the truth. But I can't do that to my son. Still, I won't defend him or stand in your way. I hope you understand."

Her pain was audible, and I didn't try to hide my anger. "Corinne, your son has put you in an impossible situation. What I understand is that you are his victim too."

"I'm glad you moved to Little Missouri, Jane."

"And I'm glad we met, Corinne. Maybe someday, we can be friends again."

"Goodbye, dear. God bless you."

I hung up and cleaned up the coffee grounds. I wanted to hate Junior for what he had done to Twila, to me, and to the women who had come forward. I wanted to hate him even more for what he had done to his mother. But I couldn't. Because from what Corinne had said, Junior was a victim of his father's refusal to acknowledge his son's needs. I still wouldn't rest until Junior had paid for his crimes. Moving forward, however, I would seek justice rather than revenge.

I looked at the clock. A half hour until weekend long-distance telephone rates started. I didn't care. After the week I'd had, I wanted to talk to my mom. I picked up the receiver and asked Betty for a long-distance connection.

I started talking the second she picked up the phone. "Mom, I have to tell you about Junior Wentworth."

The clunk and clatter on the other end of the line was deafening. "Mom, are you there?"

"Hello?"

"Dad? Is that you?"

"Affirmative."

"Where's Mom?"

"She went to the grocery store. Do you want to call back later?"

"No. I just wasn't expecting you to answer. I'd love to chat with you."

"Then shoot."

For the next ten minutes I entertained him with tales of Little Missouri. I described the vast, windswept horizon interrupted by the Long Pines and the miles and miles of gravel roads. I walked him down Main Street past the post office, the garage, The Bend, and the grocery store. He heard about meals with ranch families. He chuckled about Merle's non-skid pancakes and hooted when he learned his daughter had milked a cow, fed chickens, and cleaned up after bulls. I told him about the butterflies emerging from cocoons and setting them free, about Tiege's indefatigable energy, about being the object of Cora and Elva's worship, about Renny and Stig's horse costume, about Bennan's little cowboy swagger, and about the joy that had entered into Beau's sadness.

When I wound down, he spoke again. "You're doing good, Janie-Jo. I'm so proud—"

"Hello? Who is this?"

"Hi, Mom. It's Jane."

"Oh, my goodness gracious, Jane. What's wrong?"

"Nothing."

"But the rates haven't gone down yet. Do you have any idea what this will cost you?"

"I just wanted to hear your voice, Mom. It's been a long week."

"You know, Jane, you haven't mentioned that nice, young Junior Wentworth in a while. Is he still around?"

"He's in jail."

"Don't tease me, young lady."

"It's the truth, Mom. Sit down and I'll tell you the story from start to finish." Which I did. She didn't say a word for a full five seconds after my story ended. "Mom? Are you still there?"

"Oh, I most certainly am, Jane Josephine Newell."

I cringed and held the receiver away from my ear to be on the safe side. Mom saved my middle name for the direst of circumstances.

"I have half a mind to drive out there and haul you home by the ear."

This was going to be bad.

"And the other half of me is proud of the woman you've become."

Mom was proud of me?

"You've grown up, Jane. You don't need me to rescue you. But you already know that, don't you?"

"I may not need rescuing, but I still need you, Mom. And I love you."

"I know. And I also know this call is costing you a fortune. I'll hang up and quit spending your money."

I placed the receiver in the cradle, but my parents' words swirled around me.

You're doing good, Janie-Jo. I'm proud of you.

I'm proud of the woman you've become. You don't need me to rescue you.

Dad's illness had cost our family dearly, but my parents still found ways to give me what mattered most. Love. Approval. Stubborn perseverance. Now it was my turn to live in a way that would make them proud of who they had raised me to be. I was Harold and Doris Newell's daughter. They were made of stern stuff. So was I. And that should make Junior Wentworth tremble in his boots.

Chapter 53

Saturday, I called Lacey Jo. She had just had a cancellation, and if I could be at the beauty salon in half an hour, she could get me in. I ran to the Beetle and drove to Tipperary, rejoicing because the last-minute appointment left little time to speculate about whether the woman who had dated Junior—and was about to cut my hair with sharp scissors—was angry about the charges I'd filed against him.

Lacey Jo didn't act like she was holding a grudge. When she finished my cut, I walked across the street and purchased stationery at the drugstore. I'd written only one short note to my parents in the past two and half months. From now on, I planned to write every week and send pictures my students drew for them too.

Next, I bought four folding chairs, a deck of Uno cards, two decks of playing cards, and several board games at the hardware store. My final stop was the grocery store, where I bought food for the guests I would invite to supper in the next few weeks. First on the list were return invitations to Merle, the Barkleys, the Sternquists, and the McDonalds. Then the families of my other students until all of them had enjoyed a meal and game night with their teacher.

I stopped at the post office in Little Missouri and sorted through the mail on the way to the Beetle. A couple bills. Another letter from Uncle Tim and Aunt Wanda—I needed to write to them too. And a postcard. I let out a whoop, drove to Merle's house, and pounded on his door.

He shuffled through the mudroom. "What kinda bee you got in that bonnet of yours?"

"This kind." I waved the postcard at him.

He snatched it out of my hand and studied the photograph of the Fort Walsh National Historic Site in Saskatchewan, Canada. He turned it over and read aloud the single sentence written there. "Having a wonderful time. I be wishing you was here."

Our eyes met. I wrapped my arms around Merle's neck and planted a kiss on his bristly cheek. I laughed as a slow blush crept up his neck.

"Arvid made it, Merle. He flew the coop. He's free."

***

That night Merle ate supper at my house. I had prepared way too much food and invited Velma on a whim. She accepted and devoured huge helpings of pot roast, gravy, roasted potatoes, carrots, and onions. When she wasn't eating, she glared at Merle. He glared right back.

I wanted to ask if they had ever resolved their country school feuds. But in the interest of staying alive long enough to see Junior Wentworth go to prison, I kept my mouth shut.

Homemade apple pie and ice cream went a long way toward thawing their ill will, as did several hands of gin rummy and second helpings of pie. When they left, each with aluminum-foil-wrapped packets of leftover pie, they bid good-night without growling.

I watched them walk away. Velma to her smoke-filled trailer and Hollywood Squares. Merle to Snippy, the cats, and his chickens. Why had it taken me so long to invite them over? The answer, full of grace and truth, came in my mother's voice.

You needed to grow up first, Jane.

I stepped inside and closed the door with infinite care. You're right, Mom. And I did.

Chapter 54

Before church the following morning, I heeded Bud's advice and dressed in warm layers. Then I laced hiking boots over a pair of sensible, thick socks. I was putting on a down vest when enthusiastic pounding at the apartment door threatened to knock it down. I ran to see who it was.

Tiege stood on the landing. His words came out in an unbroken stream. "Mom-says-sorry. We're-early. Are-you-ready-for-church? If-you-need-more-time-Dad-will-come-back-in-ten-minutes."

"Well, good morning to you too, Tiege." I locked the door and followed him to the Sternquist's truck. We got in the back of the crew cab, and Tiege closed the door.

"So what's the surprise?"

"Ah, ah, ah." Cookie waggled a finger at her son. "Remember what I said to you earlier? Not a word."

Tiege shut his mouth and refused to speak. When Bud parked outside the church, the little boy vaulted out of the cab and ran inside.

Bud cut the engine. “Keeping a secret is a trial for him.”

The three of us entered the foyer together. Cookie bustled to the piano and began practicing. I paged through a hymnal until the Barkleys rushed through the door. Pam asked me to help prepare communion in the kitchen.

She fitted plastic cups into the communion platter’s circular slots and handed me a loaf of bread. “Will you cut the crusts off a few slices and cube them while I pour the cranberry juice?”

“Not grape juice?”

“Nope.” She began filling the tiny cups. “Somebody’s allergic to it.” Once we were done, Pam took the platter of bread and tray of juice to the altar.

When Pastor Petersen arrived, he asked Tiege and Cora Barkley to ring the bell. They rushed to the little door cut into the paneling behind the altar, stooped to enter the small space beyond it, and yanked a dangling rope. Clear tones rang out, jewels of sound carried through the town on the morning wind.

I hadn’t noticed the door or the bell until today. I’d been too busy looking down my nose at this crumpled building and its tiny congregation. Too busy belittling the mysterious and faithful poverty of this place. The mismatched pews in the sanctuary. The ancient linoleum dusted with clumps of dirt from the boots of worshipers. The cheap tapestry of Jesus tacked to the church wall. The crooked, dark paneling that lined the wall behind the sanctuary. The realization shamed me.

My gaze traveled from person to person in the congregation during the service. I had no inkling of what brought people to this dreary place. Pastor Petersen's sermon offered no explanation. Even so, an almost palpable peace enveloped Bud and Cookie, the sheriff, and the Barkleys as they received communion. They were intelligent people. I respected them. Yet their faith made no sense.

I left with the Sternquists after the service. Tiege was mute on the ride to the ranch. Cookie pointed out the remains of original barns and shacks built by homesteaders in the early 1900s.

Bud spoke when he passed the Drent place. "Ain't a day I pass this place but I wonder where Arvid got to and pray to God he ain't dead."

"I miss that old man." Cookie sniffled and blew her nose.

I stared at the jumble of buildings. "I miss him too." My stomach clenched at the secret Rick and I had to hide from Bud, Cookie, and everyone else who cared about Arvid.

Bud drove down their lane and parked in front of the house. "Cookie, I forgot to tell you that Rick's coming for dinner. Hope you made enough to go around."

She swatted his arm. "You know I always do. When will he get here?"

Tiege scrambled onto his knees and twisted around so he faced the rear window. "He's coming down the lane now."

Cookie and I walked to the porch as Rick parked and got out. Then she turned and hollered to the others. "Jane and me'll have everything ready in a bit."

The sheriff wrangled with Tiege who was trying to climb onto his back. "Mom, could you spare Miss Newell for a few minutes?"

"Sure. Bud, could you and Tiege give me a hand?"

Bud pulled Tiege off his brother and wedged him under his arm. Tiege protested as his father hauled him into the house.

Rick cleared his throat. "Does he act that way at school?"

"He saves it all for his parents. They deserve sainthood."

"They do." He took off his hat and rubbed the back of his neck. "So do you."

"When did aiding and abetting a blackmailer, breaking and entering, and tampering with evidence become grounds for sainthood?"

"You have a point." He put on his hat. "Sainthood is probably out. Would you accept an apology instead?"

"What for?"

"For arresting Brock after he was framed. For not anticipating Junior would bring a gun to your apartment. For only being able to arrest him for assaulting you and not for Twila's murder. For wanting to give you a piece of my mind when you leaked the story to the media." He paused. "You can stop me any time."

"I accept your apology. Just don't expect me to apologize for talking to that reporter. I'm not sorry about strengthening the case we can make against Junior. The only thing I'm sorry about is that I'll never see Arvid again." Hot tears scalded my cheeks. "But I am angry."

"At me?"

"No." I wiped at my tears with a shirt cuff. "I'm angry at the God you believe in. If he's everything you seem to think he is, why didn't he let Twila live instead of making Beau an orphan? Watching him missing her hurts so much."

"It does hurt. But the pain'll eat you alive if you hold onto it. It pretty much devoured me after Larch died. I clutched it with both fists until Tiege came along. That little baby deserved a brother as much as Larch had. It took a long time for me to let go of the hate and bitterness I'd been hanging onto.

"I finally settled on something Mom told me after Larch died. She said that when she held me for the first time, she began to understand what it means to say God is love. She said his love sent Jesus into our dark world. He gave his Son for people who never gave him the time of day. When Mom said, 'God knows my pain and yours too, Rick. He chose our pain for himself,' I knew it was time to lay down hate and choose love."

"But what about justice?"

"It'll come." He spoke with conviction. "If not in this world, then in the next."

The front door swung open and Cookie called, "Dinner's ready!"

We went inside and took our places at the table. After Bud said grace, Tiege shoveled his food so fast he made my stomach hurt.

After a few minutes of steady eating, he laid his silverware on his plate. "Okay. I'm done. Can I show Miss Newell now?"

Rick pointed a fork at Tiege and then at his chair. "Sit back down and let her finish eating."

The kid was going to explode if I made him wait much longer. I laid down my fork and knife. "I'm done."

Tiege was halfway across the living room before anyone could protest. "You want to come with us, Rick? You helped with the surprise too."

The sheriff winked. "You did most of the work. Can you reach the keys?"

Tiege jingled them in answer.

I raised my eyebrows at Rick. "He can drive?"

"Since he was four. I taught him."

"I'm ready, Miss Newell. Are you?"

I was not. But the county sheriff didn't seem concerned about this illegal activity, so what was I supposed to do? Put a seven-year-old under citizen's arrest?

I screwed up my courage and took Tiege's outstretched hand. "As ready as I'll ever be."

Chapter 55

Tiege drove through the pasture toward a small rise about a mile straight east of the house. His bottom rested on the edge of the seat. His eyes peered over the steering wheel. Just barely. His foot stretched to reach the accelerator. I fervently hoped he could reach the brake pedal too.

He stopped at a fence. "Passenger has to open the gate." He flashed a mischievous grin. "You don't have to close it until we go back."

I had never opened a livestock gate in my life, but I wasn't about to admit that to Tiege. Instead, I hopped out and studied the latch. Aha! If I pressed here and pushed there, then it should . . . it worked! I dragged the fence open and Tiege drove through. I got in beside him and we bumped across the pasture until we arrived at another gate. I jumped out again and opened this one like a pro. Practice did make perfect.

I got in the truck again. Tiege drove a little further and braked in front of a third gate. I got out and opened it. By the time we reached the huge stock tank and shiny new windmill at the top of the rise, I had opened six gates. My arm muscles burned.

Tiege patted the side of the tank, then ran to the windmill and scaled a few rungs. "Well, what do you think?"

I thought he had no business climbing it like a monkey. But that wasn't the answer he was looking for. So I pulled a question out of my teacher bag of tricks. "What can you tell me about it?"

It was the right thing to say. Soon I knew more about windmills and stock tanks than I knew what to do with.

"Why did you decide to build it?"

"Rick talked about it all summer. He said it would make it easier to run more cattle. So this fall he taught me to weld, and we done it together."

"Do you mean to say that you really can weld?"

"Almost as good as him. I practiced a lot, 'cause with the helmet on, I couldn't hear his questions." He took my hand and we walked to the truck. "He kept asking about you."

I turned away and grinned. Tiege could weld. And he could drive. But like every other seven-year-old I knew, he couldn't keep his mouth shut.

We got into the truck. He backed around until it was pointed at the house. "Remember, you got to shut the gates on the way back."

I did so without complaint. As I latched the last gate, he gunned the engine and sped off with a wave and a honk. The insolence of the child! I'd lived through some unbelievable things since moving to Tipperary County, but this might top them all.

I plucked a stalk of prairie grass and chewed it, thinking of the people I'd met in Tipperary County. Tiege and his classmates. Their parents. Merle and Arvid. The McDonalds. Velma. The sheriff. Junior Wentworth. I pictured bulls, buckles, and butterflies.

I looked to the east and south, and Iowa tugged at my heart. I saw Mom going to work every day and Dad's smile when she came home each afternoon. Someday I would tell them about being outfoxed by a seven-year-old driver. Not over the phone. In person when I went back for a visit. I wanted to see them laugh.

The October prairie stretched miles in every direction—vast and beautiful and terrible. The sky above was bright blue and cloudless. A breeze ruffled my hair. Standing there, I sensed a change, like a light flickering on. I couldn't pinpoint its location until my breathing slowed and my thoughts stilled.

The change was inside of me. I was no longer tethered to my parents, but to this place. I belonged here, wrapped in the protection of an old man with a cow, a kind-eyed sheriff, and the secret we could never reveal. Watched over by a blind man and his invisible wife. Gossamer threads bound my heart to seven boys and girls who were the center of my life. I was surrounded by friends, in love with the small community where I lived.

I hiked across the prairie toward the Sternquists' home. My arms ached and my legs would be sore tonight, physical evidence of the unseen changes in my heart. As much as I wanted to scold Tiege for abandoning me in this wild vista of sun and wind and sky, that wouldn't be wise. If that cheeky, impulsive boy gained an inkling of what he had set in motion, he would be insufferable.

One day, when he was older, I would tell him about what I'd discovered when he left me stranded on the prairie. I was not the same person who had come to Tipperary County a few short months ago. I was courageous. I was resilient. I was done running.

I was home.

Merle Laird's Non-Skid Pancakes

1. *Separate 3 eggs.*
2. *In a medium bowl, beat egg whites until stiff peaks form. Set aside.*
3. *In a large bowl, combine:*

    2 1/2 cups milk
    3 egg yolks
    1/3 cup vegetable oil
    Add dry ingredients:
    3 cups flour
    3 tablespoons sugar
    4 teaspoons baking powder
    1 teaspoon salt

4. *Fold in egg whites.*
5. *Cook in waffle iron until golden brown.*

Serves five.

About the Author

Jolene Philo discovered Laura Ingalls Wilder and Encyclopedia Brown in elementary school and has been fascinated by the prairie and mysteries ever since. She's a voracious reader of fiction, biography, and creative non-fiction. Imagine her surprise when she became the author of several non-fiction books for the special needs and disability community. The *West River Mystery Series* combines her love of mysteries and northwest South Dakota's short grass prairie, where she and her husband Hiram lived for seven years when they were first married. Jolene and Hiram live in central Iowa with their daughter, son-in-law, and their two children. Jolene instills book love into her grandchildren by reading to them as often as she can. You can keep up with her reading and writing adventures at her website, www.jolenephilo.com.

Made in the USA
Coppell, TX
06 November 2023

23870221R10204